MONEY TROUBLES

Recent Titles by Elisabeth McNeill from Severn House

DUSTY LETTERS
TURN BACK TIME

MONEY TROUBLES

Elisabeth McNeill

severn House

This first world edition published in Great Britain 1999 by
SEVERN HOUSE PUBLISHERS LTD of
9–15 High Street, Sutton, Surrey SM1 1DF.
This title first published in the U.S.A. 1999 by
SEVERN HOUSE PUBLISHERS INC of
595 Madison Avenue, New York, N.Y. 10022.

British Library Cataloguing in Publication Data

McNeill, Elisabeth
    Money troubles
    I.   Title
    823.9'14 [F]

    ISBN 0 7278 5443 7

Typeset by Palimpsest Book Production Ltd
Polmont, Stirlingshire, Scotland.
Printed and bound in Great Britain by
MPG Books Ltd, Bodmin, Cornwall.

GATES, ALBERT GEORGE, 'HOWIE' – Peacefully at his home Castledevon, Galashiels, on April 23rd, 1936, Albert George 'Howie' Gates, aged 84, deeply mourned by his only daughter Helen and son-in-law Reginald Hunt. Funeral service at St Paul's Church, Galashiels, 2 p.m., April 28th, followed by interment at Galashiels burial ground.

One

"Well, goodness me! I thought he'd be awa' years ago," said Mrs Lilian Grossett with a detectable note of satisfaction in her voice as she smoothed out the crumpled pages of a *Scotsman* that her daughter Phemie had brought home from the wastepaper basket of an architect's office in Shandwick Place where she worked as a cleaner.

"Who?" asked Phemie. A gaunt, life-soured woman in her thirties, she was peeling potatoes in the sink beneath the window of their miserable flat overlooking Leith Walk.

"Howie Gates, an awkward old sod if there ever was one," shouted Mrs Grossett, who was so crippled with arthritis that she couldn't turn her head to speak to her daughter but directed her utterances loudly at the opposite wall.

"Never heard of him," said Phemie shortly, throwing the potatoes into a battered pot and furiously pouring cold water over them. She always acted as if everything that happened was calculated to annoy her but tonight she was especially tired and more than usually exasperated with her mother's obsessive interest in the Births, Marriages and Deaths – but most of all, the Deaths – column of the newspaper.

"But I have, and you'd be interested too if you kent what I ken . . ." Mrs Grossett had a sharply malevolent intelligence and enjoyed taunting her daughter.

3

"Would I?" said Phemie in a sarcastic tone but it was obvious from the way she was standing at the sink staring out of the window that she was waiting to be told what it was her mother knew. Mrs Grossett wasn't going to satisfy her curiosity too swiftly, however.

"Oh aye, I ken a bit about Mr Howie Gates and his *only daughter*, Helen," she said and rustled the sheets of the newspaper resentfully as if she'd caught it out in a huge lie.

"Let's see," said Phemie, rising to the bait and walking across the lino-covered floor to where her mother sat hunched up in a fraying wickerwork chair. The flat was chilly, dark and poorly furnished, the home of two bitter women who were only scraping a living in a hard world.

"There it is," said the mother, pointing to the entry headed 'GATES', "That's him. Mair money than he could ever spend . . . rolling in it. Where's the other yin I wonder?"

Phemie took the paper and read the entry aloud emphasising some words and muttering others . . . "*Gates*. At his home . . . *Castledevon* . . . *Helen* . . . That seems ordinary enough. What other yin?"

Her mother gave a lopsided grin as she took the newspaper back. "His other lassie, the one I kent. And Mrs Maitland kent her too. I wonder if Maitland's seen this?"

"She's like you, she doesnae miss much." A note of interest had entered Phemie's voice and she stood waiting for more information but her mother was out to tantalise, and, shaking the newspaper sheets out, pretended to become absorbed in the Stock Market report.

Phemie gave in. "Was she one of Maitland's clients? Is that what you're saying?"

"Aye, she was."

"No' this daughter?" Phemie leaned over and put her

4

index finger on the name *Helen* in the notice. "No' her?"

Mrs Grossett shook her head. "No' her, another yin wi' a fancy name – Leonie. I've aye minded it . . . She came to Mrs Maitland's."

"But it says here this Helen's his only daughter."

"Then it's wrong, because he had another yin and her name was Leonie. I mind her fine. A bonny lassie wi' yellow hair."

Phemie's eyes were round with interest now. "What happened?"

"She brought a bairn to Maitland, and Maitland found a place for it."

"Where did it go? It might still be alive. If this Howie Gates was as rich as you say, that bairn could be in line for some money."

"I dinna ken where it went." A shuttered look came over the old woman's face.

"Was it a boy or a girl?"

"It was a wee laddie."

"You're sure?"

"Of course I'm sure. My mind's no' gone yet."

During this conversation, years seemed to drop off Phemie. Roughly she shook her mother's shoulder, saying, "Come on. Think hard. What year was it?" The old woman frowned for a bit before she said, "It was the time my sister Jeannie got married and you came back to live with me."

"I came back to you when I was eleven . . . at the beginning of 1915. I'd been wi' auntie Jean for three years. That means if the bairn's still alive he'll be twenty-one. That's old enough to claim any money his grandfather left. I wish I could find him!"

Helen Gates, petite, timidly ladylike and dressed in funereal black, was sitting in the window of the Castledevon drawing

5

room staring out over rain-soaked gardens when her husband Reggie came in and handed her *The Scotsman*.

"Have you seen the notice?" he asked in a low voice, gently laying one hand on his wife's thin shoulder.

She looked up out of swollen eyes. "Not yet. Is it all right?"

"Yes, I just thought you'd want to see it . . ."

She unfolded the paper and ran her eye down the Deaths column till she came to GATES.

"It seems very dignified, but perhaps we should have mentioned Leonie as well as me – 'and the late Leonie', something like that," she whispered after reading the entry.

Reggie snorted. "Come on, Helen, Leonie's been dead for over twenty years. From the day she was buried, your father never mentioned her name. Most people who read that notice won't even have heard of her. Don't worry about it, my dear."

"All right, Reggie," she said meekly.

Her husband put an arm around her and gave her a tentative hug. "You've had a bad time," he said, "but it's over now."

She gave a little sob and tears slid down her cheeks. "I've still to get through the funeral, Reggie, I'm dreading it. I'm so nervous."

Her husband assumed the attitude of lord and master. "There's nothing to be nervous about, my dear, everything's arranged and I'll be there. You can rely on me," he told her.

Eyes swimming, she looked up at him. "Can I? Can I really?"

Embarrassed, he shuffled his feet on the carpet, dropped his arm from her shoulder and stood back. "Of course, of course," he said, and then, muttering something about business, made a speedy retreat.

When he had gone, walking with exaggerated care,

putting each foot down as soundlessly as possible, almost tiptoeing in fact, Helen resumed her vigil at the window but she was not seeing the vista of trees and river in front of her, instead she was remembering her father's last days. How difficult he'd been, and how angry.

Old Howie Gates had taken a long time to die from the stroke that felled him. During his last weeks, he could not speak, but his ferocious stares were as terrifying as ever. They even made his lawyer stammer as he said, "Don't worry about anything, Mr Gates. Your will's perfectly in order and up to date," for he knew Howie cared more about his money than about anything else in the world.

Helen remembered how her father spat in contempt, a foam of spittle forming round his cracked blue lips. Obviously there was something he wanted to say but he couldn't get the words out.

On the last day, feeling her father's angry eyes fixed on her, Helen had bent down and whispered, "Is there anything I can do for you, Father?"

His chest heaved and his useless hands fretted at the edge of the sheet as he struggled to find words. She forced herself to put her ear beside his mouth. "Find Leonie's boy . . ." he had groaned with an immense effort. It was the first time he had uttered his elder daughter's name since she died, and tears sprang into Helen's eyes when she heard him.

Within minutes he was dead.

The next morning, before it was light, Phemie Grossett was up and bustling about. She roused her mother by putting a cup of tea on the window ledge beside her bed and said, "Drink that. I'm going out."

"At this time o' the morning? Where to?"

"To my work. I want to get finished early. There's somebody I want to see."

Besides cleaning the architect's office at night, Phemie

went out early every morning to polish the door brasses of several lawyers' offices in Queen Street.

Her mother groaned as she levered herself up in the bed and took the teacup in her gnarled hand. "Where are ye goin' Phemie? It's no' about the Gates bairn is it? I wish I hadnae telt you about that. You'd best leave it alane. Dinna meddle in it!" Her voice trembled as if she was afraid.

Her daughter folded her arms and glared. "Dinna be daft. This is maybe oor big chance. We might make a bit o' money and by God we could do wi' it. I'm fed up rubbing brass and sweeping floors. If this man Gates had a grandson and if I find him, he'll be glad to pay me for putting him in the way of his inheritance, won't he?"

Mrs Grossett shook her grey head, "Listen to me Phemie, forget it. You dinna ken what you're meddling wi'. Mrs Maitland'll no' tak kindly to you askin' questions . . ."

"I'm no' feared for her!" exclaimed Phemie boldly.

"Well you should be. Dinna go, Phem," said her mother fervently. She didn't listen.

Even at that early hour Leith Walk was busy with brightly lit tram cars jangling up and down, sparks flying from their overhead wires, and crowds of hurrying people on foot, making their way to work.

In her worn dark coat and shabby felt hat, Phemie, with yesterday's *Scotsman* in her pocket, joined the throng, slipping between groups of them like a snake. Her white face was set and determined and as she walked she rehearsed in her mind what she was going to say to Cynthia Maitland.

In Queen Street she worked quickly, moving from office to office with her cleaning things and not lingering to admire her gleaming handwork when she'd finished. By the time she gave the last brass nameplate a final buffing, it was nine o'clock and the clerks were already in their desks in the offices behind tall windows overlooking the street.

It was quite a long walk to St Bernard's Crescent in Stockbridge. Eventually she found herself on the doorstep of number six, a grim-faced building with wrought-iron first-floor balconies held up by deeply grooved Grecian-style pillars. Remembering her mother's warning, Phemie's legs were trembling nervously and her heart racing, but she gave the brass knocker an authoritative thud that echoed in the cavernous hall. After what seemed a very long time, the door was opened by a small fat maid in a white pinafore and frilled cap.

"Yes?" she challenged, glaring at Phemie, who she could see at a glance was not a person of quality.

"I want to see Mrs Maitland."

"She's maybe no' in."

"At this time of the morning? Of course she's in. Tell her Phemie Grossett, Lilian Grossett's daughter, wants to speak to her."

"I'll see if she's in," said the maid and closed the door again. The next time it opened a different woman stood in the hall. She was extremely tall, thin, carefully made-up and well coiffed, even at that early hour, with her greying hair set in deeply marcelled ridges.

"What do you want coming here at this hour of the day?" she said to Phemie in a voice that was excessively haughty and cultured.

"Let me in and I'll tell you. Or do you want me to talk about it out here on the step?"

Reluctantly Mrs Maitland stood aside while Phemie entered. Then she closed the door and led the way to the drawing room on the right of the hall. The room was cold because there was no fire burning.

Once they were safely inside with that door closed too, she turned to her visitor and said, "Out with it. It's a long time since I've seen you and every time you or your mother come here you've got your hands out after something. Is it money you want? If it is you're out of luck."

9

Phemie shook her head. "No, I'm trying to find some-body. My mother minds you having a bairn called Gates to place. I'm trying to find him."

Cynthia Maitland's eyes went like steel but she managed a cold smile. "Why would you be wanting to find that bairn?" she asked in a silky tone.

"He's related to us," lied Phemie.

"You're a damned liar," snapped Cynthia. "You're not the only one that reads *The Scotsman*. I saw the bit about Howie Gates too. Away home and tell your mother that."

"My mother says his daughter had a baby and you got it."

"I got lots of babies, as your mother knows very well."

"Where did his one go?" asked Phemie boldly.

Mrs Maitland threw back her head and gave a scornful laugh. "I don't believe this. Here I am standing in my own house with *you* throwing questions at me. What business is it of yours where it went anyway?"

"It could be in line to get a lot of money. It probably doesn't know anything about this . . ." Phemie waved the paper about as she spoke.

Cynthia Maitland laughed, "I thought so. You're out for money. If anybody's going to claim a reward for telling the Gates bairn who he is, why shouldn't it be me?"

Phemie's face was set. "My mother says you won't get yourself mixed up in it. She says there's things you want to forget."

The other woman stiffened and she took a step forward as if to threaten Phemie but changed her mind. "I hope you're not trying to threaten me. That wouldn't be a good idea. Tell your mother that if this is her idea, she'll live to regret it." She was rattled now and her agitation showed in her accent which was no longer Morningside genteel but pure Stockbridge.

"It's not my mother's idea, it's mine."

"Well it's a bloody bad one."

"Is it? My mother knows about that baby and other ones as well. What would happen if she talked about them? What would happen to the fine Mrs Maitland who's so very respectable nowadays? I'm not asking *you* for money. I just want to know what happened to that bairn. My mother looked after it for a bit, she says and she was fond of it so she wants to know."

"Was she hell fond of it!" Mrs Maitland had thrown away all pretensions at gentility by this time. "All she was fond of was the money she got for working for me. Tell her that if I get into trouble, she will too."

Phemie was standing her ground however and refusing to be intimidated. "If you don't tell me where that bairn went I'll go to the Gates family and tell them what I know."

"You don't imagine they'll be glad to hear your story, do you?"

"They might. They'd make you tell what happened to it anyway."

Cynthia Maitland walked over the floor to the fireplace and took a cigarette out of a silver box, lighting it from a big table lighter. Inhaling deeply, she turned back to Phemie and said in a different tone, "I can't remember that baby in particular. I found homes for dozens of bairns over the years, why should I remember that one?"

"You kept records. You had to inform the authorities. I could go to them." Phemie felt she was at an advantage now.

"I never liked you, Phemie Grossett, not even when you were a wee girl. You were always sly," said Cynthia in an almost friendly voice.

"I don't care a lot for you either," replied Phemie.

Her antagonist laughed, but it was not a pleasant sound. "It was a long time ago," she said.

11

"It was early 1915."

"As far back as that!"

"Gates' baby'll be over twenty-one now. Old enough to inherit his share of the old man's estate."

"Lucky baby," said Cynthia drawing on her cigarette.

"Who got it? What happened to it? Did it *survive*?" The last word hung between them like a threat.

"Of course it survived! At least it survived as long as I had it. But it's a long time ago. I'd have to look it up and that might take time. I'll let you know." Cynthia Maitland's voice was almost cordial by now.

"I'm not for waiting," said Phemie firmly, "I'll go to the authorities if I have to wait."

"Dear me, what a terrible hurry you're in. Just stay here then and I'll go upstairs to look it up. But like I said it's a long time ago . . ."

She was away for over half an hour and during that time Phemie sat shivering in the freezing drawing room which was incongruously furnished with expensive, modern, blond-wood furniture built in curving sculptured lines. A deadly chill gripped her for though the fire was made up, it was unlit. In one corner a vast cocktail cabinet stood open, its interior enticingly full of sparkling glasses and gilt-trimmed decanters. Phemie looked at them longingly, wondering if Mrs Maitland would notice if she helped herself to a glass of something that would warm her up, but she didn't dare.

Shuddering she drew her coat lapels up round her neck and clasped her hands under her arms, a picture of misery which made Mrs Maitland smile with cruel satisfaction when she finally returned.

"Here you are," she said, holding out a slip of paper. "This is what you want."

Phemie read what was written on the paper. There was a surname – Cameron – and an address in Leith.

"Is this him?" she asked. Cynthia Maitland walked over to the door and held it open.

"I think so. I placed five bairns in the spring of 1915. The papers have got a bit mixed up but I think this is the Gates bairn. You've got the name. That's what you came for, wasn't it?"

Phemie stared at the paper for a few seconds. Then she nodded and went out into the street with her ungloved hand gripping the slip of paper in her pocket and her face troubled. She could not understand why Cynthia Maitland had capitulated so easily.

Two

Shivering with nerves and biting her lip, a damp
handkerchief crumpled in her black gloved hand,
Helen Hunt looked the image of daughterly grief as
she sat with her husband Reggie in the front pew of
Galashiels' red sandstone church dedicated to St Paul.

She felt slightly drunk, though not a drop of alcohol had
passed her lips, and the booming throb of the organ music
seemed to pulse like blood through her veins. Her temples
ached and her throat felt raw and sore. The intensity of her
grief surprised her because there had never been any real
love or closeness between her and her father. All her life
she had felt that she was a deep disappointment to him.

Her husband was worried about her, watching anxiously,
fearful that she might faint or burst into wailing tears
at any moment. He wondered if he should reach out
to hold her hand but knew that such a public gesture
of tenderness would embarrass her, for Helen was not
a very tactile person. So he just sat back and closed his
pouched eyes because he too was unwell, but in his case
he was suffering from a thundering headache, the result of
too many brandies with his brother the previous evening.
His mouth was dry, and his tongue like sandpaper. What
I'd give for a brandy now! he thought wistfully.

There was a silver flask full of the stuff in the pocket of
his overcoat but it was impossible to fish it out and take a
swig with everybody watching. All he could do was think
about it, savour it in his imagination. To summon up the

14

taste of liquor was about the extent of Reggie's limited imaginative powers.

Howie's impressive black coffin dominated the space in front of the altar table. *Is he really in there?* his daughter wondered. *Is he really dead?* She had a sudden vision of her father lying in his best dark suit, with his hands folded on his chest, biding his time till he would suddenly sit up and terrify the gathering with one of his cruel remarks. This made her give a convulsive gulping sob that jerked Reggie upright in his seat as if he'd been pulled by a string from the ceiling.

"All right, darling?" he whispered, but she only shook her head and sobbed again.

The church was packed with people who had come in order to be seen at the biggest funeral for years, to mingle with the richest members of local society, and to make it known they were on friendly terms with one of the most important men in the Borders. There were others, especially his business rivals, who had turned up to reassure themselves that the old devil really was dead. Like his daughter, they wouldn't put it past him to hop out of the coffin and announce he'd fooled them.

The minister, entering from the vestry at that very moment of Helen's deepest sob, caught the full force of the air of anticipation building up among the congregation and hastened to begin the service. It wouldn't do to upset young Mrs Hunt, who looked on the point of collapse, any longer than was absolutely necessary because he had great hopes of her future patronage. The steeple needed re-pointing and the cost of that would be trivial for such a rich woman if she could be persuaded to subsidise the project in memory of her late father.

To everyone's relief the doleful funeral service droned to its end without Helen fainting and when she stepped out towards the car that was to take her to the burying ground, she realised with a rush of surprise that spring had crept up on the world almost unnoticed. The sloping banks of grass at the cemetery gates were carpeted with yellow and white daffodils and a mild wind was blowing off the river Gala, making hazel catkins wave playfully about like little furry banners. Banks of fluffy clouds were sailing slowly across across a pale blue sky. If Howie had been a man given to appreciating the beauties of nature, he would have been flattered that the town where he had made his fortune was looking so good for his final appearance.

After the coffin was safely settled in the ground, the minister announced to the people at the graveside that they were invited for 'refreshments' to Castledevon, Howie Gates' fabulous mansion that stood, battlemented and turreted on a slope of high ground outside the town. The house had been built by Helen's grandfather David Benjamin, whose favourite daughter Milly had married Howie Gates when he was forty-one and she was twenty. Like his son-in-law, David was a self-made man, rising from obscure beginnings as the illegitimate son of an itinerant navvy who'd come to the Borders to help build the railways. The navvy's grimly ambitious son went on to rise from an obscure position as a weaving-mill office clerk to owning that mill and several others.

A socially advantageous marriage in middle life with the daughter of a small landowner provided him with three daughters and one son, but the boy was killed in a train derailment and David lost his spirit after that. When the up-and-coming Howie Gates showed interest in buying his mills, he threw in his daughter Milly as well and when he died he left the couple the mansion that he had built in the days when his fortune and optimism ran high.

There was almost a party atmosphere among the crowds of people who made their way to Castledevon after Howie was buried. Many of them were curious; the dead man had not been hospitable and rarely entertained, so local curiosity ran high about his mansion.

The people at his wake were not disappointed for the butler ushered them into a forty-foot long drawing room with one wall taken up by four tall windows staring out across manicured lawns. The other walls were lined with immense gilt-framed mirrors that doubled, tripled, quadrupled the room's interior. Three enormous crystal chandeliers like cascades of glittering teardrops hung from plaster bosses of lifelike flowers and fruit in the ceiling.

For no expense had been spared in the creation of Castledevon. The architect had been imported from France; the plasterers from Italy; the interior decorators from London and New York. The carpets were commissioned in Turkey, the silk curtains woven in China. The floors were laid with planks of exotic woods and the front doorstep covered with an enormous plate of beaten brass that two housemaids had to kneel and burnish every day. This was Galashiels' version of Versailles, as remote from the lives of the people who manned the looms of the Gates' mills as Marie Antionette's court was to the *sans culottes*.

The new owner of all the magnificence, little Helen Hunt stood in the middle of the floor accepting condolences.

Few things make a person more attractive to their peers than the sudden possession of a vast amount of money, and everybody at Howie's funeral reception wanted to speak to his daughter. Other mill owners and their families crowded round her, curiosity in their eyes. No textile firm in the Borders was owned by a woman and this scrap of a thing didn't look promising. Her husband was no competition either for he was well known to be bluff and pleasant but stupid, so business rivals privately speculated, 'How long will it be before she sells up?' Several of them were already working out ways of raising the cash to buy this or that bit of Howie's vast empire.

After what seemed like an eternity to Helen the room

began to empty, since it was bad form to stay too long at funeral receptions. Finally, when one or two determined stragglers were ushered to the door by Reggie and his brother Colin, only close family remained. Then Helen felt a hand on her arm and the voice of her kindly lawyer, Mr Stevens, saying, "We should go to the library now, Mrs Hunt, for the reading of your father's will. You look tired so you go first and sit down by the fire while I tell the others."

He did not have much rounding up to do because the word that the reading of the will was about to take place flew round the family like wildfire.

When they were all seated Helen stretched out her transparent-looking hands to the flames in the hearth and watched as Mr Stevens carefully took his gold-rimmed spectacles out of their case and perched them on his nose. Then he cleared his throat and began to read the will which was very formal and correct.

The bulk of the estate went to Helen, but Reggie got Howie's horses and Colin his guns. Aunt Liza, Helen's mother's only remaining sister, who had not attended the funeral, was left money and a pair of diamond bracelets, and there were surprisingly generous legacies to the domestic employees and a few of Howie's most trusted mill managers.

When everyone thought the reading was over, the lawyer lifted his head and said, "There's one more clause that your father insisted on putting in, Mrs Hunt. He stipulated that if any male heir presents himself within two years and can prove his link, legitimate or illegitimate, with Howie Gates you are to pass over half of the ownership of the mills to him. If no one makes a claim within that period of time, the mills are entirely yours."

Beside her Helen heard Reggie gasp. "Half of all the mills?" he asked in disbelief. In the Gates empire there were four mills, all large and prosperous, all working round the clock six days a week and all worth upwards of a million pounds.

The lawyer nodded. "I'm afraid so. And he stipulates that no part of the business can be sold before the two years are up to give an heir time to appear. We have been instructed to advertise for anyone with a claim and investigate the applicants thoroughly . . ."

At this everyone in the room began speaking at once – everyone except Helen whose mind went back to her father's last words. She'd not thought about them much because they didn't make sense and she'd dismissed them as a dying man's ramblings. Now she knew that he'd been trying to tell her to find a male heir for his empire because of his contempt for her. She was only a woman and not good enough to take over, as far as he was concerned, and he'd always scoffed at Reggie who was totally uninterested in business.

It was her husband who voiced her next thought. "But he only ever had two daughters and his other daughter Leonie never had any children, had she? She was only eighteen when she died and never married."

"That's true as far as we know," said Mr Stevens carefully.

"Then how could there be a male heir? It's nonsense," snapped Colin, Reggie's brother, a prosperous doctor in Leeds who had inherited his brother's share of the family brains as well as his own.

Mr Stevens folded his papers. "All I can say is that my client Mr Gates insisted on putting in this clause. Perhaps he hoped that Mrs Hunt would have a son." The lawyer knew this to be Howie's greatest desire, for his late client had frequently voiced annoyance at his daughter and her husband because of their failure to produce a child.

"So if Reggie and Helen have a son he gets half the mills in his own right. There's no forgotten male nephews or anyone else with a claim likely to hop out of the woodwork, is there?" said Colin again, looking at his brother and thinking it was up to Reggie to make damned sure that Helen produced a child as soon as possible.

"As far as I knew Mr Gates had no living relatives except his daughter, Mrs Hunt, and any child of hers will certainly inherit without question. Then the problem would be at an end," said the lawyer.

"No," said a voice from the back of the room, "no, it isnae as simple as that."

Everyone turned in their seats and stared at the speaker who was standing with his back to the closed door. He was a rough-looking, dark-haired young man who grinned cheekily when he saw that he'd got the room's astonished attention.

"It's not as simple as that," he said again, enunciating his words more clearly this time as he began to make his way forward through the chairs.

"Who the hell are you and how did you get in here?" asked Colin who seemed to have taken over management of the gathering.

"I told the servant at the door I'm Howie Gates' grandson. I'm Mrs Hunt's nephew. I'm the son of her sister Leonie," said the stranger.

With her heart beating fast, Helen stood up from the chair where she sat and watched the young stranger walk down through the room towards her.

He was not very prepossessing – coarse of face with thick lips and a nose with a reddened, raised bridge that looked as if it had once been broken. His dark hair was plastered down on his head from a centre parting that didn't suit him and gave him an unreliable air.

His clothes were cheap but clean and obviously new; his boots the sort that carters wore. He was completely confident, however, and it was obvious that he was enjoying the sensation he'd caused.

Outraged, Reggie stood up too and walked over to his

wife as if to protect her from the stranger. "What the hell is going on?" he blustered.

Helen patted his hand. "It's all right, Reggie," she said, for to her own surprise she felt more intrigued than frightened. She held out her hand to the stranger, "How do you do," she said politely. "I'm Helen Hunt."

He took it. "I'm Billy Cameron," he told her.

"And you say that my sister Leonie was your mother?" said Helen sweetly.

"Aye, she was."

"How do you know that?"

"I've got witnesses."

Colin was spluttering beside Helen, red-faced and furious. "How come you turn up now? Why haven't any of us heard about you before?" he hissed.

"Because I've only just heard about my grandfather's death – and the friend who told me was the same one that told me I really am Billy Gates."

"A friend told you!" sneered Colin. "Where is this knowledgeable friend?"

"She's outside. The servant wouldnae let her in. She's waiting for me."

Helen acted now. Pulling on the bell rope at the side of the fire to summon Simes the butler, she told him, "Please bring in the person who arrived with Mr Cameron."

"Very good, madam," said the imperturbable Simes and in a few seconds he was back, ushering in a thin woman with a pinched white face, pale eyelashes, no eyebrows and a red-tipped twitching nose that made her look like an albino rabbit. Her clothes were markedly shabby – a threadbare dark coat and an out-of-shape felt hat. Clutched on her stomach was a worn leather handbag which she carried with both hands as if it contained the crown jewels.

"Please sit down and tell us who you are," said Helen, showing the woman to the chair that had been vacated by Reggie who now stood in evident confusion, not quite knowing what to do.

The newcomer had a whining, complaining sort of voice. "I'm Euphemia Grossett," she said.

Helen extended her hand again. "How do you do, Mrs Grossett," she said.

"*Miss* Grossett," said Phemie.

Mr Stevens took over at this stage. "I think it would be best if we discussed this privately, don't you? Let's go through to another room," he said. Trailed by Reggie, the persistent Colin and Helen he led the way into the hall.

"We can go into my parlour," said Helen and opened the door of her private sanctum where another cheerful fire was burning and her dog, a Border terrier called Tikki, slept on the seat of one of the chintz-covered armchairs. When he saw Billy Cameron he sprang to his feet, hair bristling and eyes flashing, growling fiercely.

"Ignore him. I'll ring for some tea," said Helen. The sang-froid of the woman she'd hoped to take by surprise disconcerted Phemie Grossett, who didn't know whether to sit down or stay standing. When she saw Billy throw himself onto the sofa, she did the same with ill grace.

The strangers looked around with open curiosity, and on Phemie's part with envy, at a well stocked fireplace, vases of spring flowers, pictures, books, magazines, a half-finished embroidery and a pet dog. These were the trappings of a comfortable life that contrasted cruelly with the miserable existence Phemie shared with her mother. Her cold stare betrayed some of her loathing to Helen who shivered slightly when she saw it. She had never been so openly hated before.

Colin was about to speak but Mr Stevens held up one hand to stop him. "We'd better get this sorted out properly," he said to Billy Cameron. "Perhaps you could tell us why you think you have a claim to be related to the late Mr Gates."

"I've told you, haven't I?" he said.

Phemie snapped at the same time, "He's Leonie Gates' bairn all right."

Mr Stevens looked coldly at her. "If you don't mind I'd prefer to let Mr Cameron tell me his story himself," he said. Unwillingly, she lapsed into sullen silence.

Billy leaned foward and recited as if he was reeling off a lesson: "My mother was Leonie Gates and she had me in January 1915. Then when I was a week old she gave me to a woman called Mrs Maitland who found homes for unwanted babies. Miss Grossett's mother looked after me for a wee while and then I was given to a couple called Cameron and I stayed with them till I was eighteen."

"And how did you find out you were really Billy Gates?"

"Phemie came down to Leith to tell me two days ago. And she brought a bit of paper from Mrs Maitland saying Leonie Gates was my mother."

"Really," drawled Mr Stevens. "And you believed her?"

At this point Phemie Grossett could stay silent no longer. "Yes, he does," she almost shouted. "I've got the paper here from Mrs Maitland. She told me where to find him. Leonie Gates was the mother . . . My mother minds her coming with the bairn and giving it up. Her father was there too. I've a statement here from my mother. Look for yourself."

She snapped open the tarnished gilt clips of her handbag and pulled out two sheets of paper, which she handed over to the lawyer. He perused them for a long time before passing them to Colin and Reggie.

"Proves nothing," said Colin shortly.

"We'll keep them anyway," said Mr Stevens reaching for them again. Meanwhile a heavily loaded tea tray was borne in and set out on a side table by vastly intrigued servants, so everyone stayed silent till they had left. The moment the door closed, however, Colin burst out angrily to Billy, "But these bits of paper could belong to anyone. How do we know they're yours?"

"They just are," was Billy's reply. "I'm Billy Cameron and the man who brought me up got me from Mrs Maitland because he couldnae have any bairns himself."

"You mean you were sold to Mr Cameron."

The young man grinned. "I suppose I was. They wanted a wee laddie and Mrs Maitland came up wi' me."

"How much did you cost?" sneered Colin.

"Twenty quid," said Billy, grinning. "A bargain, eh?"

"Have you always known this?" asked Mr Stevens. "If you have, why do you call yourself Cameron?"

"I told you. The Camerons adopted me. They called me Cameron but they didn't make any secret of how they got me. I didn't know my real name though till Phemie here got in touch with me two days ago and told me my grandfather had died and I might be due for a bit of money. Mrs Maitland gave her my address."

When he said this Phemie sighed and Mr Stevens' eyes sought her out. "So you alerted Mr Cameron to the possibility of an inheritance. How did you know about it?"

"My mother read old Gates' death notice in the paper and told me she'd looked after his grandson when he was a baby. She was fond of the wee laddie."

"Really? And how did she know the baby was Mr Gates' daughter's child?"

"Because she was there when the mother handed the baby over."

When she heard this Helen felt an agonising stab of pity in her heart for the sister she could barely remember. How awful that Leonie had to give away her baby!

"This Mrs Maitland, did she run a baby farm or something?" asked Mr Stevens.

"She found homes for babies that the mothers couldn't

24

keep but didn't want to go into orphanages or foundling homes."

"And presumably the mothers, the fathers or their parents paid for this service?"

"Why not?" snapped Phemie. "Mrs Maitland only worked for the best people."

Helen shivered again in spite of the heat from the fire and looked at Billy Cameron. How old would Leonie be when he was born? she wondered and started to work it out. He said he was born in 1915 and Leonie was twelve years older than Helen.

"I'm twenty-six," she thought, "and it's 1936 . . . If Leonie was still alive she'd be thirty-eight so she must have been born in 1898. In 1915 she'd have been seventeen . . . so young to have a baby!"

Her thoughts were interrupted by Mr Stevens leaning forward in his chair to question Billy Cameron. "Do you have a birth certificate naming Leonie Gates as your mother?"

The young man shook his head. "No; Mr and Mrs Cameron adopted me."

"In that case your claim on Mr Gates' estate will be difficult to establish," said Mr Stevens severely. "You'll have to prove your case and we also have to advertise for a Gates heir as Mr Gates' will stipulated. Someone else might turn up with as good a claim as you."

"I'm his lassie's bairn, and I should get the money," snapped Billy. Just then Helen asked from her corner by the fire, "Can a girl legitimately marry at seventeen?"

"Yes, in Scotland they can, and a marriage verbally contracted before witnesses is legal here as well. It legitimises any children," Mr Stevens sorrowfully told her. "The witnesses to any pledged marriage entered into by Miss Leonie Gates would have to be found of course . . ." He looked grimly at Phemie Grossett when he said this.

"What about my inheritance then? How much'll I get?" asked Billy who was tiring of the legal technicalities.

"I'm afraid that there has to be a good deal more investigating before any claim can even be entertained," said Mr Stevens firmly. "We have no proof that you say you are who you claim to be. Your story is very suspect and there's a great deal to be cleared up before there is any question of your inheriting anything."

"Suspect is it?" snapped Phemie, "We'll get ourselves a lawyer and he'll tell you what's suspect. Billy here has a legitimate claim. Mrs Maitland says he's the Gates baby that was given to her in 1915 and placed by her with Mr and Mrs Cameron in Leith. Cameron will back that up too. You can't do Billy out of his due!"

"No one is trying to do Mr Cameron out of anything," said Mr Steven severely. "But his case has to be proved conclusively before I can authorise him to receive a penny of the Gates money."

"So you're sending us off empty-handed are you?" shouted Phemie. "We've laid out good money for train fares to come here and you're sending us off with nothing!"

"Damn right," said Reggie but Helen stood up and held up both hands in a placating attitude.

"Please, please," she said. "Please keep calm. Of course we're not sending you away with nothing. Reggie, give Mr Cameron and Miss Grossett five pounds each and I will also give Mr Cameron a cheque for twenty pounds to keep him going in the mean time."

As she was speaking she walked across to her writing desk and pulled open the drawer where she kept her cheque book.

"Helen!" admonished Reggie, and Mr Stevens said, "You don't have to do this, Mrs Hunt."

"But I want to. If this man is my sister's child, it's the

26

least I can do and if he isn't, it doesn't matter. What's twenty pounds to me?"

"My God, Helen, you were marvellous!" Reggie looked at his wife with incredulous admiration in his eyes when Phemie Grossett and Billy Cameron were finally shown the door by a grim-faced Simes.

His astonishment was shared by his brother, who had till then felt little respect for Reggie's frail and fey wife whose only redeeming feature as far as Colin was concerned was her money and the expectation of her inheriting even more.

"Was I?" she asked in genuine surprise for she had acted without any artifice and listened only to her instincts when handling Billy Cameron.

"That was a master stroke, paying him off with twenty pounds. It's probably nineteen more than he expected to gain from this surprise visit," said Colin.

"But I only gave them money because I felt sorry for them. They both looked so *poor*. I thought if he's really Leonie's son, it's a tragedy for him to be so very poor."

"My dear girl," said Colin, his usual exasperation against Helen returning, "they're just a pair of crooks. They were damned lucky we didn't call the police and have them arrested, though it did cross my mind, I have to admit."

"But he had those papers," she protested.

"Forgeries," said Colin confidently. "You wait and see. They'll turn out to be as false as a three-pound note. If that young hooligan is your sister's child, I'm Father Christmas."

But Helen shook her head. "They sounded so sure, so confident and the woman said her mother remembers Leonie . . ."

As she spoke she thought that if Miss Grossett's mother remembered her sister it was more than she did herself, for all she knew was that she'd had a sister called Leonie who had died young and left only a vague sadness and very few memories behind her.

"Do most people have vivid memories of when they were five or six?" she suddenly asked Colin, who was a specialist in diseases of the brain.

He stared at her as if she'd really lost her mind. "What do you mean?" he asked.

"I mean how much can you remember of what happened to you when you were five years old? What about you, Reggie?" she added turning to her husband.

"Not much," they both admitted, and she nodded with relief. "Then it's not just me who has a poor memory. I can't even remember what Leonie looked like. Come to that I can't remember much about my mother either. And I was about five when Leonie died and my mother went away the same year."

Colin glanced at his brother. "Very sad, but we're getting off the point, I'm afraid. Decisions have to be taken about what's to be done about this Will of your father's."

Helen looked at her lawyer who said, "We'll do what he asked us to do. We'll advertise for an heir and wait to find out if the Cameron boy can establish a serious claim."

"If you advertise," said Colin, "every dishonest hopeful in Scotland who's ever heard of Gates' Mills will be down here with a good story and his hand held out. If Helen gives each of them twenty pounds it's going to cost her thousands. I think old Gates put that clause into his will to force her and Reggie into having a baby." He switched his glance to Reggie. "Sorry to be brutal, old boy, but it's time you set about it. It's your duty!"

Helen flushed scarlet and Reggie, seeing her confusion, interrupted his brother. "Come on Colin, don't say things like that. You'll upset Helen."

"It's about time somebody did some straight talking

28

around here. There's nothing physically wrong with either of you and there's no reason why you can't have a child. It's what your father wanted, Helen. You wouldn't be advertising for your sister's bastard if you'd had a son, and you know that as well as me," an unrepentant Colin told her.

The embarrassed Mr Stevens, who was gathering up his papers in preparation for leaving, coughed and said, "I'll draft a discreet advertisement, Mrs Hunt. We'll put it in *The Scotsman* and *The Times* . . ."

Colin sneered. "Hardly likely to catch the eyes of the Mr Camerons of this world in those newspapers, is it? But perhaps that's the idea."

Mr Stevens did not reply but kept looking at Helen. "And, if you like, I'll engage a private investigator to enquire into Mr Cameron's claim," he said.

"That's a very good idea," she told him.

A short time later, while her husband was seeing his brother and the rest of the family out of the house, Helen sat staring into the parlour fire, fighting against an unaccustomed tide of rage that was rising in her.

'It's not fair, it's not fair,' she told herself. 'Colin obviously blames me for not having a baby but it's really Reggie's fault. Does Colin know that his brother has a mistress in Edinburgh that he visits once a week – and more often if he gets the chance? Does he know that when Reggie's at home he drinks himself almost insensible at dinner and is no more capable of giving me a child than he is of flying to the moon? Am I supposed to welcome him into my bed in spite of those things?'

For the first time in six years she openly faced the fact that her marriage was a sham. Till then she'd pretended to herself and the rest of the world that the lack of passion between her and Reggie didn't matter because the act of sex repelled her and she was terrified at the idea of giving birth to a baby.

Yet, when she first married, she'd really thought she was in love with him and was immensely flattered that he'd chosen her for his wife. In those days he'd been a dashing, sports-car driving playboy, public school educated by ambitious parents who looked down their noses at Howie Gates' daughter as a consort for their glamorous son.

Like Howie, they'd been mill owners too but their fortune had been established for three generations and they'd reached the stage of thinking themselves well-born people who didn't want their sons sullying their hands with trade. Clever Colin had gone into medicine and Reggie tried the army, but came home again in search of a rich bride when it became obvious that the family fortunes were on the wane.

Helen Gates filled his bill perfectly for she was young, pretty enough, totally malleable and *rich*. To do him justice, the fact that she would one day be extremely rich did not weigh as heavily with Reggie as it did with the rest of his family.

Howie Gates had consented to the match with a certain amount of grim satisfaction. He knew very well that the lordly Hunts looked down on him as a rough and ready Johnny-come-lately and now they needed his money. So he gave Reggie a sinecure job in the management of his mills but no real power, because he was a shrewd judge of men and could tell that running a successful business was not within his new son-in-law's capacities. That was left to Howie's trusted managers and all Reggie had to do was walk about looking important – and produce a child with Helen, ideally a son to carry on the business. In that last requirement, however, he failed completely.

As Helen stared angrily into the fire she felt little Tikki creep up beside her feet, wagging his tail so hard that it beat a tattoo of love and devotion on the hearthrug.

30

"Darling Tikki," she said patting his rough-haired head, "you love me, don't you?"

At that moment Reggie came through the door and coughed. "I love you too, Helen," he said.

She looked across at him, wondering where the handsome man she'd married had gone. Now his fine figure had thickened with years of good living, his paunch stuck out and his cheeks had become like turkey wattles. He looked like a Roman emperor gone to seed.

"Do you really, Reggie?" she asked.

"Of course I do."

"Then why do you keep a mistress?"

He gaped at her in undisguised amazement. "A mistress?" he asked in a questioning voice, but he was only playing for time.

"Yes, a mistress called Mrs Eleanor Wishart who lives in Edinburgh. A very pleasant person I believe."

"Who told you?"

"I've known for ages. One of my friends told me and her husband told her. He's a friend of Mrs Wishart's brother."

He rolled his eyes in panic. "Eleanor is an old friend. I've known her longer than I've known you."

"But she's a widow now, isn't she? My friend said her husband died last year. Do you want to leave me, Reggie?"

"Of course not, Helen. I've told you. I love you. If you want me to, I'll stop seeing Eleanor."

In his own way he was telling the truth, for he was genuinely fond of his wife and not just because his life at Castledevon was so very comfortable. Helen was such a funny little thing, scared of life, timid, almost virginal. He thought of himself as her protector because she was so vulnerable. When her horrible old father was alive, it was Reggie who protected her from Howie's evil temper and cruel tongue, and now he was dead, Reggie was ready

31

to take upon himself the mission of protecting her from villains like Cameron.

He walked across to the fireplace and bent down beside her. "I really love you, Helen. Maybe Colin's right. Maybe we should try again, try living like ordinary married people . . ."

She looked up at him. "You mean we should sleep together. We haven't done that for at least four years, have we?"

He nodded. "Shall we try? Do you want me to stop seeing Eleanor?"

"I don't know. It all seems rather artificial, doesn't it, us sleeping together because of Father's will? I'm not actually very sure that I want a baby, you see . . ."

"And you're not very sure that you want to sleep with me either, are you?"

"I wanted to once," she told him.

"Will we try again?" he asked.

She looked back into the fire. Reggie was really a decent man at heart, she realised, and what had gone wrong between them was probably her fault as much as his, but what she said was, "Sometime, perhaps, but not now. Don't worry, though, Reggie, I don't want to leave you. Things can just go on as they've always done."

On the way back to Edinburgh on the train Phemie was jubilant.

"They're scared. You've got them scared!" she hissed to Billy, glad that they had managed to find an empty compartment and could talk. "Did you see that house? You could be living in a place like that soon."

He squinted sceptically at her. "I wouldnae want it," he said.

"You'd get used to it. My word, you've got them on the run or they wouldn't have given you all that money."

32

"Twenty quid's all they gave me – and a fiver each," said Billy.

"That's only a start. What we need now is a lawyer. We need somebody to fight our case for us."

"*We?*"

She bristled. "Dinna forget if it wasnae for me you'd never have heard a word about Howie Gates. We've done a deal, mind, half for me and half for you."

"Half?" asked Billy.

"That's what we agreed."

"That was before I saw the place. Half could be an awful lot."

"Let's settle this before we go any farther," she said turning towards him. "I'll settle for ten thousand."

"You're being awful reasonable," said Billy sarcastically. "A thousand's more like it."

"No, ten, and I want it written down. I'll find us a lawyer and we can do it right."

Billy sighed and closed his eyes, thinking of how he was going to spend his five-pound note in the bars of Leith that night.

"Go ahead," he said for he didn't really think the affair would go any farther. He'd got twenty-five quid out of it and to him that seemed a small fortune. It didn't really matter if he didn't get another penny. He'd never been entirely convinced by Phemie's story anyway when she turned up at the Leith docks where he was working in the ice factory and said he was the heir to a fortune.

"Give me that cheque," she said when they disembarked from their carriage in Waverley Station.

"Eh?" He looked blank.

"Give me the cheque. We need the money so's we can hire that lawyer."

He glowered, dreams of a week on the beer fading. "It's my money. She gave it to me," he protested.

"You'll get a damned sight more than twenty quid if

33

you play your cards right," said the pest of a woman.

"Och, it's all nonsense," said he.

"It's not. There's a fortune at stake and if you go along
with me, you can have it."

He threw back his black head and laughed. "You're
daft," he said.

"I'm no' daft. It's you that's daft if you throw this
chance away." She grasped the cloth of his coat and said
urgently, "I'm telling you this'll work. They'll pay you
off even if they don't give you half the mills. They'll
have to give you at least a hundred thousand. I asked
one of the men in a lawyer's office where I clean what
Howie Gates' mills would be worth and he said probably
a million. I just about died when I heard that lawyer say
you'd get half of it. They'll be happy to settle for a
hundred thousand."

He wrinkled his brows and stared at her. It was glar-
ingly obvious that she was totally sincere and believed
what she said. Billy was lazy and greedy, as well as
not being too intelligent, and the prospect she dangled
before him seemed *perhaps* attainable, just as it had
done when he'd agreed to accompany her to Castledevon
Even if he wasn't Gates' grandson, surely he could
pretend to be? The ethics of the affair didn't bother
him a bit.

"Give me the cheque," she said again.

"It's mine," he protested once more.

"You'll no' be able to get a bank to cash it. One look
at you and they'll think you've stolen it."

He took the folded slip of paper out of his pocket
and stared at it. He'd never handled a cheque before
and didn't know that 'Pay Bearer' meant he could cash
it even if he hadn't a bank account. Moreover, he'd
been in trouble with the police in the past and didn't
want to go through the experience again. If the bank

called in the law, one of the bobbies might recognise him and would be only too ready to think he'd stolen the cheque.

Phemie brandished her five-pound note beneath his nose. "Take this and give me the cheque. I'll use it to get us a lawyer," she wheedled. He gave in.

One of the lawyers' offices that Phemie worked for was a firm called Wedderburn and Casson, though – as was the way with many legal firms – there was neither a Wedderburn nor a Casson still in the office. One of the partners a few years ago had been a man called Herbert Johnstone, who had recently served a period in prison and was forbidden to practise law any longer for systematically swindling his clients out of money which he'd squandered on drink and high living.

His case had greatly entertained Phemie and her mother, both of whom enjoyed the spectacle of seeing the great brought low – especially when it was someone they knew vaguely. They had avidly followed its progress in *The Scotsman*'s legal reports.

By coincidence, a few weeks before Howie Gates' death, Phemie had caught sight of Mr Johnstone shuffling down Leith Walk, obviously a broken man. Out of malicious curiosity, she'd followed at a distance and watched him disappear into the main door of a foetid tenement at the bottom of the Walk. It gave her and her mother considerable pleasure to know that the once prosperous lawyer, who'd had a house in Moray Place, now lived in conditions worse than their own.

It was to that same tenement that she headed the evening she got off the train from Galashiels. Mr Johnstone's new home was a ramshackle, paint-peeling building, the ground floor of which was occupied by a public house called the Three Bells. It was the lowest kind of pub, with sawdust on the floor and a foul smell of stale beer filling the air. When Phemie first entered, her courage almost failed her, but she braved the hostile male eyes at the bar and said,

"I'm looking for Herbert Johnstone. I wondered if you knew which floor he lives on."

"He's in the snug," said the barman, pointing to a partition which was fenced off the far end of the room.

Herbert Johnstone, unshaven and dishevelled, was sitting alone at a table staring morosely into an empty glass. He did not look up when she stood beside him.

"Mr Johnstone, d'ye mind me? I used to shine the brass at Wedderburn and Casson . . ."

"Yes, I remember you." His glance slid over her indifferently.

She pulled over a rickety chair and sat down, clutching her handbag as she always did. "I've a proposition for you, Mr Johnstone." He looked almost scared as she said this so she hastened to add, "I want some advice and I'll pay for it."

"I don't practise any longer," he said.

"I know that, but I mind when you were the cleverest man at Wedderburn's. Maybe you could advise me and a friend of mine about a claim he's making to a fortune . . ." She launched into the story of Billy Cameron.

When she finished he shoved his empty glass at her and said, "Fill that for me, please."

She scrabbled in her bag to find enough small change to buy him a whisky and as it was laid in front of him, he said, "You say Mrs Maitland who used to live in George Square placed the child with a family called Cameron in Leith. You're sure of that?"

"She told me herself."

"And it was Leonie Gates' child?"

"Yes."

"And the Camerons corroborate this?"

"Mrs Cameron's dead but I found Billy by going to see Mr Cameron and he said that he'd got the boy from Mrs

Maitland." She didn't add that Mr Cameron had also said that he never wanted to see his adopted son again because the boy had turned out to be a 'bad one'. He knew where Billy was working – in the nearby ice factory – and that was all Phemie needed.

Johnstone took a draw at his whisky and sighed. "Mrs Maitland's a dangerous woman to get involved with. She's got quite a reputation, you know."

Phemie opened her eyes wide. "Has she? My mother used to work for her and she's never said anything like that."

"Take it from me, she has. She found homes for unwanted babies maybe, but she also lends money at high rates of interest and she owns a lot of property in Edinburgh. If her tenants don't pay their rents, they sometimes have accidents . . . She's not a woman to cross."

"I'm no' wanting to cross her. If Billy Cameron gets his due, he'll see she gets her share and she knows that."

"So she'll back him up in his claim?"

"Oh yes," said Phemie, keeping her fingers crossed.

"What do you want me to do?"

"We need a lawyer, someone who can tell us the best way to go about getting Billy's claim accepted and also to draw up a contract between me and Billy. I dinna trust him to keep his bargain with me."

He looked searchingly at her and shoved his glass in her direction again so that she was forced to spend her last coppers on another whisky.

"I'll think about it," he said, "Bring Cameron to see me here tomorrow night."

Three

After a sleepless night during which she was beleagured by tearful thoughts about the dead sister she barely remembered, Helen decided to pay a visit to her aunt Liza who lived in grim state in an imposing house in Rosewell's most exclusive road. She stared balefully at her niece when Helen was shown in, but being Liza, she took the initiative.

"What's this I hear about someone claiming to be your sister's child turning up at the funeral yesterday?" she demanded, laying down her embroidery.

"Irene and Alice were there. They must have told you what happened," countered Helen. Irene and Alice were her cousins, Liza's daughters, who had been at the will reading. They would certainly have hot-footed it back to their mother with the news after leaving Castledevon.

"I want to hear your version," said Liza.

"A man called Billy Cameron walked in and said he's my sister Leonie's illegitimate child," Helen told her rather snappily. She added, "I've come to ask you what you know about my sister. Did she really have an illegitimate baby? Reggie thinks the man's an imposter."

"I'm afraid he could be your sister's child."

"You mean Leonie did have a baby?"

"I mean she got herself in trouble. I never saw any baby, but your mother and father took care of that."

Helen remembered her father's last words . . . *find Leonie's boy* . . . He hadn't been rambling at all.

"When did she have it?" she asked in a shocked whisper, all her bravado gone.

Liza lifted the embroidery off her chair arm and made a careful stitch. "Nineteen-fifteen," she said.

"That's the year he said he was born. What else do you know about it?" persisted Helen, who realised information would have to be extracted from Liza like teeth. Secrets were the lifeblood of her world.

"Nothing really. Milly, your mother, was always so secretive. It was only by accident that I even discovered the girl was pregnant – and I was her aunt, for goodness' sake! Milly just told me they were sending her to Italy to be finished, and that's what they did but before she went she saw my doctor and his wife let slip the secret to me. Leonie was pregnant and they were sending her away to have the baby."

"Was it born in Italy then?" Helen's head was swimming.

"No. Because there was so much talk of war that summer, Milly went to Italy and brought the girl back but she didn't bring her to Castledevon. Though it wasn't the shooting season they went to the Highlands, to a sporting lodge our father took every year and when they came back Leonie looked perfectly normal and the matter was never referred to again. It must have been born up in Argyll but, as I've told you, Milly didn't take me into her confidence. We were not close."

"Do you think they told Aunt Agnes?" Helen asked. Agnes, a much more sweet-natured woman than Liza, her sister, had brought Helen up after the disappearance of her mother. All Helen's memories of her other aunt were sweet ones and she had grieved sorely when Agnes died just months before Helen's marriage.

"No, she didn't or Agnes would have told me. We talked about it a lot and she knew no more than I did. If Milly talked to anyone, it was to that crony of hers over in Falconwood, that Lady Rutherford. They were as thick as thieves."

Lady Kitty Rutherford of Falconwood, whom Helen had never actually met, was a well-known local character loathed by the ultra-respectable ladies of the mill magnate society because of her chequered past and obscure origins. Rumour had it she was the illegitimate daughter of a bondaged farm worker and an Irish navvy, who had by some means inherited a fortune and married well. Money and a good marriage were not enough, however, for the wives and daughters of the mill owners to overlook her beginnings. Socially she was beyond the pale as far as they were concerned – title or no title.

"I could go over to Falconwood and ask Lady Rutherford about it," said Helen.

"Is that wise?" asked Liza. "You don't want to go around discussing family business with people like her, surely?"

"Well, I've got to get to the bottom of this. I've got to find out if this man Cameron is Leonie's child. Surely if Lady Rutherford knows anything she'll tell me."

Liza pursed her lips and stabbed her needle into the embroidery canvas. "Well, when you're at it, you might ask her where your mother is now," she said vindictively.

Helen stared at her, genuinely astonished. "But my mother's dead. Agnes told me that long ago, when I was small."

"Agnes told you a lie. She wanted to spare your feelings. Your mother bolted and left you and your father after Leonie died . . ."

"I knew she went away when I was five, but Agnes said that she was ill and had to go to live in a sunny climate. Some time later she told me she'd died."

"Agnes was sparing you. Milly just took off and we've never heard from her again, but I know she draws a small annuity from our father's estate and if she had died we'd have heard about it. The lawyer pays her money into a London bank but we have no idea where she's living. She's so hard-hearted! I know she was my sister but that doesn't mean that I wasn't aware of her faults. Your mother was a very selfish woman who never gave a thought to anyone else but herself."

"Why?" Helen gasped.

"Why what?"

"Why did she run away? Was she unhappy?"

"She went after Leonie drowned herself. That hit her hard. Your father was broken-hearted too, but Milly never gave him a thought. Off she went to the station in her carriage with four cabin trunks, a big box of jewellery and a maid when he was out at business and when he came back all he found was a note from her. I never cared for Howie, I have to admit, but I was sorry for him that day."

Helen was staring in consternation at the stitching woman. "What did you say just now?" she whispered. There was a funny singing in her ears and she felt faint.

Liza paused. "Didn't you hear anything I said? You never listen, Helen."

"What did you say about Leonie drowning herself? I thought she got ill and died. That's what Agnes said . . ."

A look of uncertainty crossed Liza's face. She'd said too much and she realised it now. "Oh, you must have heard about that," she blustered. "She went fishing in the Tweed and she was drowned. I didn't mean she actually drowned *herself* – it was an accident of course. That's what the inquiry said."

"Inquiry? Fishing?" As far as she knew none of the women of Helen's family had ever fished, though the men did.

"Well not fishing exactly, paddling really . . ."

"Paddling?"

41

"Do stop repeating what I say. The important thing was that she drowned."

"How awful. Why has no one ever told me this before?"

"I suppose they kept it from you because you were so young and afterwards it just wasn't talked about."

That was true. Helen had no memory of her father even mentioning his elder daughter's name. Suddenly she wanted to escape from Aunt Liza. She wanted to be alone so that she could think. So much was happenng, she was learning too many things all at once. She must be alone so she could sit down and think about them.

"I'm going now," she said, standing up. There was a gleam of malice in Liza's eyes as she looked up at her niece and Helen realised with a sinking heart that her new accession to wealth had alienated her mother's sister.

"I hope you're going home to have dinner with Reggie. The pair of you are hardly ever together those days. If you were nicer to him he wouldn't be rushing off to Edinburgh so often."

So she knows about Reggie's mistress as well, thought Helen, but said nothing. Before she left the room, however, she suddenly turned and asked her aunt, "Who was the father of Leonie's baby?"

Liza gave a little cry as her needle stabbed into her finger. "Look what you've made me do!" she exclaimed, brandishing a thumb spotted with a ruby of blood.

"Who was the father?" Helen asked again.

"I have absolutely no idea," said Liza firmly – too firmly – and Helen knew that what Liza was concealing was one of those sacrosanct family secrets that she would never divulge.

"What a terrible family this is for keeping secrets," she said, turning to go away.

One of the unexpected things about shy, retiring Helen Hunt was that she liked to drive her own car. While other

42

women of her society preferred to be driven here and there by uniformed chauffeurs, Helen had learned to drive and often took the wheel herself, ignoring the protests of her husband who disapproved of women drivers. It was the only unusual, rebellious thing she ever did.

She also drove fast. Perched up in her roaring Lanchester, she tore along quiet roads, scattering squawking hens who wandered about around farm steadings. As she drove away from her aunt's house that morning, she looked at her watch and noticed it was nearly eleven o'clock. There was still time to find out about Leonie's death before lunch if she drove even faster than usual.

The office and printing works of the local newspaper, which reported every event of significance in the district from flower shows to funerals, was situated in an old building facing the square in the heart of the town of Selkirk.

A tiny bell tinkled when Helen pushed open the street door that had the newspaper's name written on it in cursive gold embossed lettering and found herself in a sparsely furnished room with a long pine-topped counter running parallel to a back wall on which hung a red and white wall-calendar. A bentwood chair stood beside the counter but there was no sign of human life. A strong smell of tobacco, paper and printing ink hung in the air and from the back premises came the clattering and thudding of a printing press.

Then a door opened and a pleasant looking grey-haired and jacketless man with expanding metal bands around his shirt sleeves came through from the back premises. He smiled at her and asked, "What can I do for you, madam?"

She said who she was and he nodded as if he'd known that already. Then she asked if he kept back numbers of the newspaper in the office.

"Right back to 1807," he exclaimed proudly. "Imagine

that! Every week since 1807, and I'm only the fourth editor. Mackie's the name; Edward Mackie. Four editors in nearly a hundred and thirty years. It must be a healthy job I always say."

"When did you take over?" she asked.

"I became editor in 1910, but I was chief reporter before that and message laddie even earlier. I've worked here all my life and I'm seventy-two now," was the prompt reply.

She gazed at him wide-eyed as if he was the answer to a prayer. "Then you must have been editor when my sister Leonie Gates drowned. I was wondering if there was anything in the paper about it at the time. That's why I'm here now."

His wise brown eyes that scanned her face as she spoke showed pity and no longer was he lighthearted and flippant. He nodded slowly and said, "I remember when Miss Gates drowned. It was very sad."

Helen sighed. "I think so too. It was in 1915, I believe, but I'm not sure of the exact date. I'd be most obliged if you would let me see the newspapers for that year and I'll look for any report."

Like a courtier he held up a little flap at the end of the counter and gestured for her to come through. "That's no trouble at all. I've a good idea when it happened. We'll look for it together," he said.

The back copies of the newspaper were bound up in huge, leather-covered books, one for each year, and piled on the floor of a dusty room beyond the large space where the thudding press was standing. A man in a white apron was tending the press and a rumple-haired youth in wire-rimmed spectacles was standing beside him.

Introducing the youth as his chief reporter, Mr Mackie told him to get out the volume of back numbers for 1915 and put it on a trestle table. Dust flew up in the air when it was thumped down. Then the editor began ruffling the pages, muttering, "It was late summer, I'm sure . . . Yes, I'm right. They said at the inquest that she was fishing and the season had not long started. I attended the inquest myself . . ."

Helen nodded silently, remembering the large collection of unused fishing rods that always stood in a tall china container in the front hall of Castledevon. No one ever used them and she had always been forbidden to go down to the river on her own. Mr Mackie was still turning over pages and then gave a cry of triumph. "Here it is. I was right. It was the first week of September. Lovely weather, I remember."

Helen leaned over his shoulder and read where his finger was pointing. It was only a small paragraph at the bottom of a long column of jingoistic stuff about young men rushing to join the army and fight for their country. All it said was that the body of Miss Leonie Gates, 18, eldest daughter of Albert Gates of Castledevon, Galashiels, had been recovered from the River Tweed near her home. It was believed she'd drowned while fishing.

In the following week's issue, Mackie found another even smaller entry which said that at an inquest on Miss Leonie Gates a verdict of accidental death was returned.

Helen gave a little cry of relief between a gasp and a sob. "It *was* an accident," she said.

Mr Mackie closed the book with a thud and stood back shaking his head. "You're her sister. You should know the truth. I wouldn't go talking about this to other people but you're entitled to the facts. It wasn't an accident. She'd tied a rock round her waist and lain down in the water. I believe she left a note too but it wasn't mentioned at the inquest. They covered it all up. I did too. I wrote that report and I was at the inquest but everybody reckoned the family had suffered enough and she was only a lassie. It wouldn't have been fair to deny her a Christian burial . . . Some things are best glossed over."

Helen leaned her elbows on the trestle table and held her head in her hands. Warm tears slid down her cheeks and she was shaking uncontrollably. "Oh dear, oh dear," she whispered, "I had no idea. No one ever told me. I've only just found out she was drowned. Why did she do it?"

She looked up at the concerned man by her side and repeated the question, "Why did she do it?"

He shook his head. "Nobody had any idea. All the witnesses said she seemed happy before it happened. There was no sign of depression or anything like that. They said she was the last girl they'd expect to kill herself; so full of life with a lot to live for."

Helen stood up straight and asked, "Were my parents at the inquest?"

"Yes. Your father gave evidence of identifying the body and I could see he was very angry. Your mother just sat like a ghost in the front of the court through the hearing and when it was over she walked out all on her own like a character from a Greek tragedy, a tall woman, all in black. Nothing was said about the stone around the girl's waist or the note she left."

"How did you hear about them?" asked Helen.

"A friend of mine was the policeman who had to wade into the river and pull her body out. He told me about the rock, all tied up in a white scarf he said. He was the one who had to break the news to Howie, your father, and that was when the note was found in the girl's bedroom. He said when Howie read it he went mad, shouting and cursing and carrying on. He even tore the note up before anybody could stop him. Everybody decided to forget about it. The girl was dead, wasn't she? Digging things up wouldn't bring her back."

"Would your policeman friend tell me what happened if I go to see him?" Helen asked but Mr Mackie shook his head. "He's been dead for fifteen years, I'm afraid."

He was so touched by her shocked appearance and

paper-white face that he offered her a cup of tea but she declined, shook his hand and left.

"If I remember anything else, I'll let you know, Mrs Hunt," he promised as he showed her out.

It was now past twelve but she didn't go home. Instead she headed west, for the village of Camptounfoot where the house called Falconwood stood.

It was a handsome house, built at the end of the eighteenth century from golden-coloured stone and carefully situated on the top of a dominating bluff above the River Tweed. Over the years since it was built, a forest of beech, oak and chestnut trees had grown close around it, holding it safe against prying eyes.

Not for Falconwood the vainglorious turrets and spires of Castledevon; it sat low, modestly two storeyed, in a U-shape facing south, curled like a basking cat. The front door was on the top level and approached by a flight of curving stairs with iron balustrades that curved outwards to accommodate ladies in crinoline skirts.

Barely noticing the beautiful garden and the fountain in the shape of a fish with water spouting from its mouth that stood in the forecourt, Helen Hunt ran up the steps and pulled the bell that hung by the side of the door. It was too early for social calls really but she hoped that the woman who lived there would see her. According to local gossip, Lady Kitty did not stand on ceremony.

A young woman with russet-coloured hair and a freckled face answered the door. She was obviously not a servant.

"I'm so sorry to arrive on your doorstep without making an appointment first," gasped Helen. "My name's Helen Hunt from Castledevon and I'm most anxious to speak to Lady Rutherford about a private matter concerning my mother, Milly Gates . . ."

The girl in the doorway did not look too surprised but

stood back and ushered the importunate caller into a large hall with a black and white tiled floor, saying, "Wait here and I'll ask if she'll see you."

Within what was really only moments she was back, smiling and welcoming. "She can, but only for a little while because she hasn't eaten yet and she tires easily. Come this way please."

Though she'd never been close to her before Helen could see that Kitty Rutherford had once been beautiful but was now fading away with grace. Her once abundant red hair was white and sparse but her wilful spirit was unchanged and her curiosity still avid.

"So you're Milly's girl," she said, turning her gaze away from the river where a solitary heron was stalking fish in the glittering shallows. Her accent was broad Border.

"Yes, I'm Helen Gates – Helen Hunt, I mean."

"Milly and Howie's daughter, Reggie's wife," said Kitty in a slightly sceptical tone, "and very rich now that your father's dead, I believe."

The young woman pulled out a chair for Helen beside Kitty's couch and she perched awkwardly on it, wondering what to say.

"I'm so sorry to descend on you like this but I believe you were a friend of my mother," she started.

The old woman's eyes were amused as she looked at the visitor but she didn't answer Helen's question. "It's not often I get callers from Galashiels," she said. Helen flushed for she knew very well that none of her friends or relations would ever dream of dropping in at Falconwood.

Kitty saw the blush and relented. "I read about your father's death in the newspaper," she said. "I knew him when he was only a laddie and I knew your grandfather too. Do you know why your father was always called *Howie* when his real name was Albert?"

Helen shook her head. The origin of her father's nickname had never bothered her.

"It was because when he was wee he was always asking questions – How's this, how's that? So they called him Howie." Kitty Rutherford laughed.

Helen laughed too in a nervous way and said, "I never knew that!" The two women looked at each other in a more friendly way and the atmosphere in the room lightened a little.

"So you've come to see me about the naughty Milly. Why exactly?" asked the old woman and Helen, abandoning discretion, launched into the story of Billy Cameron, ending up with, "My Aunt Liza says you were friendly with my mother and you might know if she's still alive and where she is now. We've got to get to the bottom of this business and she's the only one who can tell us what happened to Leonie's baby."

"You don't want to share your father's fortune?" asked Kitty Rutherford but Helen shook her head.

"No, it's not that. I'm perfectly prepared to share it with the proper claimant, but we have to be sure. If Liza's right and my mother is still alive, I think she should have a share of father's money too . . . there's a lot involved, you see."

"That I can believe," said Lady Kitty. "Howie was very canny with money and so was David Benjamin. The trouble is that I can't really tell you much about your mother, I'm afraid. I haven't seen her for years."

Helen sat back in her chair and sighed. "Oh dear, I was hoping you could help. You see I can't remember her really. I was only five when she went away and my memories are all confused about that time . . . I've never even seen a photograph of her. It makes me very sad."

"Hardly surprising," was the sharp retort.

Helen shook her head sadly and went on, "And I can't remember much about poor Leonie either, just confused

49

things about her lovely clothes and the nice way she smelt. Only today I found out she'd killed herself. It's been an awful shock and I can't take it all in somehow."

Kitty Rutherford's eyes were scanning Helen's face. "Which one of them are you?" she said sharply. "Are you a Gates or a Benjamin? And if you're a Benjamin, which one of *them* are you – David or Marie?"

Helen shook her head in confusion. She'd never heard of any Marie. Her ignorance was obvious, so Lady Kitty explained: "David Benjamin's sister Marie was my child-hood friend. I was very fond of her but she died young. That's why I helped her niece Milly though she wasn't a Marie – much more of a David, I'm afraid."

"How did you help my mother?" asked Helen.

"When she came here saying she was going to kill herself like her daughter did, I told her not to be stupid. I told her to go to my villa in Menton and that's what she did."

"Why did *she* want to kill herself too?" whispered a shocked Helen.

"Because of what had happened. Because of Leonie dying, because her life was a mess. She felt respon-sible."

Tears pricked Helen's eyes again. "But then she left me and my father . . ."

Kitty shrugged. "It was her decision. She cut everything off. Everything and everybody. Before she left she made me promise I'd never tell any of her family where she was. I never have, though it was hard to keep my promise when your father came and asked me. I'd never seen Howie in tears before."

"Then she's not dead?" whispered Helen.

"I don't think so. I'd have heard if she was, I think, but that's all I can really tell you. She sends me postcards now and again. If I were you I'd hire an investigator to find her and to find out about the man who's claiming to be your sister's son." She sighed and closed her eyes in signal of dismissal. Helen stood up to go, recognising the interview was at an end.

"Thank you, Lady Rutherford," she said softly.

"I've not done anything," said the old woman sharply. "I'm sorry I can't."

Depressed, Helen went home but didn't go into the house. Instead she walked across the lawn to a stone-built bower in the garden when she sat on a bench with her chin on her hands. Her thoughts were confused. 'Why am I so unhappy when I am a rich woman, a young woman, a woman in good health with all my life before me? Even if I have to give away half of my mills I'll still be very rich indeed and there are people all around who would envy me, who would scorn me for the way I'm sitting here wallowing in misery . . .' The words ran through her head but failed to change her frame of mind. It was not the prospect of parting with money that worried her – there were deeper concerns. But the most unsettling was the life of Helen Hunt herself. She was surrounded by puzzles and she felt as if any certainties she'd had before had disappeared.

She was brought out of her reverie by her husband's voice.

"Don't you want any lunch, Helen?" he asked, quite gently.

She shook her head. "Not really."

"Come in and eat something. Stevens is sending a fellow over this afternoon for us to talk to him," he said.

"What about?" she asked.

"He's one Stevens thought could check up on Cameron for us. The newspaper advertisement to contact your father's heirs is in the paper today. Have you seen it? Stevens thinks it'll bring out all sorts of other crooks and they'll need to be checked up on too." Reggie was completely convinced that the claimant to Howie's fortune was an imposter and Helen envied him his certainty.

Helen sighed. "Isn't it awful having to check up on people? They'll be followed or something I expect. I'd hate that if it happened to me."

Reggie snorted. "I'd hate it far more if we had to hand out money to a bunch of crooks. I think we should see this man of Stevens and listen to what he has to say."

She looked up at him and said sharply, "Reggie, why have you never told me my sister killed herself?"

He looked genuinely surprised. "It wasn't my place to tell you that, and anyway, I thought you knew. I don't think we ever talked about her, did we?"

"That's true." They never talked about very much except trivialities, she reflected. "But no one ever told me. I feel as if there's lots of other things I don't know about my family. In a few days I discover my sister had an illegitimate child and that she committed suicide. That's a lot to be faced with all at once."

Reggie sat down on the bench beside her. "I didn't know your sister very well and I was away at school when she died. I just remember her at tennis parties in my parents' garden. She used to come with her governess."

Helen swung round to face him. "She had a governess! I remember that now. A tall woman with a funny voice . . ."

He laughed. "Yes, that's right. Very English and highfalutin. After your sister . . . she went to work for my mother's sister and taught her girls."

"Your Aunt Mary – the one who lives outside Edinburgh?"

"Yes."

"Would Mary know if she's still alive?"

"Perhaps. She was with my cousins for about ten years. If you like I'll ring Aunt Mary up and ask. Now please come in and have something to eat."

Mr Stevens' investigator appeared promptly at two-thirty, a mild little man in a shabby suit who looked timid and sat clutching a small attaché case to his stomach in a way that reminded Helen of Phemie Grossett and her handbag. He listened to what Reggie had to say, nodding all the time, and then asked, "If you had to pay off Cameron, Mr Hunt, how much would you consider giving him?"

Reggie glared. "Damn all. I've told you he's a rogue. You only have to look at him and the woman who came with him to see that."

"But if you had to pay them off, how much?"

"Nothing," said Reggie, standing up to end the interview. When the man had gone he said to Helen, "What's Stevens thinking about sending us somebody like that? He's given up before he started."

Helen sighed and went to lie down, pleading a headache, while Reggie telephoned to his aunt. About twenty minutes later he came tiptoeing into her bedroom to tell her, "Mary says the governess's name was Miss Cunningham and after she left, she went to work for some Lady or other in Fife. She'll try to find out where she is now and let us know."

That night when she went downstairs to dinner, Simes presented her with a paper package which had been sent over for her earlier. Reggie was absent – dining in Edinburgh, said Simes – and Helen didn't really care.

"Who's it from?" she asked turning the package over between her fingers.

"The young lady who brought it said it was from Lady Rutherford," was the reply.

"Lady Rutherford! Goodness me," she said, tearing the package open. Inside was a photograph set in a cardboard mount and a single sheet of paper covered with spidery writing.

She looked at the photograph first. Smiling at the

camera, in the middle of a flower-filled garden, was a beautiful woman in a large hat and flowing gown with an older man who she recognised from other photographs in Castledevon as her grandfather, David Benjamin. Hanging onto the woman's hand was a sulky-looking child in a sun-bonnet and lace-edged dress. Dangling from the hand that held the woman's was a cloth doll and it looked as if they were fighting for possession of it.

Helen unfolded the note. There was no formal beginning – just the words:

> I'm sorry I was so short with you today. The photograph enclosed was taken by my husband at a garden fete here in 1900. The woman is your mother, the child your sister and the older man your grandfather. I've kept it all those years to remind me of Marie's family but I don't need reminding any more.
>
> If you're serious about finding out your sister's child, you'll need good professional help. I can recommend a firm who have worked for me in the past. The man I used was Mr Sutherland and he was very good but I'm not sure he's still alive – nobody I used to know still is, I'm afraid.

The name written after that was Sutherland, Ross and McQueen and the address was in Queen Street, Edinburgh.

Helen stared at the photograph avidly. So the smiling woman was her mother, beautiful, carefree. Why could she not remember her? Why, whenever she thought of her, did a shadow seem to cross her mind?

And the child. That was Leonie, who also seemed like a wraith in Helen's memory – represented by a scent of violets, a rustle of starched skirts, a cool hand, the twang of tennis rackets and laughter on sunny afternoons. Frowning out of the photograph over the years she looked petulant and spoiled.

Helen laid the picture down and determined that tomorrow she would telephone Sutherland, Ross and McQueen and engage them sight unseen. But after a few minutes consideration she decided that was not the right thing to do. She wanted to choose the person to whom she would entrust this delicate investigation. She wanted to watch the candidate's face, to try to judge his probity by how he looked and what he said before she committed her secrets to him. She'd not liked the man who had been recommended by Stevens but this time she hoped the shrewd Lady Rutherford would come up with someone better.

So it was necessary to go to Edinburgh and speak to Mr Sutherland if he was still alive. She'd do it alone, without consulting Reggie because she knew he'd want to take it over and would be sure to consider the finding of an agent an unsuitable job for a woman. She began to feel a little better and was surprised at how her headache had disappeared now that she'd decided to take independent action.

Four

" Aw my God Phemie, I telt you to keep oot o' that!"
wailed Mrs Grossett when her daughter presented
her with a written statement about the Gates baby and
asked her to sign it.

"Why? It was the truth you told me, wasn't it? You
were there when Leonie Gates and her father brought the
baby to Mrs Maitland's."

"But I dinna want to sign anything. I'm feared o'
Maitland. She'll no' like it." Mrs Grossett sounded genuinely afraid.

"I've been to see her and she told me where she'd
placed the bairn. It was through her I was able to find
him and he's going to claim a fortune. I tell you, mother,
he'll see us right," said Phemie.

"Away ye go!" exclaimed her mother, obviously surprised. "Maitland told you where he was! What's she
getting oot of it?"

"He'll give her something when he gets his money,"
said Phemie, "but before he does we've got to have
everything in writing. I've found a lawyer and he'll fight
the case for Billy."

"Aw my God lassie, watch yersel. I hope you ken whit
ye're dae'in'," wailed her mother but Phemie's patience
snapped. "Dinna be so daft. Now listen to me. I need
as many witnesses as I can get. Who else kent about
that bairn?"

"I dinna mind."

"Think. You were aye gossiping wi' your friends then. Think . . . Did you tell anybody?"

"There was that Mrs Kennedy. You mind her? She started to work for Maitland about the same time the Gates brought in that bairn. She was fond of it, I mind. Aye pickin' it up and cuddlin' it. She knew whose bairn it was."

"Kennedy. The big woman that lived up in the Lawnmarket? You and she used to be very thick."

Mrs Grossett nodded. "Aye we were, till she took to the drink and spent her time in pubs greeting aboot her brother who was killed in the war." Both of the Grossetts were puritanically against women who drank.

"Is she still in the Lawnmarket?" asked Phemie.

"How do I ken? Ye'll hae to go up there and find oot."

Georgina Kennedy was a large, powerfully built woman who looked as if her bones were sunk inside layers of lard that wobbled every time she moved. Rolls of fat hung over her wrists and ankles, her flushed cheeks drooped and her pendulous breasts swung low beneath her half-buttoned coat.

She was climbing up twenty flights of worn stone stairs, carrying a canvas bag that clinked whenever she laid it down so she could lean against the wall and draw a wheezing breath. When she stooped to pick up her burden after the fifth stop, she muttered aloud to herself in a surprisingly refined voice, "Oh my God, these stairs get steeper every day. I'll have to move . . . I canna go on like this . . . Oh my God!"

A skinny young woman who was going down the stairs when Georgina was going up squeezed past her huge frame irritably and snapped, "It'd be easier if you didnae bring a' these bottles back wi' you every night."

"Mind yer ain business," said Georgina, her accent coarser this time.

57

At last she reached the top landing where there were two paint-blistered doors. Hers was the one without a lock. She put her shoulder against it and shoved it open to reveal a low-ceilinged room with a tiny window looking out into an expanse of grey sky, the bleakness of which reflected the misery of the room which was only furnished with a truckle bed, a table and one chair. Cold ashes were heaped in the black iron fireplace.

A woman was sitting in the chair, eyes on the door, and when Georgina struggled in, she made no effort to get up and help her.

"Jesus!" cried the fat woman, dropping her burden and laying one hand on her heart. "You gave me a real fright! What are you doing here?"

"You know who I am?" asked Phemie Grossett.

"Of course. You're Mrs Grossett's lassie. Is your mother dead? Is that what you've come to tell me?"

"My mother's fine. I've come about other business. Sit down and get your breath."

Still wearing her hat, Georgina collapsed onto the unmade bed and closed her eyes. "I'm puggled. It's the stairs. They're killing me."

"Then move," said Phemie shortly.

"Where to? I canna afford any place better. The rent here's four bob a week and what can you get for that?"

Phemie looked around and sniffed. "Four bob seems a lot for this hole. Who's your landlord?"

"Mrs Maitland."

"That's funny, in a way it's her I've come to talk to you about."

"You've come to talk about Maitland? Why?" A scared look crossed the bloated face when she heard the purpose of Phemie's visit.

"Do you mind when you worked for her and helped look after the babies?"

The look of fear deepened. "Why? What about it?"

"Do you mind her getting a bairn from a family called Gates?"

The fat woman shuddered as if she'd been dealt a blow. "I mind. Why?"

"Because old man Gates has just died and that bairn could be in line to inherit a lot of money."

Georgina seemed to collect her wits and her eyes were suddenly alight. "Is that bairn still alive?" she asked.

"It is. It's called Billy Cameron now and we're trying to prove his claim to Gates' money."

"You're sure it's the Gates bairn?"

"Aye. But he needs someone to give a statement about how he arrived at Mrs Maitland's."

"Oh, I'm glad. I was afraid . . ." the voice trailed off and the eyes went blank again till she recollected herself and asked, "What's he like?"

Phemie stared at the fat woman. "What does it matter what he's like?" she asked.

"It matters to me. He was a bonny wee bairn."

"He's a fine-looking man, big and dark haired. Strong."

"Dark haired? How dark?"

"Listen, Mrs Kennedy, I dinna ken how dark. He's got bonny hair if that's what you're worried about though God knows why. Will you give a statement about knowing the Gates gave their bairn to Mrs Maitland? I'll write it down for you. All you've got to do is sign it."

Georgina got up and groped into her canvas bag for a black bottle of beer. It was closed with a screw top which she struggled to open and when it did, a white froth spewed forth and wetted the blankets on which she sat. Ignoring this, she put the open bottle to her mouth and took a huge swallow.

When she'd finished she waved the bottle at Phemie and asked, "D'ye want one? I get them from the place I work, the bottling plant down the Canongate."

"No thanks," said Phemie, screwing up her pinched

59

nose. "Now listen. Billy Cameron'll see you all right if you help. He'd slip you a few quid. All you've got to do is sign a short statement. I've got it here and I've brought a pen and ink." She opened her handbag to take out those items, but Georgina waved them away. Her face was haggard when she said,

"I dinna want to get involved in anything to do wi' Maitland and I don't think you should either if you've got any sense."

"You don't have to get involved with her. All you've got to say is you mind him arriving at Maitland's house and that he was the Gates bairn who's in line to inherit the mills."

"The old man's mills! Are you sure?"

"According to the will. If the lost bairn's found, it gets half the mills. They're worth about a million pounds apparently."

Georgina sank her head in her hands and groaned, "Oh my God. Is it true? Are you sure he's the Gates bairn?"

"He is if we say he is. Maitland says he is and he's as likely to be as anybody else but we've got to prove it so's the lawyers cannae slip out of paying him his due, and you know what lawyers are like. His case has to be rock solid. Otherwise he'll lose his birthright."

Tears were slipping down Georgina's fat cheeks. "Lose his birthright," she sobbed. "That would be awful."

Phemie reached over and pulled another bottle out of the bag on the floor, unscrewing it and passing it to the weeping woman. "Have another swig and think about it," she said. "I'll go down the street and get you a half-bottle of whisky if you'll sign."

She deliberately stayed away for over an hour and sat on a wall in a corner of the yard outside the building before she returned. By that time it was growing dark. The door was still unlocked and Georgina was drunk, lying fully dressed in her foul bed with empty beer bottles tumbled on the floor beside her.

Phemie, making sounds of annoyance, looked around for a candle and found one on the mantelshelf beside a box of matches. She lit it and took it over to the bed to shake the fat shoulder and to say in a loud voice, "Wake up. Listen to me. Sit up. Here's the paper for you to sign."

Georgina opened her eyes and gazed around befuddled. Her hat, which had been skewered to her hair by a long hat-pin, slipped to the back of her head and her abundant, grey-streaked black hair fell around her face. When Phemie shook her again, however, she seemed to come to herself and asked, "Where's the whisky?"

Phemie said, "Sign this first. I've written it out. Just write your name there." She spread out the sheet of paper on the table, lifted the pen and pulled the half-bottle of whisky out of her bag to show it to the woman on the bed. "Write your name and this is yours," she told her.

Georgina took the pen and said with a sob, "Oh my God. What have I come to!"

Helen did not travel to Edinburgh the next day because she was laid low by one of the feverish headaches to which she was prone.

Looking solicitous, Reggie stood at the foot of her bed. "Feeling bad, my dear?" he asked.

"Awful," she groaned.

"I was wondering if, when you're better, you might like a little trip to Biarritz. A sort of second honeymoon . . . ?"

She stared at him in astonishment. "Biarritz? When all this is going on about Leonie's son? Don't be silly, Reggie."

"Just an idea," he said abashed. "You don't mind if I go out for a round of golf, do you?"

"I don't care if you play ten rounds," she said shortly and shut her eyes.

She was still feeling poorly in the afternoon when her Aunt Liza arrived. "You look absolutely washed out. You're not pregnant, are you?" she asked.

"Of course not."

"You're sure?"

"Absolutely certain." How could I be pregnant when my husband and I haven't shared a bed for years? thought Helen.

"Pity," said Liza. "It would solve a lot of problems."

"Please go away, Liza," said Helen. "I think I'm going to be sick."

She was beginning to feel better by the evening of the second day, and was sitting up in bed nibbling at some toast when Reggie appeared again.

"Just came to tell you that Stevens has had a phone message from that Cameron fellow. He and his lawyer want to meet us in the North British Hotel tomorrow afternoon. I said I'd go up with him. They're not wasting time, are they?"

Helen swung her feet over the edge of the bed. "In the N.B.? I'll come too!"

Her husband looked shocked. "That's not necessary. You've been ill. You shouldn't be going out."

"Nonsense. I'm much better. And anyway, it's my money that's at stake. I want to know what's going on." Even she was surprised by how energetic she suddenly felt.

Next afternoon their party was seated at an opulently laid out tea table in the large salon overlooking the entrance hall of the big hotel when a solemn-toned clock struck three. Reggie, who had placed his seat so that he was looking straight at the front door while the others had their backs to it, raised his eyebrows as the last tones of the clock died away.

"They're coming," he hissed.

A disapproving waiter appeared by the table ushering another trio of people, very different to those awaiting them. Phemie, still in rusty black, clutched her handbag and sniffed and Billy Cameron looked shifty, as if he expected to be ejected any moment: The third member of their party, Herbert Johnstone, who had been familiar with such places in his glory days, was the only one who walked across the deep-piled carpet with any assurance, but his suit was baggy and stained and his shoes in need of mending, details which did not escape the waiter's eagle eye, for there are few people in the world more snobbish about accoutrements than waiters.

Reggie, always polite, stood up and ushered his guests to their chairs before enquiring if they would take tea. They accepted and Helen busied herself with the enormous silver teapot while Johnstone delved into his pocket and produced a little sheaf of cards which he distributed around, one to each of them. 'Herbert Johnstone, 375 Leith Walk, Leith', they said. There was no mention of his qualifications and no telephone number.

"I represent Mr Cameron," he said grandly. Mr Stevens, who knew of Johnstone's past, bit his tongue. Instead he asked, "Exactly what do you want to speak to us about?"

"Mr Cameron is prepared to negotiate," said Johnstone.

"Oh yes?"

"He'll settle for a hundred thousand pounds."

"Will he really?" said Stevens while Reggie let out a hiss of outrage. Helen, who had come equipped with a notepad and several sharp pencils, flipped back the first page and carefully wrote down the figure.

"He is being very reasonable because if he pursues his claim, it is most likely that he would be able to claim at least five hundred thousand. However, he would prefer not to have to go through the time- and money-consuming exercise of going to court."

63

It was obviously difficult for Reggie to keep silent but he managed and it was Mr Stevens who replied: "There is no guarantee that Mr Cameron's claim would stand up in court."

At this Phemie cracked. "Oh yes there is. We've got our witnesses and they've made their statements. Show them, Mr Johnstone."

He went on, "I have signed statements from Mrs Lilian Grossett and Mrs Georgina Kennedy testifying that the baby Mrs Cynthia Maitland got from Miss Leonie Gates and her father, Mr Howie Gates, was given to a Mr and Mrs Albert Cameron of Salamander Street, Leith. I have copies of all the statements here."

He laid three sheets of paper on the tea table and Helen reached out for them. They were short and to the point and when she finished reading she carefully copied down the names and addresses of the witnesses before passing the papers over to her lawyer who folded them and put them in his briefcase.

"We will enquire into them," he said.

Phemie, who felt that things were not going well enough, leaned forward and said, "And dinna forget that Mrs Maitland's sworn Billy's the Gates bairn, and she's the one that would know."

Mr Stevens gave her a considering stare before he said, "I feel it is only fair to tell you that there could be other claimants to Mr Gates' estate. We are advertising for them at the moment."

Phemie's white face went even whiter and a grey tinge crept into her lips. "You'll not find anybody with a better claim than Billy," she said.

Mr Stevens sighed. "We're as anxious as you are to get to the bottom of this business and will be making our own enquiries. We'll get in touch with you as soon as possible. In the meantime I'll just leave Mr Cameron's offer of settling for a hundred thousand on the table."

At twenty past three the meeting was over. When Billy, Phemie and Johnstone crossed the road and walked to the top of Leith Walk, Billy suddenly said, "Och, let's forget the whole thing. They're no' going to pay us. I'm fed up wi' it."

Phemie was not for giving up, however, and neither was Johnstone. "Why don't we let them know we'll settle for less. Maybe twenty thousand?" said Phemie, who dreaded her dreams of financial independence vanishing.

Johnstone shook his head. "If we did that they'd know we were beaten. No, we stick it out. Maybe I could go to see Mrs Maitland to get her to harden up her statement. Money counts with her."

"Mair than anything," said Phemie bitterly. "She'll do anything for money."

Back in the hotel Reggie and Helen lingered over the tea table with Mr Stevens till he looked at his watch and said, "I'd like to catch the three forty-five back to Gala, if you don't mind."

Reggie looked at his wife. "Will you be travelling back with Mr Stevens, dear?"

Helen shook her head, for all of a sudden she'd made up her mind. She was going to the offices of Sutherland, Ross and McQueen. Now more than ever she wanted to get her teeth into the problem and suspected that Mr Stevens was far too polite and orthodox for the job.

"I'll go back later," she said, and Reggie sighed which gave her a clue that he too had plans for the rest of the afternoon which did not include her. She leaned across and patted his arm. "I'm only going shopping, darling, and don't want anyone's company," she said with a smile.

Before she left the hotel she went into the ladies room and removed the most obvious items of jewellery she was wearing – her diamond earrings and the magnificent emerald engagement ring Reggie had given her. She was glad that, for fear of exacerbating Phemie Grossett's dislike and cupidity, she'd taken the care to dress soberly and had left her car at home, because to these new lawyers she intended to present the appearance of a woman of fairly limited means, at least until she decided whether to hire them or not. One look at her car would have shown up that pretence completely.

She headed for Queen Street, walking slowly along the pavement reading the brass plates – which, had she known it, were polished daily by Phemie Grossett – and was pleasantly surprised to find the firm she was seeking quite easily. 'Sutherland, Ross and McQueen' was inscribed on a brass plate by the door of a tall, thin house just along from Hanover Street.

Until she found herself on the pavement outside the office, she had not been entirely sure of what she was going to do, but now she was sure, so she rang the bell and said to the clerk who answered the door, "Is there still a Mr Sutherland practising in this firm?"

"Yes'm. There's two, old Mr Sutherland and young Mr Sutherland."

"I suspect I'm looking for old Mr Sutherland. Would it be possible to see him?"

Normally such a request from someone arriving off the pavement would be rebuffed but there was an air of status and money about Helen, even though she was trying to appear innocuous, which made the clerk open the door wider and invite her inside. The woman, he had noted, was well shod, for he always looked at the clients' feet to ascertain their financial status. He'd take a chance on her.

Old Mr Sutherland was so old that he looked as if he had been a grown man when Howie was a boy and he peered at Helen with milky-lensed eyes while she told him her name and explained the reason for her call.

"I have a rather delicate matter that I want investigated. There's a young man claiming to be related to me, my sister's illegitimate son in fact. I've come to you to ask for advice in checking him out because you were recommended by a friend, Lady Rutherford of Falconwood . . ."

"Oh my goodness, Lady Rutherford! I remember her well. She was involved in a case about a will, and a treasure trove, Roman silver I believe . . . a very interesting business. Is she still alive?" he asked, brightening visibly.

"Yes, she is. She told me to come to you. This is about an inheritance too, you see. If what the man says is true, he'll inherit a large part of my late father's estate. I just want to be sure that it's going to the right person."

The word 'inheritance' obviously interested him too and his eyes lit up, remembering the days when he was young and entranced by the charismatic, red-haired Kitty, but seconds later reality returned, and he shook his head. "My dear young lady, I'm an old man now. I'm not up to taking on complicated cases any more."

Helen smiled. "I'm sure Lady Rutherford realised that, but she has great confidence in your firm, and I believe she thought you would recommend someone else for me . . ."

"Well there's my son . . . but he's not so curious as I was. I think the man you need is our young fellow, if he'll take you on. He's always busy but if he gets interested in a case he's very good, even though I say it myself."

Helen positively sparkled at him. "I'd be so grateful if I could see him," she breathed.

She was left for about ten minutes in the waiting room with huge, dark Victorian portraits of previous partners in the firm staring down from the walls while the other staff member was summoned. When the door finally opened, she looked up with expectation in her eyes but it very quickly died, because the man who peered in at her was totally unlike anything she had expected, and certainly unlike the other investigator who had already been presented to her.

He was a tall, thin man about five or six years older than herself with a sharp, bony face that made her think of an intelligent dog, and his dark hair was fairly long and wavy, like an artist's. It was his clothes that were wrong as far as she was concerned for, instead of sporting a proper business suit, he was dressed in a loose jacket and a floppy red tie, and his grey flannel trousers were baggy and very crumpled.

"You Mrs Hunt?" he asked abruptly, without smiling.

Her face took on a stony look. Mentally she blackmarked him because of his discourtesy. "Yes. I'm Helen Hunt," she said.

"Valentine McDermot," he said, pointing at his own chest.

"Really?"

"Re-ally," he said. Was he mimicking her voice or was that the way he normally spoke?

He walked across the floor towards her without speaking and paused in front of her, taking her in. She glared and he glared back.

"You want someone investigated? Who is it?"

"It's three people actually. A Mr Cameron, a Mrs Kennedy and a Miss Grossett."

"Is it a matrimonial matter?"

"What do you mean?"

"Are you trying to find the women because of your husband? Are you trying to prove adultery to get a divorce or something?"

"Goodness gracious, no."

"What's it about then? People only go looking for other people when there's either money or marriage involved, I find."

She sighed, thinking 'another dead loss, but I might

as well go through the motions of this interview'. "It's money," she said.

"Do they owe you money? I don't like dunning."

"No, it's nothing like that. It's about a will. My father died two weeks ago and his will stated that if a male heir turns up, he's to inherit our weaving mills. My father was a very prosperous businessman in the Borders, you see . . ."

"Really?" he said again. His eyes scrutinised her, making her stammer and feel foolish, but she pressed on. "At the will reading a stranger appeared and said he was my sister's son who'd been given away for fostering when he was a baby . . ."

"What did your sister say to that?"

"My sister is dead, unfortunately."

"And you're the sole heir – heiress – to the estate?"

"Yes."

"So you don't want to share your inheritance with a claimant?"

"It's not that. If Leonie had a son, I'd be happy for him to have his due. It's just that I have to be sure, but there's more to it than that. I want to find out about my sister and I want to find my mother. They're more important than the money as far as I'm concerned."

"Complicated," he said. "You said your sister's dead so you won't be able to find her . . . I take it your mother's still alive. Doesn't she get a share of your father's fortune?"

"She ran away when I was a little girl – and my sister committed suicide after the baby was born. I want to find out as much as I can about her and her baby and if my mother can be found, I want to share some of my inheritance with her as well."

"Very generous," he said sceptically.

She wished she hadn't revealed herself so much to him.

"Do you think the claimant is genuine?" he asked.

"I've no idea. The more I think about it, the more I'm convinced that he's not. I know now that my sister did have a secret baby but . . ." She felt her face going red and wished this man was not making her so angry and defensive. "I'm not greedy. It's not that I want to keep the money to myself. It's just that I want it to go to the right person. Do you think I'm'wasting my time, Mr Mc—?"

"Dermot. McDermot."

"Would you act for me in a case like this? Or do you think I should pay him off and forget the whole thing?"

"Could you afford to do that?"

"Probably," she said cautiously.

"Why did you come here for advice? You're not one of the old boy's regular clients. Most of them are in their dotage."

"I came because your firm was recommended to me by an old client of Mr Sutherland's, a woman for whom I have a great deal of respect, and I'm prepared to pay well for the service if it's performed satisfactorily."

She knew as soon as she'd said it that her words sounded pompous and saw by the look that crossed his face that they cut little ice with him.

"I have a lot of work on at the moment and your business sounds pretty straightforward. Why don't you take it to an investigation agency and not a legal firm?"

She shook her head. "I prefer dealing with professionals. Please consider it," she said on impulse and saw him soften.

"I'll think about it. But I'll need all the details you can lay your hands on."

She opened her handbag and said, "Well, I've got something for you to start on," as she took out her notebook with the names and addresses of the people who'd made statements about Billy Cameron. She explained who they were as she passed over the relevant pages.

He ran his eye across the lines and a smile appeared on his face.

"What's funny?" she asked, defensive again.

"Nothing," he told her, folding the page over.

When she left the office, he wondered if he should have stuffed the notebook page into his waste-paper basket, for the haughty little woman had not impressed him. She had been very sharp in her manner and he also felt that she had more money than was good for her, though she'd been trying to pretend not to be rich.

What changed his mind was the same thing as had made him smile – the name and address of one of the witnesses. "Mrs Georgina Kennedy, top floor, Bailey's Building, the Lawnmarket."

Seeing that he had almost laughed aloud for he knew Bailey's Buildings. How could anyone in that warren be involved with the very precise and ladylike Mrs Hunt who sat eyeing him cautiously across the table?

When he read Georgina Kennedy's short testimony his curiosity was sharpened even more. Then after a few moments of sitting thinking in his chair, he got up and wandered into the senior Mr Sutherland's room.

The old man should have been retired years ago but could not abide staying at home in an empty house, for he was a widower with no other interests outside his work. He had been taking a pleasant little nap in his leather armchair, but pretended that he'd been reading the paper when Val walked through his door without knocking.

"Remember that Mrs Hunt you passed on to me?" he asked without preamble as was his wont.

"Yes, Lady Rutherford's friend," said Mr Sutherland, blinking.

"The business she wants investigated has something to do with that woman Maitland, the one who was suspected about ten years ago of being a baby farmer. Do you remember her?"

"There was never anything illegal proved against her. Her business was all above board if I remember rightly."

"Yes, it was, but the police were interested at one time if I'm not mistaken. I've heard talk about it," said Val.

"They never brought any charges though. She's a clever and careful woman is Mrs Maitland."

"And now she serves on charity committees and goes to official receptions."

"Does she? I know she's made a good bit of money one way or another." The old man heard all sorts of gossip from his cronies in the New Club.

"Yes, she has and there's quite a few stories about how she's done it. apparently she owns a good bit of property in the Old Town and is a very tough landlord, and I've also heard she's a money lender . . . but again, she keeps on the right side of the law. Just. I thought it was interesting that her name crops up with the Hunt business."

Mr Sutherland said, "I'm sure Mrs Hunt is as respectable as she looks. She's a friend of Lady Rutherford after all. I could ring her up and ask about Mrs Hunt if you like . . ." He was looking forward to talking to Kitty Rutherford again for he'd never forgotten her. When he got through to her on the phone, Val was amused to see how courtly he became in his manner.

Kitty had not forgotten how to enchant either and it took a fairly long exchange of compliments before they got down to discussing the matter in hand.

"Helen Hunt?" said Kitty. "Dear Mr Sutherland, she is quite the nicest person. Do try to help her. She had a terrible father and I know her mother who, I'm afraid, is more than a little scatterbrained. She ran away from home when Helen was only a baby and has never shown the least curiosity about her child. Helen's absolutely genuine and the terrible business about her sister killing herself after having to give away her baby has really upset her. Do help if you can . . . For old times' sake, please do."

When he put down the receiver, Mr Sutherland looked at Val. "Did you hear any of that?" he asked.

"She has a rather penetrating voice," Val admitted and laughed. "I take it you'd like me to look into the case?" In fact, he was becoming rather interested himself.

Bailey's Buildings was a ramshackle tenement standing at the back of a rubbish-littered courtyard just off the Lawnmarket. An arched alleyway led into the south side of the courtyard from the High Street and another flight of steep stairs led from the north side onto the Mound. The entrance to the building was a battered wooden door threateningly studded all over with big nail heads. It swung on only one hinge, however, so it couldn't have kept anyone out. The narrow vestibule that was revealed when the door was shouldered open by Val smelt horribly of damp and stale urine. It was very dark but he knew his way about and headed for the stairs, the stone steps of which were deeply worn down in the middle by the many feet that had gone up and down them over the centuries.

There were no landings and the flight rose in a spiral with mysterious doors opening directly off it every now and again. At the third door McDermot stopped and thumped with his fist. Almost at once it opened and a dirty-faced little girl glared out into the gloom and said, "Whae is it? My ma's oot."

"No she isn't. I heard her voice. Tell her it's Val."

From the gloom behind the child came a roar. "It's you! Come awa' ben. I thought it was that rent man."

He stepped into a low-ceilinged room with a single window overlooking the street. On a table in the middle of the floor was an empty milk bottle and a loaf of bread. A tall woman was standing beside the fireplace and the half-naked child ran over and clung to her skirt. A cat slept on the window ledge in the sunshine and there was a body lying in bed in a recess next to the hearth. Val knew he was witnessing the sort of domestic tableau that had been enacted in that room for centuries, for Bailey's Buildings had been the home of hundreds of families – some of them, in earlier times, people of great status, as the roof beams decorated with painted armorial bearings testified.

The woman, an old friend of Val's called Mags MacInnes, pushed a wooden chair forward and gestured to him to sit down as she said, "You're no' in your workin' claes, Val, are you? Whit's up? It's no' one o' the laddies again, is it?"

He didn't take the chair but leaned smiling against the table with his hands in his pockets and said, "No, no, Mags, don't worry, it's nothing like that. I've not been up in the court and since I'm on the hunt for information, you're the best place to find it. Do you know anything about one of your neighbours, a woman who lives on the top floor here? She's called Georgina Kennedy."

She stared at him. Her eyes were very black and her eyebrows thick and widely arching. She was a handsome woman but none too clean. "Ina? Of course I ken her. She's been living here for years. The laddies were only wee when she first came."

Val nodded, encouraging her to go on. They knew each other well because she often provided him with information about people who lived in the High Street, and he was also called on from time to time to plead in court for her grown-up sons who had fiery natures and tended to fall foul of the police on Saturday nights after they'd been drinking.

"Let me think. What would you like to ken aboot her? When she arrived she had another woman wi' her. A peely wally sort that was aye coughing but she deed and the Kennedy woman's been on her ain ever since. Funny you should ask about her because there's been a fair stream of folk going up to see her over the last couple o'days. For years she didnae see a sowel and now they're a' coming at once. Has she inherited money or something?" asked Mags.

"Who's been to see her?" Val knew that nothing that went on in that stair missed this woman.

"Weell, first of all it was a skinny woman in a black coat wi' a big handbag, and then she went awa' but a man cam'yesterday, a shabby looking kind. Then, this morning Mrs Maitland's Danny went up the stairs but the Kennedy woman was oot at her work and he didnae get her."

"Mrs Maitland's Danny? Who's he?"

"He's the one that collects Maitland's rents. I thought you were Danny the noo when you rattled on the door. I'm a couple o' days late in paying and Danny's a bit rough wi' folk that dinna pay on time. Kennedy's no' usually late though. I think she's feared o' Danny and she aye has her money ready."

"How much do you owe Danny, Mags?" Val asked.

She bridled. "I didnae tell you that because I was asking for money."

"I know you didn't, but I'll give you some. I suspect the person I'm doing this job for spends more money in a day than you'll put through your hands in three months and she'll not notice if I charge your rent to expenses. Here's two pounds. Will that cover it?"

He laid the money on the table and the nimble child shot over and scooped it up before her mother could refuse this bounty. While this was going on, the body in the bed heaved and a voice croaked, "I want my tea!"

"Aw my God, you would, granny," snapped Mags, and then to the child she said, "Awa doon to the shop and get some milk for granny's tea." Jingling Val's money, the child went.

Val looked at his watch and asked, "Will Mrs Kennedy be in yet?"

Mags shook her head. "She's no' gone up the stairs.

I'd hae heard her. She makes a hell of a noise, jingling beer bottles and peching like a grampus. She works in the bottlin' plant doon the Canongate and she takes maist o' her wages in brown ale, puir sowel."

"What time does she get back?"

"About half six but she'll be blootered. She aye is. You'll no' get ony sense oot o' her."

"It's ten to six now. Can I wait?"

"You're welcome," laughed Mags and produced a beer bottle from a cupboard beneath the sink, saying, "Have a drink, unless you want to wait for granny's tea."

He took the beer and sat conversing with his hostess about various court cases, prison sentences and offending neighbours while the child held a cup of tea up to the lips of an ancient woman in the box bed. It was nearly half-past six when they heard feet slowly mounting the stair in a shuffling sort of way.

"There she is noo," whispered Mags, pointing with her chin towards the door.

McDermot shot out and took the arm of a stout woman who seemed to be weighed down with bags and was struggling painfully up the steep steps. "Let me help you, Mrs Kennedy," he said.

"I'm awful hot," she muttered.

"Come on, it'll be cooler upstairs," he said, putting a reassuring hand on the broad back. The woman's face was purple and she seemed to be on the verge of collapse but with his help she finally made it to her door.

The day had been spring-like and sunny and her room was stiflingly hot for it was tucked under the eaves of the building, eight floors from the ground. Val was struck by the poverty in which she lived – and not only poverty but complete lack of any human comfort. Even in the poorest houses, he was used to seeing cheap lithographs on the walls, cracked ornaments on the mantels, but there was nothing like that here, absolutely nothing except empty beer bottles that were ranged along the wall like watching soldiers. The bags he had lugged upstairs turned out to be full of more bottles to add to the ranks.

Georgina Kennedy flopped onto the chair and fanned her face with her hand. Her eyes were closed, her cheeks scarlet and her breathing laboured but after a bit she seemed to collect herself, opened her eyes and stared at the man in her room.

"Who are you?" she asked sharply. "Are you from Phemie Grossett too?"

"I'm Val McDermot, a lawyer. I've come to ask if you can help me."

"A lawyer? Help you? How?" She was very flustered.

"With some information. I'll pay for it," he told her soothingly but she was not reassured. Her pouched eyes searched his face and he saw fear in them. "Is it about that bairn thing?" she whispered. "If it is I dinna ken anything. Please go away."

"But you've signed a statement saying you do know something about it. Are you telling me you didn't sign it?"

It seemed as if sobriety had returned to her in an instant. "Oh my God," she groaned, "I was drunk. Phemie Grossett made me sign it."

"So you were forced. Are you telling me what you said isn't true?"

"Not forced exactly . . . but I didnae think straight. My memory's not so good nowadays." Though she spoke with a local accent, her voice was more polished than Mags'. She sounded as if she'd known better things and could have passed as a lady if she tried.

"Let me go through it with you," said Val, pulling a notebook out of his jacket pocket and opening it up. She watched him with the hypnotised stare of a rabbit in front of a stoat, but she answered his questions with every appearance of honesty.

When they had finished, he said, "Let me read back what you've told me. You're Georgina Kennedy of this address and you're fifty-two years old. In 1914, you were working for Mrs Cynthia Maitland who at that time lived in George Square. You were present when a Miss Leonie Gates and her father brought a male infant to the Maitland house and gave it up for fostering . . . Is that what you said?"

She shivered though the heat was still intense. "Yes."

He pressed on, reading again from his notes. "The baby was looked after by you and your friend Mrs Lilian Grossett who now lives in Elm Row."

He stopped and stared at her again. "Did you say that?"

"Yes."

"And that child was taken away from you a few weeks later and given to a Mr and Mrs Cameron of Leith?" This was something he had not yet asked her and he saw her face close up.

"I dinna mind where it went. Phemie told me the Camerons got it. And that other man she sent said the same."

"It's very important," Val warned, "and if you were telling lies, and if Mrs Hunt goes to court, you could be charged with perjury."

Not strictly true, he knew, but enough to frighten her. She started to cry. "I mind the wee bairn going to Maitland. It was a terrible time, terrible. It was the start o' a' my trouble."

"What do you mean? Why the start of your trouble?"

"Because that was when I started to drink. That was when I got in tow with Maitland. But I couldn't help it. There was no place else for me to go. They all let me down – all of them, all of them, even though I'd helped them."

"How did you get in tow with Mrs Grossett?"

"I met her at Cynthia Maitland's. We both worked there."

"Did you keep babies up here?"

"No. I had Amy living wi' me then and she had consumption. It wasnae good for the bairns."

"Who's Amy?"

"She was my sister-in-law. Her man, my brother, was killed in the war. She died just after it finished."

"That was sad."

Her eyes sought out his and seemed to find some genuine pity in them.

"Please go away. Please dinna get me involved in this. I dinna want to have anything to do wi' it. I'm an old woman and all I want now is a bit o' peace," she pleaded.

He put the paper back in his pocket. "I'm very sorry. Truly I am, but you are involved. You've involved yourself by signing a statement. There's a lot of money at stake and the man you say is the Gates heir will use your statement to back up his claim."

"Phemie said he was Miss Leonie's bairn. Her mother says he is too and that he was given to folk called Cameron when he was very wee. Honestly, I was glad to hear that. I've always been feared it was worse." When she said this she started to cry, wiping her eyes with the back of her hand.

Val leaned forward. "Worse? What do you mean?"

"Nothing, nothing. I didn't mean it!"

He persisted, "And you called it, 'Miss Leonie's baby'. Why did you call it that?"

"Because it was."

"So how do you know that the one you say went to the Camerons was the same one as was given for fostering by Leonie Gates?"

She stood up suddenly and threw her arms in the air. "I dinna ken anything aboot it! I wish to God Phemie

Grossett had stayed oot o' this. Go away, go away. I don't want to remember it. I don't want to remember."

She was deeply distressed and also very afraid. The only thing he could do was leave, but his curiosity was well awakened. Helen Hunt had him on her case.

Five

When Valentine McDermot's curiosity was aroused he became bulldog-like in his tenacity. The morning after his meeting with Georgina Kennedy found him striding down Leith Walk in search of Herbert Johnstone, whose card Helen Hunt had given him.

As usual Johnstone, cigarette hanging from his bottom lip, was in the snug of the Three Bells with *The Scotsman* spread out on a rickety table before him.

Val remembered him from the time of his scandal and walked across to him saying, "Hello, Bert, remember me?"

"Should I?" said Johnstone, looking up indifferently.

"Val McDermot . . . Probably not. I was just starting in the courts when you got sent down."

"You a policeman?" asked Johnstone.

"A lawyer. Sutherland, Ross and McQueen," said Val.

"That's worse," was the reply but in spite of this discouragement, Val pulled a chair away from another table and sat down on it, staring at Johnstone with a friendly grin on his face. Johnstone grimaced and looked away but Val kept on smiling.

"Fancy a drink?" he asked.

"Double whisky," said Johnstone promptly.

When it was produced, Val pulled an unopened pack of cigarettes out of his pocket and, after offering one to Johnstone, who took it, left the pack on the table top.

"How're you getting on with Cameron and Grossett?"

he asked when the cigarettes were lit and going well. 'So that's what this is about,' thought Johnstone, and said, "What's it to you?"

"Just interested. I heard about the Gates business. They're advertising for an heir, I believe. I think you're a brave man though to be tangling with Mrs Maitland. You know what a reputation she's got. Are you sure your client is who he says he is, or is he cutting you in on a scam?"

Johnstone stared back, bleak eyed. "What's it to you?" he asked again.

"Mr Nosey Parker, that's me," said Val cheerfully. "I've a client with an interest too."

"Mrs Maitland?" asked Johnstone.

"No way. I'd give her a wide berth. She's a dangerous woman from what I hear. I hope you're watching your back."

"I'm not tangling with Mrs Maitland," said Johnstone. Though he'd had two double whiskies by this time, his mind was sharp as it always was when he was given a tricky problem. He guessed Val was working either for a rival claimant or the Gates estate, though he favoured the rival hypothesis because the Hunts had brought Stevens to the meeting in the N.B. as their lawyer. He sat back and prepared to listen, deciding to drink no more that morning. He wasn't convinced Billy Cameron was really the Gates child but he was long past the stage of worrying about ethics. The one who was prepared to pay him was the one he'd fight for.

Val was still talking about Mrs Maitland. "She's the only person that can authenticate any claim though. She placed the baby. Get her on your side and the others have no chance. That's right, isn't it? The Grossett woman's mother's in it for money and the woman in the Lawnmarket, Mrs Kennedy, is a drunk. It's Maitland that counts. Been to see her yet?" said Val.

"What's it got to do with you?" asked Johnstone aggressively.

"I'm interested." Val stood up, forgetting about the cigarette packet on the table, "Is there much in it for you if Cameron wins?"

"A fair bit," said Johnstone, who didn't like to be pitied.

"Then don't forget Maitland," said Val, walking away. In the mirror by the door he saw Johnstone pocketing his cigarettes and he smiled as he left the pub. "Divide and rule," he said to himself.

For the rest of that morning, with a great struggle, Johnstone stayed sober and when the one o'clock gun boomed out from the ramparts of Edinburgh Castle, he was making his way to St Bernard's Row.

He told the maid that he wished to see Mrs Maitland on business connected with the Gates baby and was admitted without too much trouble. A svelte looking Cynthia Maitland received him in her incongruously furnished drawing room and scrutinised the card he handed to her with a sceptical eye.

"Yes?" she asked abruptly without inviting him to sit down. His eye caught the glittering glasses in her cocktail cabinet and the sight of them made his mouth water.

"It's about Billy Cameron's claim to Howie Gates' estate," he said.

"Yes?"

"I believe you've been asked to make a statement supporting Billy's claim to be the Gates heir."

"Yes." A statement, not a question this time.

"And did you?"

"I said I had a baby to place from Miss Leonie Gates."

"And did you say where he went?"

"I said I thought he went to a Mr and Mrs Cameron of Leith."

"You *thought*?"

83

"It's a long time ago. I'm no longer in that business."

"But when my client makes his claim, will you back him up?"

"It depends. There could be other claimants."

"Why?"

"Because I had other babies to place at the same time and I might have got some of them mixed up."

He looked at her in pitying wonder. "Mrs Maitland, I know enough about you to be sure that you're unlikely ever to get things like that mixed up."

Her face hardened. "What do you mean?"

"I've taken the precaution of getting a list of the babies you put through your hands during the first half of 1915 from the City Chambers. There's nine of them and if necessary, I'll check up on each one."

A faint flush of colour crept up her powdered cheeks. "You're going to a lot of trouble," she said tartly.

"I've plenty of time and if I turn up something interesting it might help to reinstate me in my profession."

"I doubt it," she said. "Edinburgh people have memories like elephants as far as the mishandling of money is concerned."

"You never know. It depends on what I find out," he said. "Miss Grossett and her mother have been speaking to me and so has another interested party, Mrs Kennedy. They have information that they might give to the authorities if you don't co-operate so I think that you should give serious consideration to backing up their candidate."

In fact he was taking a shot in the dark, remembering the older women's intense reaction to any mention of Mrs Maitland. It was obvious they were terrified, and reluctant to admit to any association with her. His shot hit home. The lines down the sides of her mouth tightened and deepened and her voice went rasplike.

"You'd all better watch your step," she warned. "The

best thing you can do is get out of this business or you'll find you're in deeper than you think."

"Oh no, Mrs Maitland, it might be you that's in deep," he said.

When he left Johnstone, Val's next port of call was to Leith. The wind blowing off the river smelt of fish and he began his search on the quayside, standing with his hands in his pockets, watching men manhandling wooden fish boxes out of trawler holds. There were lots of idlers watching like himself and he asked one old man if he knew where Cameron's shop was.

"Oh aye, it's a grand shop, a good business. Been there a long time."

"Is it near here?"

"Just a bittie up the road. You cannae miss it. The name's above the door."

Cameron's grocery store was painted dark green with the name spelt out in golden script. There were two windows, one larger than the other and curving around a corner. The glass was sparkling and the pavement in front of the shop swept clean. When Val stepped inside, a bell rang above his head and a man in a pristine white apron popped up from behind a high mahogany counter. It was a high-class establishment for that part of the world.

"Would it be possible to have a word with Mr Cameron?" asked Val, at his most mannerly.

"You're not a commercial, sir, are you?"

"A commercial?" Val wrinkled his brow.

"A traveller, a representative . . ."

"Oh no. I'm not."

"I didn't think so, sir. Then I'm Mr Cameron," said the man behind the counter. Val laughed and the ice between them was broken.

Mr Cameron had a full head of thick white hair and bushy grey eyebrows above intelligent hazel eyes. He was wearing a green cotton work jacket over a white shirt and old-fashioned boiled collar that looked too tight for his neck.

"What's your business, sir," he asked.

"My name's Valentine McDermot and I'm an advocate in Edinburgh . . ."

Mr Cameron groaned. "It's not that boy again is it? I'm not going to help. I told him the last time that I'd washed my hands of him."

"Your son?"

"Unfortunately yes. It was a bad day for us the day we got him."

"Well, it is about him, but he's not in trouble. He's concerned in a matter with a client of mine. She's trying to find the lost child of her dead sister and it might be him."

"There's been a woman here already looking for him. Was that her?"

"I don't think so. My client's sent me to find out about him." Val had a pretty good idea that the first seeker after Billy was Phemie Grossett and when he questioned Mr Cameron about her, he found his suspicions to be correct.

"What I've come for," he said eventually, "is to find out what you know about Billy's origins."

Mr Cameron sighed. "That boy! The worry about him killed my wife. She had her pick of three and she took him because he was the bonniest. Big and strong. He was just what we wanted. Our own wee laddie had died the previous year, you see, and the doctor said we couldn't have any more. We heard about Mrs Maitland in George Square who arranged private adoptions and we went to see her. We had a baby inside a month and it was Billy. She said he came from good stock. Mrs Maitland did all the paper work for us and said it was quite legal."

"Did she tell you anything about his real parents?"

86

"Yes, she told us he was illegitimate but came from a good family. His grandfather was a very respectable man and his mother just a silly girl so the baby was only an embarrassment. There wasn't any danger, Mrs Maitland said, of the mother turning up again and wanting him back and we were never bothered by his real family at all. They gave him away and that was that."

"How much did you pay?"

Mr Cameron looked at Val, nodded slowly and said, "He wasn't cheap. Twenty guineas."

"A considerable sum," said Val.

"My wife was desperate. The loss of our boy nearly killed her. I'd have paid five thousand to make her happy again."

"Who told you about Mrs Maitland?"

"A lady who came into the shop, an account customer. I've a feeling she got a little girl that same way as we got Billy but I can't be sure. She's dead now. She said Mrs Maitland organised children for people who could pay . . ."

"How did Billy turn out?"

"He was a grand baby. No trouble at all after we got a good wet nurse for him because he wasn't properly weaned when we got him and my wife couldn't feed him of course. He thrived but when he got older the trouble started. He wouldn't go to school; he wouldn't help in the shop. Then he started stealing. It was just from the neighbours at first and they let me pay them back without going to the police, but he got worse.

"He was aye fighting with other lads. He split one boy's head open with an iron bar and they had him up in court for that. Then he robbed an old woman and knocked her over so that she broke her leg. He was up for that too. In 1930 he stole a car and smashed it, and he was always helping himself to cash from the shop and blaming the other assistants. In the end he took fifty pounds from

87

my safe and tried to set fire to the premises. That time I reported him to the police and he went to jail for three months. He ran away to London then and got in trouble there, too, but he was soon back and got work in the ice plant over there in the docks. What's he done now?"

"He's making a claim to a considerable sum of money, a fortune in fact. He says he's the only male heir to a rich mill owner in the Borders, and from what you tell me he may be right."

"Well that's what Mrs Maitland told us but if you asked me now where he'd came from I'd say it was the lowest of the low. In spite of what Mrs Maitland said I don't think he's got a drop of good blood in him," said Mr Cameron bitterly.

"Have you seen him recently?" asked Val who was feeling sympathy for the old man.

"No. I told him not to come back after his mother – my wife, I mean – died. He upset her so much I'm sure he made her ill."

"And when you got him, there was no clue to who his parents might have been?"

"Not a thing. The lady who got the little girl said that her child came with a wee locket round its neck but there was nothing with Billy except a tartan blanket. I thought it was a funny thing for a well-off man's daughter to have round her baby . . ."

"I don't suppose you've still got it?"

"As a matter of fact I do. We used to put it on his bed when he was wee and my wife said we should keep it for him. She used to wonder who his mother was but he's never showed any interest."

"Could I see the blanket?"

Mr Cameron looked at Val in surprise but after a moment's reflection said, "All right. It's upstairs. Come up with me and I'll get it out for you."

The flat above the shop was cheerless, missing the presence of a woman, but it was obvious that it had once been a bright and comfortable home. The old man seemed almost lost in it as he wandered around opening cupboard doors and staring into them in search of the blanket. Eventually he found it in a large cabin trunk and handed it to Val.

The material was of poor quality and very thin, and it was not a blanket but a shawl of the kind that poor women wore knotted round their bodies in cold weather. Some old ladies in the High Street could still be seen wearing them when chill winds blew in from the Forth. As he rubbed the cloth between his finger and thumb, Val reflected that it was unlikely this shawl would ever have been worn by Helen Hunt's mother or sister.

"What's the tartan?" he asked, almost speaking to himself.

"It's Campbell," said Mr Cameron, "My wife was a Campbell and she thought it was wonderful he should come wrapped up in her family tartan. Like an omen, she said. Poor soul."

Val handed the blanket back and said, "Thank you very much. You've been very helpful. I represent the side of the family whose money is being claimed by your son Billy. They are very fair and reasonable people and if he has a claim, he will be paid in full."

Mr Cameron shook his head sadly, "What a waste of good money that's going to be," he said.

As Val made his way back to Queen Street there was something niggling away in his memory that he wanted to check in his notes. The list of names of male babies registered in Edinburgh in the end of 1914, which he had sent an assistant to seek out in Register House, was lying in the litter of papers on his desk and he found it at last. Running his finger down the names, he found the one he sought – 'Thomas Campbell, born October 20th, mother

89

Mary Campbell, street hawker in High Street, Edinburgh. Father unknown.'

It was evening by the time he finished in the office but, instead of going home, he headed for the High Street and the flat of the informative Mags. He found her alone except for the comatose mother-in-law who was in bed as usual.

She was amused to see him. "Still on the trail, Val?"

He laughed. "I was wondering if you knew anything about a woman called Campbell who used to live in the High Street. She might still be here for that matter."

"There's lots o' Campbells round here. Brodie's Close is fu' o' them. Aye fighting and carrying on," said Mags.

"The one I'm looking for had a baby boy about twenty-one years ago and she gave him away for fostering. She probably carried the bairn around in a tartan shawl and she might have kept him for a bit before she gave him away . . ."

A croaking voice came from the dark recess beside the fireplace. "That's the yin that used tae tell fortunes wi' a bird. Ye mind her, Mags. She lived a wee bit up from St Giles. Ye mind her Mags. She married thon coalman that fought wi' oor Jamesie last week."

The two sitting at the table stared amazed at the bed. Mags' mother-in-law hadn't put so many words together for years. The younger woman shook her head in amazement and told Val, "If that's who granny says it is, she'll be right. She's aye right."

"Where does the coalman live?" he asked.

"I've telt you that already. Brodie's Close. Just ask for Big Tam."

Brodie's Close was on the other side of the road from Bailey's Buildings and was a narrow alley running like a rabbit hole into a mass of buildings, all huddled together and falling higgledy-piggledy down the steep hill to the Grassmarket far below.

Big Tam's household was not hard to find. The first person Val asked knew where it was, one floor up and approached by an outside staircase. There was a light in the window and a rough-looking big woman answered the door.

"I'm looking for Big Tam and his wife," said Val and met the usual High Street response of, "They're no' in. Whae wants them?"

"My name's McDermot and it's really Big Tam's wife I want to see. It's about her son . . ."

She looked scared. "Which yin? Is it Sandy? He's no' a bad lad really. Just a bit ready wi' his fists."

"No, no, there's no trouble, nothing like that. It's about another son, a boy who's twenty-one now. She had him before she was married."

She held the door wider and stared out at him, using the light from inside to scrutinise his face. "Are you from Maitland?" she asked. "I told the yin who cam' yesterday that I dinna ken onything about that bairn."

"Can I come in, Mrs . . . I'll make it worth your while," he pleaded.

"Campbell. I was a Campbell and I married a Campbell," she said, standing back to admit him and giving up all pretence of not being at home.

He explained he was a lawyer investigating the claim of a Billy Cameron to be the heir of a mill magnate called Gates. "But I've discovered that he was given up for adoption by a girl called Campbell," he said. "Was it you, Mrs Campbell?"

She folded her arms defensively over her breast and said, "It was an awfy bad year that. My mither took sick and had to go to the Infirmary. He was the grandest-lookin' bairn though! Mrs Maitland saw us on the street one day and said she'd tak' him aff my hands. She needed a wee boy for some folk she'd promised a bairn to. I dinna ken what happened to it, maybe it deed. But my bairn

91

was as strong as a horse so she took him and gave me a guinea. I was sad to part wi' him because I loved him but we hadna ony money and my mither wasnae able to work any mair. I wrapped him up in my shawl and handed him over. I mind how sore I grat that night . . . He was my first, you see."

This unvarnished account struck Val as being very pathetic and he felt sympathy for the hardened woman who told it to him.

"You've had other children since then?" he asked.

"Six, and every one o' them a heller. I married Big Tam the year after I gied the bairn away. He wasnae its fayther and he didnae care."

"When was your baby born exactly, Mrs Campbell? Do you remember his birthday?"

"Damn sure I remember. It was November the tenth. I mind my mither saying when she washed him that it was her birthday too and a grand morning."

Before he turned to go, Val paused and put another question. "You said Mrs Maitland sent somebody to see you about Billy recently?"

"This afternoon. Her laddie Danny, him that collects rents for her, cam' here. He asked me if I'd seen Billy recently. I said I hadnae seen him since the day I gied him awa' and I wouldnae ken him if I ran intae him in the street. He jist said that I was to keep it that way."

Just before lunch time the next day Val was reading the first edition of the *Evening Dispatch* when his eye caught a short report on the front page.

A body taken out of Leith Docks this morning has been identified as that of Herbert Johnstone, 57, of 375 Leith Walk. Johnstone was disbarred from practising his profession as a lawyer five years ago

*when he was convicted of embezzlement. Police say
there are no suspicious circumstances.*

Val, who had been sitting with his feet on his desk, shot
upright in his chair and reached for the phone. His call was
to Colin Anderson, a friend who worked in the police as a
detective based in the head office in the High Street.

"Colin, what's this about Herbert Johnstone drowning
himself in Leith Docks?" said Val, for he knew that
the line about 'no suspicious circumstances' was press
shorthand for suicide.

"Yes, I've just heard about him. He's the one I sent
down a few years ago, isn't he? He was on the bottle in
a big way the lads tell me."

"I spoke to him yesterday morning. He wasn't sui-
cidal then."

"He must have changed his mind. There weren't any
marks on the body and the coroner said he was drunk
when he fell in."

"What time do they think it happened?"

"Early this morning or late last night apparently. He
was drinking in his local till closing time and nobody saw
him after that. Did you know him well, Val?"

"Not really. I just met him once as I've said. He nicked
my cigarettes."

"Well you'll not get them back off him now," said
Colin with a laugh.

An hour later Val was sitting with his head in his hands
on the stairs of 375 Leith Walk when a policeman he knew
came heavily up the steps.

"Hello, Val," he said. "What're you doin' here?"

"I was waiting for someone to come along and let me
into Johnstone's flat. It'll save me breaking in."

"You've some cheek. Why do you want to go in there?"

"Because he was involved in a case I'm looking into.
He was trying to screw money out of a client of mine."

"Well, he didnae get it, did he?" The policeman was opening the door of the flat with a skeleton key as he spoke.

"No, he didn't. Are you sure he drowned himself?"

"Either that or he fell in."

As Val stepped into the flat he passed the policeman a ten-shilling note which was rapidly pocketed and they walked into the middle of a room which had a long window overlooking the street. It was surprisingly well furnished, with heavy period pieces of furniture which must have come from a more prestigious address. Against the back wall stood a high roll-topped desk with the working surface littered with papers.

As he riffled through them Val saw that some had to do with the Cameron affair. One sheet fluttered to the floor and when he bent to pick it up he saw it was a list of names and addresses . . . some of which he recognised because they were the same as the ones his assistant had got from the City records for him. Folding it up he slipped it into his pocket.

The policeman was prowling through the rooms, deliberately ignoring him.

"What are you here for?" Val asked him.

"They sent me down to see if I could find addresses of any relatives."

"Will I have a look with you?"

"Go ahead."

They found nothing. Johnstone seemed to have deliberately obliterated all signs of the past. Any relatives, wife, or children had been removed from his life. In looking for traces of them, however, Val found a dossier on Howie Gates which he would dearly loved to have removed but didn't risk it, and another on Cynthia Maitland which interested him even more. Opening it, he saw it was full of carefully written notes on squares of pasteboard, each with a different year or month on the heading. Though he drank more than was good for him, Johnstone had obviously retained the ability for doing painstaking work when he so chose.

He found the policeman in the kitchen staring bleakly at the remains of a half-eaten meal on the table. Val picked up a glass that stood beside a plate containing congealed bacon fat and a cut-open fried egg, the yolk of which had hardened into an unappetising looking paste. There was about two inches of amber liquid in the glass and when Val sniffed it he realised it was straight whisky.

"Funny," he said laying it down, "You wouldn't think a drunk going out to kill himself would leave a big slug of whisky in his glass, do you? He might leave his bacon and eggs but I doubt if he'd not finish up his whisky. And where's the bottle? It's not in the bin or in a cupboard, is it?"

The policeman, throwing open cupboard doors, shook his head.

"What was he wearing when they fished him out of the dock?" asked Val.

"An overcoat over pyjamas."

"Was he wearing shoes?"

"Socks, I know that, but no shoes. They could have come off though."

"Funny," said Val again.

Ushered out by the policeman eventually, he waited while the door was locked again.

"Dinna you try to go in again, Val," he was cautioned.

He said he wouldn't, but what he did do was knock on the doors of Johnstone's neighbours. The only one that responded was the occupant of the flat on the other side of the landing – a crabbed-looking old woman who glared at him accusingly and asked, "What?"

"I'm trying to find out about Mr Johnstone who lived next door to you," he said.

"The police've been here already asking aboot him. We dinna ken anything."

"I'm a lawyer trying to find out if he had any family who should be informed of his death."

"I dinna ken anything about his family. All I ken is that he was a nasty-tongued boozer."

"You didn't like him?"

"No, I did not and neither did my man. He was aye moaning aboot our wee dog Tommy. He said Tommy barked but that's whit dogs dae, isn't it? They bark."

"Did Tommy bark last night?"

She glared at him. "Whit if he did?"

"Nothing. I'm just wondering if Tommy wakened you at any time last night with his barking."

"As a matter of fact he did. He's a grand watchdog. I said to that man next door that he should be happy to have a dog like Tommy on the stair. He keeps away burglars."

"Did Tommy bark at people he knew?"

"No, he did not. He never barked when Johnstone came home puggled because he kent who he was."

"So if he barked last night it was probably because he'd heard somebody he didn't know."

She nodded cautiously, wondering what catch there was in the question.

"Where's Tommy now? Why didn't he bark when I knocked on your door?"

"He's out wi' my man. If he'd been here you'd never have got your hand on the knocker before he was barking."

When Val left the tenement, pulling the big street door closed behind him, he found a bent old man with a walking stick and a dog on a lead barring his way. The dog, a rough coated terrier was baring its teeth and growling ferociously. When Val looked into its eyes it let out a volley of angry barks.

96

"Hello, Tommy," he said, and then addressed the old man. "Your dog's a great guard for you, isn't he?"

"Oh aye!" Tommy's owner regarded his slavering pet with pride. He obviously enjoyed Tommy's aggression.

"He must have kicked up a row last night when the man came to see Mr Johnstone."

"He did that. I thought he was going to tear the door doon."

"Did you see who Johnstone's visitor was?"

"No, I did not. It was the middle o' the night. I just heard Tommy kicking up a din."

"There might have been nobody there then?"

"Maybe, but Tommy doesnae usually bother unless he's got good reason."

Phemie Grossett had to wait till the next day before she read about the death in a small paragraph in *The Scotsman*, which only carried it because of Johnstone's previous legal notoriety. Sitting at the table with the paper spread before her, she gave a gasp that alerted her mother who asked, "What is it? What's happened?"

"It's that lawyer that was helping us, Mr Johnstone. It says here he's been found drowned in Leith Docks."

"Oh my God. Did Maitland know he was helping you?"

"I don't know."

"I'll bet she did and she's got him. I'm warning you, Phemie, you'd best get out of this business before you're found floating face down too."

"But why, Mother? What's she got to hide that's so big?"

"Dinna ask. Just believe me it's big enough for her to want it hidden at any cost."

While the two women were arguing, Val McDermot was on his way to interview Mrs Maitland. Now he was driven not just by curiosity but by a kind of anger as well, though he was not exactly sure why it should be directed at Cynthia Maitland. When he found himself in her pretentious drawing room, his anger grew stronger and he had to fight to hide it.

She was extremely hostile and went on the attack as soon as he said he was representing Helen Hunt, daughter of Mr Gates.

"I've had about enough of this. First it was Phemie Grossett, then that disbarred lawyer and now you. If this doesn't stop I'm going to make an official complaint to the police about harrassment!" she exploded.

He stood watching her with his hands in his pockets. "Go ahead," he drawled. "All I want to know is why you've got yourself involved."

"I'm not involved!"

"You are. You've been named as a supporting witness for a man claiming to be the Gates heir. He says he was given the information by you but I happen to know he's a fake because his birthdate is wrong and he wasn't weaned when the Camerons got him. The Gates baby was weaned because the women who kept it for you weren't wet nurses. Why did you get mixed up in this messy business?"

"I thought it was Billy Cameron who was the Gates baby but then I remembered it wasn't. I'm not involved in this. Anyone can make a mistake. Now get out of my house and don't come back."

She was so scared he could almost smell her fear. Why? he wondered as he walked back up the street.

Then a second thought struck him. "I wonder if Johnstone dug up some dirt on her. Damn, I should have taken that folder from his flat yesterday. I'll have to go back and try to get it."

He went back to the office first, however, and when he returned to Leith Walk there was no policeman guarding the door. A lonely, squalid death was soon forgotten and Johnstone was simply not important enough for massive investigations. The stair was silent – Tommy must be out, thought Val. Looking surreptitiously over his shoulder, he produced a narrow-bladed penknife and slid it down the jamb of the door. The Yale lock clicked open and he was in.

The flat was in chaos. Fairly tidy when he left it, the books were tumbled over the floor and papers were scattered everywhere like a snowstorm. Even before he started searching seriously he knew that the files on Mrs Maitland and Howie Gates would not be there and he was right. They had been spirited away.

Tommy's owner was out but a younger woman with a toddler clinging to her skirt in a flat on the floor beneath nodded when he asked if she had seen anyone going into Mr Johnstone's. "Yes, his son came a wee while ago. He asked if any of us had a key. I had one that the folk who were in the flat before him gave me so I gave it to him."

"His son? Did he say what his name was?"

"He said he was called Danny. Mr Johnstone never spoke to any of us so I wasnae to know if he had a son or not. He seemed polite enough but not Johnstone's sort really. Kind of rough. A bit of a surprise."

"But you gave him the key?"

"Why not? I watched to make sure he wasnae taking away the furniture or anything like that but all he had was a bundle of papers when he went back down the stair."

"What did he look like?"

"He had very red hair, all curly, and a red face. Quite heavy built but no' all that old. Twenty-five maybe . . ."

Red haired. The dreaded debt collector who terrorised Mags and the other tenants of Bailey's Building. Mrs Maitland's Danny.

Six

Reggie's Aunt Mary came up with an address for Leonie's old governess on the same morning as a concerned-looking Mr Stevens arrived at Castledevon to announce that he had received a letter from a young man called Hugo Anderson who also claimed to be Howie Gates' illegitimate grandson.

"Another one!" exclaimed Reggie. "Twins, d'you think?"

Mr Stevens examined the letter in his hand. "I don't think so. This one has a different birthday, a week after Cameron's. Even twins aren't born a week apart."

"They're all frauds. I knew this would happen," exploded Reggie. "Get someone to investigate this new fellow, Stevens."

Helen, who had been sitting quietly listening, suddenly said, "I've already engaged an investigator. He can do it."

The men turned and stared at her as if she had suddenly sprouted a pair of horns. "Who?" said Reggie.

When she named Sutherland, Ross and McQueen, Mr Stevens gave a sigh of relief. "Very respectable," he said. "A good choice. Do you want me to contact them and tell them about this latest development?"

"That's all right. I'm going to Edinburgh today to try to find Leonie's old governess," said Helen coolly. "I'll tell him myself."

Reggie was still goggling when Stevens left. "How did you know to go to that firm?" he asked.

"Through contacts," said Helen airily, surprising herself.

Still feeling self-confident, she drove to Edinburgh and parked in Queensferry Street where she had been told that the ex-governess Miss Alice Cunningham lived in a flat belonging to one of her old employers. The building was easy to find because it was strategically placed on a corner, staring up the street towards the West End. Miss Cunningham lived on the first floor. The gods were smiling on Helen that day because when she pulled the bell, the lady herself answered the door.

The moment Helen saw her standing ramrod straight and rake thin in the doorway, a shoal of old memories came rushing back and she was five years old again. For some reason tears pricked her eyes and she felt a cold clutch of fear at her heart.

"Yes?" said the unsmiling woman in the half-open doorway. "What do you want?" Her tone, however, was not challenging, more curious, for some instinct had told Helen to dress up for this meeting. She was wearing a smartly tailored suit made from the finest material produced by her father's mill and a jaunty hat that was pulled down on one side of her head. In her ears were the diamond earrings and on her lapel was a large diamond brooch. She knew she looked rich.

"I'm Helen Hunt – I used to be Helen Gates," she said. "I wondered if you could spare a little time to talk to me about my sister Leonie."

"Little Helen!" said Miss Cunningham in astonishment. She went on more cordially, "Do come in. I saw your father's death in the paper – very sad."

"He was an old man," said Helen stepping into the dark hall and following Miss Cunningham's poker-straight back into a large drawing room with a bow window that looked down on the street. The woman who now turned to look at her was wearing a black dress with a dirty crocheted collar. Her greying hair was tied into a loose bun at the back of her neck and on her feet were worn house shoes. She had obviously been caught *en déshabille*. A forest of potted plants was arranged along the sills of the windows and on every available surface were framed photographs of men in uniform or women in court dresses and fabulous jewels.

"Do sit down," said Miss Cunningham graciously, eyeing Helen's glittering brooch. "I'm afraid my maid is out but I could make us some tea."

Judging by the untidy state of the room, Helen doubted the existence of a maid but she declined the tea and sat on a large sofa that was piled with books and newspapers.

"I won't take up too much of your time, Miss Cunningham. I'm trying to find out about my sister – I was very young when she died, you see, and I don't really remember her.

"You were her governess, I believe, and now that we meet again I do remember you."

Miss Cunningham gave a frosty smile. "You were just a little thing when I was at Castledevon, newly born when I arrived in fact. Your sister's previous governess had left under a bit of a cloud – an unsuitable liaison, I believe."

"And you stayed how long?" asked Helen.

Sharp eyes looked into her face. "Till your sister died."

"Did you go to Italy with her?" asked Helen sharply.

"Yes. She couldn't go by herself. She was extremely gauche. But we didn't get as far as Italy. We went to Cannes – a terrible trip by ship to Marseilles, it was a good thing I spoke French – and then in November when the war had started, your mother arrived and took us home again."

"You went to the Highlands with them?"

"No. Your mother took over, much to my relief, I must admit – I had no experience in that sort of thing. She and Leonie went to the Highlands, to the shooting lodge her father used, with the Castledevon housekeeper and a midwife. Your sister was very pregnant by that time and making a great fuss. She didn't want me there. I went back to Castledevon and waited for them to return because it had to look as if everything was normal afterwards . . ."

This had obviously rankled and still did.

"Then when Leonie died you went to my husband's aunt? I married Reginald Hunt," Helen explained.

"Yes, and then to Lady Amulree to tutor her daughter Annabelle. A very good family." Why don't I like you? Is it just because you're a terrible snob? wondered Helen but she hid her reactions and smiled blandly.

"Do you happen to know where the hunting lodge was?" she asked.

"Oh yes, a very remote place, most unsuitable in winter. I was glad I didn't have to go, in fact – it was bad enough in summer. All those midge things that bite! It was called Farquhar Lodge and it's in a place called Glencripsdale, miles from anywhere. You have to reach it by *boat*!"

Helen had a vague memory of a house amid tall pine trees and a glittering loch. It was like recalling a blissful dream.

"And that's where my sister had her baby," she said. Miss Cunningham did not flinch though the word 'baby' had not been mentioned between them before.

"I presume so," she said stiffly.

Helen leaned forward and clasped her ringed hands on her lap. "You see, that's what I'm trying to find out – about the baby. In his will my father left a legacy to Leonie's child. Already we have had two people trying to claim it and there may still be more. I'm anxious that the money goes to the right person."

"I have no direct knowledge of the child. I never saw it. The person who was most involved was the housekeeper, Mrs Lang. That's why they took her with them, because

103

she was going to arrange for it to be fostered. She knew some woman who found good homes for unwanted children, I believe. It's her you should be speaking to, not me."

"Mrs Lang! I remember Mrs Lang now," cried Helen. "Was she a big woman with very black hair?"

Unlike Miss Cunningham, Mrs Lang evoked warm feelings in Helen – big arms that cuddled, pockets in an apron that could always be relied on to contain something nice to eat, a red apple or a stick of barley sugar, a deep laugh.

"Yes, black hair like a gypsy. In fact, I think there was gypsy blood in the Lang family. Her brother certainly looked like one, very low class, very *animal*," she said with a sniff.

"But Mrs Lang wasn't at Castledevon when I was growing up. Did she leave too?"

"She was sent away when the baby was born. Your mother repaid people's help in a strange way. Mrs Lang was very upset by it all."

"How do you know that?"

"Because I met her on Princes Street one day. She stopped me and told me. I'm afraid she'd been drinking so I didn't waste time with her. I didn't want people to see me speaking to a person of her sort, you see."

"Was she living in Edinburgh?"

"Somewhere in the High Street, I believe, with her sister-in-law, a girl called Amy that used to work in Castledevon too as a scullery maid. A very consumptive looking person, always coughing. The brother was killed in the war . . ."

"Do you have any idea why my sister would want to kill herself?"

There was no sign of surprise from Miss Cunningham at hearing Helen knew Leonie had committed suicide. "No," she said flatly.

"What sort of girl was she?" asked Helen desperately.

"Very spoiled, very wilful, not a clever girl, no real refinement, but then . . ." Helen knew that Miss Cunningham had to bite back words that would have betrayed her feeling that the Gates' family background could hardly produce a girl of breeding and refinement.

She stood up. "Thank you for your time, Miss Cunningham," she said. "I have just one more question. Do you have any idea, any suspicion, who the father of my sister's child could have been?"

A glitter of malice showed in the other woman's eyes. She's probably not as old as she looks, thought Helen with surprise, she might still only be in her fifties. When she was living in Castledevon, she would be thirty-something . . . a young woman.

"Your sister knew a lot of young men and she was quite indiscriminate about them. She was very keen on horses and hunting and through doing that she met some strange people. But when her parents found out she was having a baby, they were so extremely angry that I suspected that the father was someone outside their social circle. A *servant* . . ."

If I were braver or more cruel I would remind this woman that she was a servant herself, thought Helen. Instead she said nothing and allowed herself to be shown out.

When Helen Hunt was shown into Val McDermot's office later that afternoon, he was in a bad mood and the sight of her in her diamonds and expensive clothes made him even more irritable. I bet when she first came here she dressed down so's we wouldn't think her rich and not charge her so much, he reflected caustically. He'd heard about those Border manufacturing families – money mad and cheese paring, the lot of them. They paid the lowest wages and dominated town councils so's no other industries would be allowed into their area and force them to pay higher wages.

"I've brought you a lot more information about my case," she said breezily, sitting down opposite him and giving him a dazzling smile.

"Indeed, and have we a business arrangement?" he asked.

Her face fell. "Don't you remember? I asked you to investigate the claimant to my father's will."

"Did we enter into a formal contract? Are you aware of our charges?"

"No, but you said . . ."

"I think we'd better put it on a regular footing," he said in a schoolmasterly tone and saw her stiffen. He wasn't going to tell her that there was no way he was going to abandon this case now because he had become personally engaged in it . . . driven on by anger and pity for Johnstone and the grocer Cameron, as well as dislike of the glacial Mrs Maitland who he was sure was not above murder. It had nothing to do with her and her petty worries about whether or not to share her vast fortune with a claimant.

"All right," she said. "Just tell me what you want me to do."

He named a rate that he knew to be exorbitant – serve her right for walking around dripping with diamonds. She flinched only slightly before she agreed to it but he saw her eyes harden, a true daughter of the Borders business magnates, he thought.

When they'd signed an agreement, he sat back and invited her to tell her tale. More sober now, she launched into it.

"A second claimant to my father's money has come forward. It's a Mr Hugo Anderson and he lives in Corstorphine. I've brought you his address. He says he was adopted at six days old and that his mother was my sister Leonie."

She passed Mr Stevens' paper over the desk to him and he dropped it negligently onto his blotter. What a horrible man, thought Helen. Why am I giving him my good money? But she'd signed the paper and had to go on with it. Besides, what would Reggie say if she went home and told him she'd become disillusioned with her enquiry agent?

"Anything else?" he asked.

"There is something. I went to see my sister's old governess today and she told me where the baby was born."

"Where?"

She dictated the address and he wrote it down.

"Was she there at the time?"

"No, but the Castledevon housekeeper was because she knew some person who would find a home for the child when it was born. Her name was Mrs Lang. The governess told me she met Mrs Lang in Edinburgh a few years ago and she was drunk but said she was living in the High Street with a consumptive sister-in-law called Amy. The sister-in-law's husband, Mrs Lang's brother, had been killed in the war . . ."

It was as if she'd fired a dart into the heart of the man on the other side of the desk. He shot upright in the chair where he had been slouching and said sharply, "Amy – drunk – High Street? It's not possible, is it? Of course it is. It fits. Maitland. It fits."

With a leap he was out of the chair and heading for the door as if she weren't there. She turned in her seat and watched him pull a raincoat off a coat-stand behind the door. "Where are you going?" she asked.

"To Bailey's Buildings."

"Where's Bailey's Buildings?"

"In the High Street. I think your mysterious Mrs Lang might be there."

"Can I come?"

He paused with one arm into the coat and glared at her. "You? In Bailey's Buildings with all those diamonds? They'd lynch you."

"I can take them off," she said, wresting the clips from her ears, "Besides, if the woman you're going to see is Mrs Lang, I think I'd recognise her. It might help if I was there."

He considered this for a minute. "All right, but take off the jewellery. And put on this raincoat. I don't really need it."

She did as she was told. The raincoat almost swept the floor when she put it on but she belted it tightly and did not complain.

Her car was standing at the pavement edge outside the office door and when she ran round to get into the driving seat, Val McDermot stopped dead and said, "Are you crazy? We can't go up there in that. We'll walk."

"At least let's take the bus. I'll pay," she pleaded.

May was a hot month that year and all through the stifling days and nights, Georgina Kennedy felt ill. She stopped going to work and took to lying all day in her tumbled bed beneath the roof tiles, tossing and sweating. Her back ached and her legs had swelled up to twice their normal size. Her skin had taken on a yellowish tinge and she was plagued by constant nausea.

She no longer yearned for beer or any alcohol. She decided that she did not have much longer to live and resigned herself to death.

After she had not been seen for several days, Mags became concerned about her and went upstairs to investigate. Though she was unsqueamish, when she pushed open the unlocked door, the smell that met her made her screw up her face in distaste.

"My God, what's happened here?" she asked, looking around in concern before she went over to the only window and threw it up to let in some fresh air.

Georgina lay on the bed, her once ample flesh sagging from her arms and legs like blubber from a whale. When she saw Mags she gave some gulping sobs. "I'm dying. I'm done for," she said.

"Nae wonder. It's amazing you've no' been gassed, the stink that's in here," said Mags. "What's wrang wi' you?"

"I dinna ken. I've been vomiting something terrible."

"It's a doctor you need," said Mags, looking sharply at the woman on the bed. "I'll send one o' the bairns for Dr Sharp up in Johnstone Terrace."

"I canna pay for a doctor, Mags. I've no money."

"He's a decent man. When he sees how bad you are, he'll maybe no' ask you for onything."

When the doctor came, he toiled grunting up the many, many stairs and then frowned when he saw the state of the woman on the bed. "Are you still drinking?" he asked as he palpated her swollen belly.

"No, doctor," she said humbly, "I've not had a drink for a couple of weeks now. I havenae felt like it."

"I think we'd better get you into the Infirmary where they can have a real look at you and feed you up a wee bit. You've not been eating either, have you?"

"No, doctor."

When he went back downstairs Mags stopped him and asked, "How is she, Dr Sharp?"

"I'm sending her to the Infirmary, Mags. There's something wrong with her liver. They'll fetch her away this afternoon."

Before the ambulance arrived, however, Val and Helen appeared in the stair and were met by Mags on her way down from the top storey.

"That woman on oor top flair. She's being taken to the Infirmary," she told him.

"Why?"

"The doctor says there's something wrang wi' her liver."

"Can't say I'm surprised. Thanks for telling me, Mags. It's her we've come to see actually," he told her.

"Well, you'd better hurry up. The ambulance'll be here soon."

They saw her through the open door, lying parchment-faced on an unmade bed. She turned her head when she heard them coming and stared straight at Helen.

Though it was more than twenty years since they last saw each other, Helen recognised her at once.

"Mrs Lang!" she cried.

The sick woman groaned, "My name's Kennedy. I married him in 1915 . . ."

Unmindful of the pitiable state of the room, Helen ran across the floor and took the woman's hand. "But you used to be Lang. It's Helen Gates. Wee Helen."

"Helen! Oh you wee soul! What are you doing here?"

Helen was kneeling by the bed. "I've come to see you about Leonie's baby. I'm trying to find him."

"You too? You'll no' find him, Helen. He's gone."

"Gone? What do you mean? Where's he gone?"

"He's gone and it's my fault. I didnae realise . . . Go away Helen, dinna get mixed up in it. It's bad. They're a' bad." Tears were sliding down the furrowed cheeks and the sick woman's voice faltered. Helen desperately chafed her hands. "Tell me where the baby went, Mrs Lang. Just tell me."

"I dinna ken. Go away, Helen."

At the door of the room there was a thunderous knock and three men with a stretcher stood there. "Is it her?" they asked Val, pointing to the woman on the bed. He nodded.

110

They loaded her onto the stretcher and groaned and moaned all their way down the stairs. The neighbours were out at their doors to watch the procession go by and Mags patted Georgina's hand before she was unceremoniously loaded into the back of the ambulance.

Before she was taken away she whispered, "Mags, you know Miss Grossett who sometimes comes to see me? She lives in Elm Row, number twelve. Could you send someone to tell her about me being ill?"

"I'll send the bairn, dinna worry. You're going to be all right."

When the ambulance drove away to take their patient to the charity ward of the Royal Infirmary, Mags said to Val, "She was awful worried that the Grossett woman should know where she's gone."

Val tapped his teeth with his fingernail. "Really. Do you want me to let her know?"

"That's fine then. I'll leave it to you."

When Val and Helen were walking back down the Mound, she took off the raincoat and handed it to him. "I don't need this now that I'm no longer in disguise," she said.

He took it and slung it over his arm. "That didn't get us very far," he said.

"At least it confirmed that the woman who calls herself Kennedy is really our old housekeeper Mrs Lang and she was involved with the giving away of my sister's baby," said Helen.

"She called you Little Helen," said Val.

"That's what she called me when I was a child. I remember her. She was kind."

"Very feudal," he said.

She bristled. "I can't understand you. You seem to dislike everything I stand for but you're not averse to taking my money."

111

"Well, if I didn't somebody else would. You may rest assured I'll put it to good use."

"Like what? Political causes probably. Are you a Communist or something?"

He whipped the end of his red tie out of his jacket and waggled it at her. "How did you guess?" he jeered.

They did not speak again until they reached her car. She climbed into it and was greatly relieved when its engine fired immediately without her having recourse to the starting handle. He stood on the pavement and watched impassively as she carelessly ground the edge of the running board against the kerbstones. "Nice car," he said. "Pity about the driver."

"I hate you McDermot," she shouted over the noise of the engine as she drove away.

When Val reached the flat in Elm Row he found that Phemie was out at work. The door was unlocked, however, so he pushed it ajar and went in. A crumpled-faced old woman was sitting in a basket chair beside the table. Her pouched eyes were staring at him and her swollen hands clutched and unclutched at the blanket that covered her knees.

"I'm sorry if I frightened you. I'm looking for your daughter," he said loudly.

"She's oot . . ." It took a long time for the words to come but they were clear enough.

"You're Mrs Grossett?" he asked and she nodded.

"Can I wait?" She nodded again.

"I'm Valentine McDermot and I'm acting for Mrs Hunt. Her sister was Leonie Gates whom I believe you knew."

The lumpy old body leaned forward in the chair and she mumbled, "Puir lassie."

"Was she?"

"Oh aye. Greetin' for her bairn. Puir lassie."

"What happened to the baby?"

"Maitland got it. She took lots o' bairns. A baby farm."

"A baby farm?" exclaimed Val. It was the first time in this inquiry someone had described Mrs Maitland's operation so baldly. Mrs Grossett was struggling for words and it was obvious that she was enjoying his interest.

"Lots o' them. Best families . . . lots o' money."

"Where did the babies go? She couldn't keep them all – the law wouldn't allow it – and it must have been hard to find homes for them all."

She sat back and a shuttered look came over her face. "I dinna ken that," she muttered.

Val leaned forward. "Tell me where Leonie Gates' baby went, Mrs Grossett. It's not Billy Cameron, I know that now. Where's the real Gates baby? And what about Mrs Kennedy? What's her story?"

He did not hear Phemie Grossett coming silently through the open door but he saw her mother's gaze shifting over his shoulder and turned round to see her watching him with a look of sheer hate on her face.

"What are you doing here? I'll get the polis man to you," she snapped.

"I knocked on the door and asked your mother if I could come in. She said yes."

"She cannae talk."

"She can. She's been talking to me about the Gates baby. I came to tell you two things: first that your friend Mrs Kennedy – or is it Lang? – is in the Infirmary and wants you to go to see her; and second that I have proof that your friend Billy Cameron is not Howie Gates' grandson and has no claim to the old man's estate. You've been trying to perpetrate a fraud and if you persist in it, I'll have you charged."

"Did my mother tell you he's not the right one? She's lost her mind. She doesnae ken what's she's saying."

Val looked at the old woman and could see quite clearly

that she knew perfectly well what was going on. "No, she didn't tell me. I knew he wasn't right before I came here. I have cast-iron proof. But she knows, doesn't she? You'd better call the whole thing off now."

Phemie Grossett said nothing, only stared at him till he turned and left the flat. As he went back down the stairs he heard her shouting at the old woman in the basket chair.

That's it then, he thought. That part of it's over. She'll get in touch with Cameron and they'll abandon their little scheme. Mrs Kennedy hopefully keeps her liver; Phemie Grossett keeps her mother and perhaps her temper. What Cameron would keep was anyone's guess. And Val McDermot? I'll keep my nose to the grindstone and keep on trying to find out what's behind this puzzle. There's a lot more to come, he thought as he walked along.

Back in his office he telephoned Mrs Cynthia Maitland and when he spoke to her he was at his most charming: smiling, polite, and very correct. His innocuous manner almost disarmed her – but only almost.

"My client Mrs Helen Hunt has been having the most upsetting time," he said. "People have been turning up claiming to be her sister's illegitimate sons."

"*People?*" asked Mrs Maitland in surprise.

He nodded. "We thought you might be able to cast some light on the subject because they claim to have been given away as babies by you."

There was a pause and he could almost hear her thinking. Then she said, "I used to find good homes for unwanted children from time to time. That's not a crime."

Val smiled. "Of course not. Such arrangements used to be quite common, I believe, but the Infant Life Protection Act of 1908 attempted to regularise the position. The local authority became involved then, didn't it?"

He sounded mild and slightly confused as he went on, "Mr Cameron of Leith said you gave him the choice of three children in 1915 when he chose the boy called Billy."

"He's mistaken."

"Of course he is an old man. Memories fail, don't they?"

She said nothing. Then he asked, "How many people did you tell that their babies were the child of Leonie Gates?"

"Memories fail," she said sharply.

"Did people like to think their children came from respectable homes? Was that how you got good money for them? Were you selling them like puppies?"

"Of course not. People were anxious to get good children. They wanted to know something about the circumstances of the birth, naturally."

"Especially if they were paying a lot of money," added Val smoothly. "It must have been a lucrative business. Real parents paid to have their children looked after and adoptive parents paid to be given a child. Howie Gates paid for his grandchild to be placed, didn't he? Did he ever ask for details about how it was getting on? It could have been dead for all he knew."

It was as if he'd stung her over the distance. She hissed, "I hope you're not making accusations. You'd better not be. I'm a respectable woman who provided a service for the best families."

"Unfortunately the sort of service you provided is not one they'd be prepared to give you a testimonial for doing," said Val, "but perhaps you can give me some names of satisfied adoptive parents. What about Mrs Anderson whose son also thinks he's Howie Gates' grandson? Are there many more of them? You were required by the law to provide the authorities with written information of where each child came from and where it eventually went, weren't you? Have you kept your records?"

"If I have they're my property."

"You could be made to produce them in a court of law," Val reminded her.

He was hardly off the phone when Mr Maitland's adopted son Danny emerged from her house and strode off in the direction of Leith Walk. In her stuffy room Phemie Grossett was washing clothes in a tin basin and hanging them out of the window on a sort of wire pulley. When she saw him shouldering his way through her narrow door, she paled.

"C'mon," he said taking her roughly by the shoulder.

"Where to?"

"You ken fine where to. She's hopping mad at you."

"I canna leave my mother."

Danny flexed his fists. "If you dinna come noo, your mither'll be on her ain for ever."

Nobody looked at them as they hurried through the streets, the big man hauling along a reluctant woman. Sights like that were fairly common in Leith Walk.

Mrs Maitland's first greeting for Phemie was to slap her on the face.

"You fool. You shouldn't have got involved in this Gates thing. Are you involved with the other one too?"

"What one?"

"Mrs Anderson's boy."

"Is he Howie Gates' heir?"

"Of course not, but I might have mentioned the name to Mrs Anderson and she's a terrible snob who never forgets a thing."

"Honest, I haven't anything to do wi' that."

"Well the best thing to do is let the whole thing drop. It's been a bad idea from the beginning."

A sly look came into Phemie Grossett's eyes for, since she had realised that Mrs Maitland was rattled, she was recovering her composure. "You're awful keen to wash your hands of it. Are you scared they'll find out more

than is good for you? There's a lot of folk still about that
could talk, you know."

"Like who? You and your mother."

"And Kennedy. She's in the hospital greeting and
moaning."

"How much will it cost to keep her quiet?"

"Well, she's not working any more. She won't have
any money she hasn't drunk. Maybe forty pounds."

"And you and your old bat of a mother?"

"Fifty – each."

"And that'll be the end of it? You'll get out of that flat
and disappear?"

Phemie nodded. "Aye. My mother's brother lives in
Cowdenbeath. We'll go there."

"I can only give you twenty pounds now. That's all
I've got in the house, but I'll send Danny with the rest
tomorrow and you make sure you stay settled in Fife."
Mrs Maitland walked over to her desk and pulled out a
drawer containing a small roll of pound notes. When she
counted out twenty, Phemie Grossett took the money and
tucked it into the waistband of her skirt. "I'll not let you
down," she promised.

"You'd better not," said Mrs Maitland.

Val McDermot borrowed old Mr Sutherland's car to go
to Corstorphine in order to interview Hugo Anderson,
another claimant for Howie Gates' fortune.

He sprawled awkwardly in the back seat feeling resent-
ful because McDonald, the stiff chauffeur, did not like
anyone riding in front with him. The car was a massive
machine with deep plush covered seats and a speaking tube. It brought out all Val's most rabid political
prejudices.

The Corstorphine address given by Anderson was in
an estate of recently built semi-detached houses with
minute front gardens and wooden rustic-style gates built

117

on the slope of a south-facing hill not far from the zoo. Val had sent a message asking for an interview at 11 a.m. and he was obviously expected for the front door was opened before he even descended from the car.

"I will wait here for you, Mr McDermot," said McDonald gravely as he held the car door open for Val who stumbled out shamefaced.

A red-haired young man welcomed him with an out-stretched hand. "I'm Hugo Anderson. Do come in. You're the lawyer from my grandfather's family, aren't you?"

There was a very genteel tea tray laid out in the small front room and a fussy-looking woman wearing pince-nez spectacles asked him if he preferred tea or coffee, "or something stronger, a sherry perhaps?" He declined all the offers and said he would like to get the business done as quickly as possible because he had other appointments for the afternoon.

They understood pefectly and settled themselves beam-ing in two armchairs after ushering Val into a rounded sofa which was extremely uncomfortable. He opened his briefcase and said, "I represent Mrs Helen Hunt, the daughter of Mr Albert Gates."

"My esteemed grandfather," carolled Hugo who was a strongly built young man with startlingly red hair. As he followed him into the sitting room Val had noticed that though he looked muscular and sporty, Mr Anderson walked with a very obvious limp.

"Perhaps you would like to tell me why you claim Mr Gates as your grandfather?"

Hugo looked fondly at the lady with the pince-nez. "My mother – my adoptive mother – noticed his death in the newspaper and said to me that she had reason to believe he was my grandfather. The lady who found me for her had told her so."

Val switched his gaze to Mrs Anderson who nodded

enthuiastically. "I got Hugo from Mrs Maitland of George Square who was one of my pianoforte pupils . . ."

Here Hugo interrupted again. "My mother is very highly regarded as a piano teacher in Edinburgh and she frequently gives well-attended recitals. Perhaps you have heard her?"

Val shook his head.

"That can be rectified," said Hugo Anderson grandly. "She would be happy to play for you. You have a pianoforte, I presume?"

"No, actually I don't, but what proof exactly . . . ? You see, you are not the only claimant." Val was becoming impatient.

Hugo adopted a solemn expression and said, "I'm sure I am a genuine Gates. When I was adopted by my mother, as I call her, her friend Mrs Maitland told her that my mother was a Miss Gates, the daughter of a very rich mill owner in the Borders. We would have made an effort to attend his funeral if we had heard of his death in time but soon after we saw his death notice, we read another advertisement asking for his heirs to contact his lawyers in Galashiels and that was what I did. I presume you have come here as a result of that."

"Yes," said Val. "But have you any written documentation for your claim?"

"No, just Mrs Maitland's word. She lives in Stockbridge now and I'm sure she will recall what she said to my mother."

Huh, thought Val, will she though?

"Have you a birth certificate?" he asked.

"Yes, one filed by my present mother because I was only a few days old when she got me. The mother's name is given as unknown as if I were a foundling. Mrs Maitland said that was perfectly legal and the Gates family wanted it that way. There was a Mr Anderson then too, of course, but unfortunately he is now deceased."

"Can I take it?"

"Of course," said Hugo and handed it over.

"There are other claimants to Mr Gates' estate, I'm afraid," said Val, "and we have to investigate every claim, but we will be in touch with you as soon as possible." Then he stood up to go and Hugo stood up with him, lurching slightly on his bad leg.

"I hope you don't mind my asking, but have you suffered an injury?" he asked.

Normally he would not draw attention to a person's disabilities but he knew this was significant for he suddenly realised that one of the young man's legs was shorter than the other and his left shoe was built up by about two inches.

Hugo's bombast did not leave him as he shook his head. "Oh no. I was born with what is called a club foot, I'm afraid. Fortunately it does not curtail me in any way."

Seven

For days Helen Hunt had been silent and abstracted with her husband, hardly seeming to notice when he addressed a remark to her.

Eventually he became petulant, thinking of his affectionate, motherly mistress in Edinburgh who he had decided to give up in order to make an effort to mend his marriage. His brother had been most vehement on the subject. "For God's sake Reg, get your wife pregnant and then this bother about missing heirs will disappear. Why should you pay out thousands of pounds to some bastard when your own son could have it?"

But how, thought Reggie, watching his wan-faced wife who sat at the opposite end of their dining table shoving food aimlessly around her plate, how did you get a woman pregnant when she wouldn't even speak to you? His idea of going to France had not even been considered by her and he wasn't the sort to break into her bedroom at night and impregnate her by force. It took him all his time to manage it with Eleanor and she was more than willing.

He lowered his eyebrows and glared at Helen. "What is the matter with you? Are you ill? Do you want me to call a doctor?"

She looked genuinely surprised. "Ill? No, I don't think so. I'm just sad – and very confused, confused and sad."

Reggie was a decent chap and he immediately sympathised with this, becoming contrite as he said, "Of course, my dear, you've just lost your father and all the bother about the will has been very upsetting, but I don't want you to worry about a thing. I don't like to see you miserable. We really ought to try to sort things out between us. We live like strangers but we're husband and wife!"

"I thought that was the way you wanted it."

"No, it isn't. I want to make a new start. I want to go back to the beginning. I want us to be a family!"

"A family," she repeated. "Children."

"If you want."

"For the money?"

"Not just for that. We married each other, we made promises and vows. Let's try again."

"It's not me that has a lover in Edinburgh, Reggie."

"That's over. I've finished it. I really have. Please forgive me, Helen."

She stared at him with rising dread and realised how well it had suited her for Reggie to have a mistress and leave her to her own devices. "I can't forget the past just like that, Reggie."

"I know. That's why I wanted us to go away to France."

"I can't. Not yet. You don't understand. It's not just my father dying that's making me unhappy. It's more what I've found out about Leonie. I think she must have drowned herself because she had to give away her baby and that's so tragic. Every time I look down at the river I imagine how she felt that day . . ." Her voice broke and she put her face in her hands, a gesture that got Reggie out of his chair and up to her side.

"Oh Helen, I'm sorry. I didn't think. Of course you must be sad. I didn't realise what it meant to you."

He knelt by her chair and put his arms around her. It was the first time they'd touched for a very long time.

Sobbing, she clung to him. "And it's not just Leonie though that's bad enough. It's my mother too. She's probably still alive, you know, Reggie. But she's made no move to come back now Father's dead. Anyway, she couldn't have cared a jot for me or she wouldn't have left me behind when she ran away. I don't think anyone has ever really loved me in my entire life . . ."

He clutched her tighter. She was such a little thing, like a bird. Eleanor was a well-built woman, not much smaller than Reggie himself, and he wasn't used to handling someone as fragile as Helen. "*I* love you, Helen," he offered but she shook her head.

"No, you love your lady in Edinburgh. Nobody loves me," she told him.

She was wiping her eyes when there was a deliberate noise at the door and the normally silent Simes entered – after giving them time to compose themselves, for he'd heard the sound of weeping from inside.

"Someone is on the telephone for you, madam." he told Helen. "A gentleman from Edinburgh called McDermot."

She looked at her wrist watch. "At this time?"

"He is most insistent that he speak to you," said Simes who had tried very hard to deter the caller but to no avail.

She went into the hall where a tall black telephone stood on a pedestal table and held the listening trumpet to her ear while she said, "Hello?"

"Val McDermot here. I've found out something rather interesting."

"It's rather late, Mr McDermot."

"Is it? It's only half-past seven. I'm still in the office. Listen, Mrs Hunt, that man Anderson who wrote to your father's lawyer making a claim has a club foot."

Helen perked up. "A club foot? He'd have been born with that."

"Exactly. He said he was. If you could locate your missing mother she'd know if your sister's baby had a damaged foot, wouldn't she?"

123

"Yes, if I could find her."

"I'm going to the Highlands tomorrow, to that lodge where your sister's baby was born. But before I go any farther I want you to now that this could prove to be an expensive job. Are you sure you want to go on with it? It might just be cheaper to pay off Cameron and Anderson and forget all about them."

She sounded outraged. "Of course I want to go on. I can't give up now. Leonie's real baby is out there somewhere and I want to find him."

"It could cost you a good deal of money, I'm afraid," Val warned.

"I can afford it," said Helen stiffly.

"In that case, what about advertising for your mother to get in touch with you? Do you think she reads *The Times*?"

"Probably. I've no idea really."

"It's worth a try," said Val. "I'll put it in for you if you want me to . . ."

"I'd appreciate that. Just send me the bill," said Helen and regretted the words the moment they were out of her mouth for something told her that Val McDermot had pulled a face when he heard her say them.

That night, Reggie came knocking at her bedroom door for the first time in years. She let him in but warned him that there was no way she was going to let him make love to her.

"Just lie down beside me, Reggie, and we'll talk," she said. Docilely he did what he was told and it struck her, not for the first time, that he was a very nice man indeed. She was fond of him in the same way as one became fond of an over-affectionate, gambolling dog. It wasn't his fault that he drank – he had nothing else to do really – and he couldn't be blamed for the mistress. They chatted about insignificant things, deliberately avoiding the issues that engrossed them both, till he fell asleep by her side and when she woke in the morning, he was gone.

As she looked at the mark his head had made on the pillow beside her, it struck her that her life was remarkably passionless. She could hardly believe that people would do outrageous things for love. But living without passion was how she preferred it. She did not want a ferment of emotion.

What is passion *like*? she wondered. How could one abandon oneself completely? What impulse made her sister take a lover, have his child and then kill herself? Was that passion? She shivered and, although the morning was warm, pulled the quilted bedspread over her shoulders for she thought she could feel the chill waters of the Tweed lapping against her, rising round her waist and closing over her head.

It took Val a day and a half by rail, rowing boat and foot to get to Farquhar Lodge, a remote house tucked into the side of a heather-covered hill on the Glencripsdale peninsula in Argyllshire. When he eventually found it, it was shut up, the windows shuttered and grass growing through the gravel of the drive, but an old man and woman were living as caretakers in the kitchen quarters at the back. The man came wandering round to the front when he heard the hammering on the door and asked in a soft lilting accent that delighted Val's heart, "What's your business, sir?"

There was a camaraderie among Highlanders and Val, as one of them, knew how to present himself by announcing his antecedents first, rather like a medieval knight declaring his allegiance. "I'm Valentine McDermot, second son of Roderick McDermot of Glenfashie," he said.

The response was immediate. "Oh indeed, indeed. You have a look of your father. I was in the same regiment as him in the war. How is he these days?"

"He's very well but getting older."

125

"We are all getting older. The master's away in London but come in to meet the wife and have a wee dram."

The lodge kitchen was huge, its ceiling stained with smoke. A line of dull copper moulds that reflected what little light there was hung along a rail above the fireplace.

The dram of whisky they poured for Val was enormous. Then they gave him another and a meal of fish caught from their own stretch of loch that shimmered in the distance behind a belt of fir trees. Darkness was drawing in before he got round to telling them why he'd come, that he was seeking information about Mrs Gates, her daughter and an unwanted baby who was born in the lodge over twenty years before.

"I remember them fine," said the old lady. "Mrs Gates had been here before – her father used to rent the house every year – and the girl used to come too when she was little. They were both very beautiful with lovely yellow hair but though they were mother and daughter they did nothing but fight and shout at each other. Even when she was in labour, the girl was shouting. They had a mean-looking wee midwife and a sort of a maid, very grand and ladylike, a big woman with black, black hair like a gypsy, but I had to do all the running up and down stairs with pails and jugs of hot water. They left a terrible mess when they went away."

"How long did they stay?"

"Only a few weeks. The baby was just a few days old when they left and we thought it was a scandal moving a girl so soon after she'd had a baby, but she seemed strong enough. There was a fine big boat here then and a carriage on the other side of the loch. It took them to the station twenty miles away. I was glad to see the back of them."

"Can you remember what happened when the baby was born? What was the date?"

"Indeed, I remember that because it was my birthday,

December eighteenth. Poor little scrap. The midwife told me it was going to be given to a woman who found new homes for unwanted babies. Isn't that a terrible thing to do a baby?"

Val sipped his whisky and shook his head. "At least in the Highlands we keep our bairns, bastards or otherwise. Was it a healthy baby?" he asked and the old woman nodded vigorously. "It was perfect. A wee laddie with yellow hair like his mother."

"Yellow? Not red, not black?"

"Yellow. I mind washing him and thinking what fine hair he had."

"What about his legs and feet?"

She looked at him quizzically. "Legs? Feet?" she asked.

"What were they like?"

She laughed, thinking he was joking. "Like any bairn's legs and feet."

"He wasn't going to be a cripple?"

Her laughter died away. "Of course he wasn't," she said stoutly.

They put him up for the night, which was just as well because after the amount of whisky he'd drunk, he would have found it difficult to walk back to the landing stage.

Next day as he chugged towards Edinburgh in the train, he went over in his mind what he'd been told – a perfect blond-haired baby, a mean-looking wee midwife and a big, black haired maid that looked like a gypsy . . . The last bits fitted Mrs Kennedy and Phemie Grossett's mother. He'd have to go to see both of them again.

It was Reggie who first noticed the notice in the Personal Column of *The Times*. He came into the breakfast room with the newspaper flapping from his hand and said to Helen, "Look at this. Milly Gates was your mother's name, wasn't it?"

Helen read the entry. "Milly Gates, previously of Castledevon, Galashiels, or anyone knowing her whereabouts, please contact Sutherland, Ross and McQueen, Queen Street, Edinburgh. Privacy ensured."

"That's your mother they're after," repeated Reggie.

"Yes, I know. I'm trying to find her."

"What's this about Sutherland, Ross and McQueen?"

"I told you, I'd engaged them as agents in Edinburgh. They're acting for me."

"What's wrong with Mr Stevens?" Reggie asked.

"Nothing. I just wanted a separate investigation. Two heads being better than one, something like that. I've engaged a man called Valentine McDermot. I told you already."

"Valentine? He sounds like a bloody actor," said her husband as he stumped away muttering, "This business about your mother and your sister is becoming a fixation. If you ask me neither of them are worth it."

After breakfast she set out to call again on her Aunt Liza whom she found engaged in her perpetual embroidery. She looked up when Helen walked into her sunny drawing room.

"Goodness me, I hardly recognised you. You do look ill," she said complacently.

Then, bitting off a length of silk, she added, "You're not pregnant at last, are you? About time, I'd say."

"No, I'm not pregnant."

"You're sure?"

"I'm certain." Absolutely certain. She resented the fixation shared by all the women of her acquaintance, not about *if* but *when* she was going to become pregnant.

"Sit down then. I'm just about to have a sherry. Would you like one or would it upset you?" Exasperating Liza seemed to have made up her mind that Helen was pregnant and denying it.

"I'll have a sherry. I'll have two sherries. I'll have a bottle of sherry . . ." she snapped.

Liza looked at her over the top of half-spectacles. "There's no need to go to extremes," she said. Liza never had any sense of humour, thought Helen. I wonder if my mother had a sense of humour? I do hope so.

She sat down and said, "Do you take *The Times*, Aunt Liza?"

"Of course. Which other newspaper should I take?"

"Did you notice the item about Milly Gates in today's Personal Column?"

"Milly Gates? Your *mother*?"

"Yes. I put it in asking her to contact my lawyers if she's still alive."

"Oh, you shouldn't have done that. Everyone will see it. There's going to be so much *talk*."

"Who's going to care, for heaven's sake?"

"Everybody. All the local families. Imagine advertising in a newspaper for your own *mother*!"

"But I've been trying to find her for ages. It seemed a good way."

"You silly girl! I doubt very much if it'll do you any good though. Milly was never one for reading newspapers."

By the time she drove back to Castledevon, Helen was in a state of deep depression that even a riotous welcome from Tikki failed to lift.

"What do I expect to happen?" she asked herself. "Do I really think my mother who has ignored me for over twenty years will contact me now? And if she does, what difference will it make? My life won't change overnight . . ."

But she hoped that one thing would happen, that the cloud of dread that filled her mind whenever she thought about her mother and Leonie would be dispersed. She hoped that the baffling lack of memory about them that came over her whenever she tried to cast her mind back would be lifted and she would at least be able to remember something happy about them.

In a steely dawn Val McDermot rode back into Edinburgh on board a train from Perth. Swaying on his feet with tiredness he stared up at the outline of the jagged buildings of the Old Town rising above Waverley Station and weighed up his options.

The idea of going home to bed seemed most seductive but his mind was teeming with ideas which meant he probably wouldn't sleep so, instead, he set off to walk to the Royal Infirmary, stopping only for breakfast in a little cabman's tearoom tucked away in a close off the Royal Mile.

When he arrived in the grim, grey stone buildings that looked like barracks, he wandered the corridors with their mingled smells of antiseptic, anaesthetic and panic till he found a woman's charity ward. A pretty nurse told him that Mrs Georgina Kennedy was indeed a patient there but he couldn't see her because it wasn't visiting time for another five hours. He bent his head, proffered one of his cards and whispered, "It's terribly urgent, nurse. I'm her lawyer. She wants me to make her will."

The girl's forehead wrinkled. She knew the woman was ill but not exactly how badly. "She's desperately worried she's going to die without a will," whispered Val again. "It won't take long."

"All right. I'll put a screen round her bed but you must be quick. If matron comes round and sees you, she'll kill me."

Georgina was dozing and opened her eyes to see the tall lawyer friend of Mags hovering over her bed. "Oh my word, I hope you didna gie that Billy any money. He's not Miss Leonie's laddie," she said.

"I know," said Val sitting down on the bed. "I've come to ask you, did the Gates baby have a club foot?"

"Of course not. It was a perfect child." Spoken with a kind of pride, as if she was responsible for it.

"How do you know?"

"Because I saw it."

"You saw it? Where?"

"When it was born. I was there."

Val nodded, unsurprised. "At Farquhar Lodge. You were the servant. I thought as much. What happened after you went there?"

"It was me that told Mrs Gates about Mrs Maitland. She and Grossett worked as a team, you see. Another lady I'd worked for once got rid of her daughter's baby to them."

The little nurse poked her face through a gap in the screens at this point and Val waved a hand at her, while pretending to be scribbling on a piece of paper as he did so. She went away.

"What happened after you left the Highlands?" asked Val.

"We went to Edinburgh, to a hotel. Mr Gates arrived and I took Miss Leonie and him with the bairn to Mrs Maitland's. She lived in George Square then. Mrs Maitland was keeping the baby for a specially good home, she said."

"How did the mother, Miss Leonie, react to giving her baby up?"

Mrs Kennedy's face hardened. "Her mother had got round her. She did what she was told – for once. I think in a way she was relieved really. She wasnae old enough to be a mother. She was a silly lassie, I'm sorry to say."

"Where did the baby go? Who got it in the end?"

"I don't know. I asked Maitland once but she said there had never been a Gates baby. I'd been drinking a bit you see, and couldn't argue because nobody would believe my word over hers. I've always wondered about the bairn but when I saw that Billy Cameron I knew it wasn't him. He wasn't fine enough."

Val knew his time was running out but he couldn't resist asking, "What do you mean by 'fine'?"

"Sort of delicate – genteel – the sort of wee baby you can almost see through if you know what I mean. The kind that needs a lot of looking after."

"But not club-footed?"

"No, certainly not."

"Who was the father?" Val suddenly asked leaning towards the woman in the bed.

She shrank away from him and whispered, "You dinna ken, do you? Well I'll not be the one that tells you."

Before he left the hospital Val sought out the ward sister and charmed her to such an extent that she let him see Mrs Kennedy's medical notes. "Her liver's gone, I'm afraid," she said. "She's been drinking for years, you see."

"Is it bad?"

She nodded. "Six months at the most the doctor thinks, but she doesn't know so don't say anything, will you?"

He felt sad as he walked away from the hospital, and before he turned the corner he paused and looked back at the huge pile of the Infirmary. To his surprise he saw Phemie Grossett hurrying past the doorman's lodge, on her way, he was sure, to visit Mrs Lang who was about to have her second visitor that morning.

Inside the hospital, Phemie, in a great state of nerves, beseeched the nurse to let her speak to her friend and eventually prevailed too.

The screens were still up round Georgina and Phemie leaned over the bed to whisper, "Cynthia Maitland's got the wind up. She's offered me money to leave Edinburgh but I don't trust her. You and me know too much for our own good. She's going to give you something to keep your mouth shut. But when you get the money, as soon as you can, get away."

Georgina sighed. "It doesn't matter about me any more." Then she grabbed Phemie's hand and said urgently, "There's one thing I want to know. Where's the bairn?"

Phemie stared down at the raddled face. "Aw Georgina, you ken fine where it is. My mother told me all about it. It's where all the other wee sick ones went."

Mrs Kennedy turned her face to the pillow and sobbed. "That's what I was feared for. God's given me a terrible punishment."

Knowing that Phemie was in the hospital and would probably be there for some time, Val headed next for Elm Row. He took his time as he strolled, confident that if he could get the old woman alone while her daughter was out she would tell him more about the Gates baby.

The door of the flat was swinging open and he went cautiously in to find the room empty. The basket chair stood where he had last seen it and the blanket that normally covered Mrs Grossett's legs was tumbled on the floor. The window was open and a line of washing fluttered in the wind. There was a puddle of soapy water on the floor as if someone had inadvertently put a foot into a washing basin that stood, half full of water, beneath the window frame.

A cold hand gripped Val's heart and he went slowly to the door that led to the only other room. It too was ajar and he pushed it with one hand so that it swung fully open. Old Mrs Grossett lay fully dressed, as if thrown down like a rag doll, in a high double bed in a disorderly pile with one arm dangling. A pillow had fallen onto the floor by the bedside.

In his heart he knew she was dead even before he reached the bedside but still he had to try to help her. He pulled her up into a sitting position and felt her cheeks with his hands. She was still warm so he rushed over to the dressing table and lifted a hand mirror which he held to her mouth but no mist of breathing appeared on the glass.

"Mrs Grossett, Mrs Grossett," he cried out, frantically shaking her so that her head wobbled about on her neck. Then, realising that his efforts were in vain, he gently laid her down and crossed her hands on her breast. Her eyes were staring open and that disturbed him so he was trying to close the lids when Phemie, who hadn't wasted much time with Mrs Kennedy, came in and began screaming.

"Oh my God, oh my God. You've killed my mother. You're a madman. You've killed my mother!"

He went towards her with his hands outspread, telling her, "I didn't, I didn't. I found her like this. She's been smothered I think." But she kept backing away and screaming, "Get away from me, get away!" too hysterical to listen to what he was saying.

The neighbours started coming out of their flats and crowded up the stairs to gape through the door at the dead woman on the bed. "Get the polis, get the polis," screamed Phemie. "This bastard's killed my ma."

Two big police constables came pounding up the stairs and stood confused when they saw the dead body. Phemie pointed at Val. "I found him in the room beside the bed. He was touching her face. He killed her. He's been bothering us. He was here before."

The biggest policeman grabbed Val's arm. "Come on, son, you're coming with us," he said.

They took him to the police station in the High Street where lots of the men on duty knew him, having seen him many times in court, joked with him, had him grill them in the witness box, and fulminated against him when he got some villain off though they knew he was guilty.

"Hey, Val, you're in big trouble this time," said Sergeant Stanley Henderson, an old opponent.

"For God's sake, Stanley, you know I didn't kill that old woman. She was dead when I went into the flat."

"What were you doing going in there anyway? That could be called breaking and entering."

"No it couldn't. The door was wide open."

"We've only got your word for that. Into the cells, lad, till the Inspector makes up his mind what to do with you."

It was Colin they called, which was fortunate. He stood at the cell door with his arms crossed and a grin on his face looking at the prisoner who lay flat on his back on the plank bed with his arms crossed behind his head.

"Let's hear it then, Mr McDermot," he said.

Val sat up and replied, "I didn't kill that old woman. She was dead when I arrived in the flat, Colin."

"But she'd been alive only a little while before. One of the neighbours heard her speaking to somebody."

"Did they? They didn't see who it was I suppose. She certainly didn't speak to me."

"Let's have a look at your hands."

Val held them out and turned them under the other man's gaze.

"Let's see your face . . ." It was turned towards the grey light coming through the tiny cell window and scrutinised. Then the Inspector said, "You're clean. Whoever killed her would be badly scratched. She had blood in her finger nails. The poor old soul must have put up a fight."

Val sat down heavily on the bed. "Thank God for that," he said.

His friend sat beside him. "Now tell me why you went there. The Grossett women aren't your normal kind of clients."

The tale took a bit of telling but he went through it from the beginning, starting with Helen Hunt's first visit to his office and ending with his discovery that Mrs Maitland

135

had run a baby farm. The Inspector nodded with interest and when the recital was finished, he said, "I know that Maitland woman. She's attracted a bit of interest from us from time to time. You're working for a Mrs Hunt, you say. She can verify that I presume?"

"I'm sure she will. But she lives forty-odd miles away."

"I suppose a lady with a fortune like she apparently possesses will have a telephone?"

"Of course."

"Then I'll ring her up to vouch for you."

Reggie was alone in Castledevon when the call arrived and Simes the butler oiled smoothly through the hall to tell him that the police from Edinburgh were on the line asking to speak to madam.

"Good God! What about?" he asked, sitting bolt upright in the library chair.

"I cannot say, sir."

While Reggie was speaking on the instrument, the butler noticed that his face was becoming redder and redder. "What? Where? Murder? My wife? Good God. Good God. I don't know anything about it. *I* can't vouch for the man, I've never met him. My wife has a bit of a thing about her sister, I'm afraid, but I don't think it's gone as far as murder."

When he hung up Simes asked, "I hope madam is all right, sir?"

Reggie glared. "As far as I know. She's out somewhere, isn't she? When is she due back?"

"She said she'd be here for lunch at one, sir."

Reggie was stumping up and down the hall. "I'll phone her Aunt Liza," he said and was about to pick up the phone again when Helen came in.

"What's the matter?" she asked when she saw the two men staring at her as if she was a ghost.

"The police from the High Street police station in

Edinburgh have been on the telephone asking for you," said Reggie. "It's about your lawyer."

"Val McDermot?" She felt very weak and had to sit down in the ornate porter's chair that stood against the wall. "Is he all right?"

"He's in jail," said Reggie, "in connection with some old woman being murdered today. The police want to know if what he said about being your lawyer is correct."

"What old woman? Of course he didn't murder anybody. I hope you vouched for him," she replied sharply. They were both so agitated that they completely forgot about the presence of the butler.

"How could I vouch for the man? I've never seen him. You've never told me anything about him or what he's meant to be doing for you. That policeman on the telephone knew more about it than I do. I think it's about time this nonsense finished, Helen. If you're being bothered by false claimants for your father's estate, we should put the matter in the hands of the family lawyers and leave it to them to sort it out. They'll spend a couple of thousand, pay those people off and we'll have no more trouble."

She flared up as if he'd set a light to her. "Don't tell me what to do! You don't understand. I want to know the truth about Leonie's baby. I want to find it wherever and whoever it is. And Val McDermot is working for me. You should have told the police that, because you knew perfectly well. You're just being bloody-minded, Reggie."

Then she grabbed her handbag and gloves off the floor by the porter's chair and headed for the front door. "Where are you going?" shouted Reggie.

"Edinburgh!" she yelled back and disappeared. Seconds later they heard the car engine roar into life and a wild spattering of gravel as she set off down the drive.

The butler looked at his employer. "Should I tell Cook there will only be one for dinner?" he asked.

Helen covered forty-odd miles in just over an hour and drew up in the High Street at half-past two. "Where's the police station?" she shouted to a group of men standing outside a public house and they pointed across the road to an arched entrance leading to a dark and narrow vennel. "Doon there," said one of the men.

She leaped out of the car and ran across the road in the direction of the pointing finger. An enormous sergeant was standing behind a high wooden desk and there was a flap-topped counter on his right. He stared at her when she walked in and said in a tone pregnant with suspicion, "Yes, madam?"

"Where's Val McDermot?" she asked.

"Oh, you're his lady," said the sergeant with a suspicion of a smile.

"I'm his employer," said Helen stiffly. "I've come to confirm that with you and to tell you that I'm sure he didn't kill anybody."

The sergeant lifted the wooden flap. "Come this way," he said.

The Inspector and a police clerk interviewed her in a bleak room with green painted walls and wire mesh over the window. He took her name, her maiden name, her age in spite of her protests, her address, and then asked her to relate how she came to know McDermot and why she had hired him to work for her. It was all very solemn and intimidating and Helen began to be afraid that she was under suspicion as well. What would Reggie say, she thought with trepidation, if he had to come up to the city and bail her out?

"Do you know a woman called Lilian Grossett?" she was asked eventually.

"I know a woman called Phemie Grosset. She came to my house with the man called Billy Cameron that I've told you about . . ."

"Lilian Grossett was her mother."

138

"I've heard about her mother but I've never met her. You said 'was' her mother. Is she the person who's been murdered?"

He didn't answer that question. "There would be no advantage to either you or Mr McDermot if Mrs Grossett died, would there?"

"Quite the opposite. I was hoping she'd be able to tell us more about the circumstances of the birth, that sort of thing."

The Inspector leaned back. "Well, that's more or less what Mr McDermot told us. He's free to go, but of course he'll be an important witness so he can't go far away. You're not planning on sending him far afield in search of information, are you?"

She shook her head. Her mouth was dry and she was longing for a cup of tea.

"Thank you, Mrs Hunt," said the Inspector, standing up.

She stood up too. "Are you going to let him out then?"

"He's out already, Mrs Hunt. After he made his statement he was free to go. He left here about half an hour before you arrived. It was good of you to come so promptly."

"But the phone call to my home? Why didn't you ring and tell me not to come?"

"We didn't know you intended to come."

She looked at her watch. It was nearly four o'clock and the offices of Sutherland, Ross and McQueen would still be open. "Do you know where Mr McDermot went when he left here?" she asked.

But Inspector Brand said he had no idea.

She went to his office and he was not there, but the clerk said he might be at home and, surprisingly, gave her his address. She'd never wondered where or how he lived but when she stopped the car in front of the number

139

she had been given in India Street she looked up at the long, elegant windows of the first floor with surprise. The house faced into the steepest part of the street, a flight of steps led to the front door, and a line of spear-topped iron railings fenced off the basement area. She dropped the brass knocker into its bed and stood back to wait.

The door was opened by a pretty young woman in a lilac-coloured sweater and a checked skirt who smiled when she saw Helen on the step. "I expect you're looking for Val," she said. "But he's not back yet."

"Has he been in touch with you?" asked Helen.

"Not since the day before yesterday."

"So you don't know about the murder."

This did not seem to worry the girl to any great extent. "A murder? That'll please him. I thought he was working for some rich old woman who's worried about people trying to take her fortune off her." Then she held the door wider. "Do come in. Don't stand out there. He'll be back any minute. We're going to a concert tonight in the Usher Hall at seven o'clock."

Helen stepped into the hall and looked curiously around. There was a marble statue of a naked Greek god with a discus in his hand standing in an alcove. Someone had put a top hat on his head and there was a knotted tie round his neck. She recognised it as the red tie Val McDermot had worn on the day she accused him of being a Communist.

The girl was walking towards a room on her left. "What's your name?" she asked.

'Helen Hunt' obviously meant nothing to the girl for she went on, "How are you involved with the murder? Val'll do his best for you. He's very good."

"I'm not. He is. The police had him in custody this morning because a woman called Mrs Grossett had been murdered."

The girl turned with consternation on her face. "They arrested Val? How ridiculous."

Who is this girl, Helen wondered. Is she his girlfriend, his fiancée, his wife perhaps? She certainly seemed very much at home in his house.

"He got out though. I went up there to corroborate his story."

"Did you? That was kind. How exactly . . . ?"

"I'm the rich old woman who's worried about her fortune and Mrs Grossett was involved in that business."

"Oh, I am sorry. Val didn't exactly say you were old. I just thought you were from his description . . . I don't mean that . . . from what he said about the circumstances, I mean. I thought just now you were one of his ladies, they're always turning up. He doesn't discuss his cases with me really. I'm only a little sister as far as he's concerned." The words came tumbling out in obvious embarrassment.

His sister! Helen felt a strange sense of relief. The girl put out a hand and indicated a chair for Helen to sit on. It was the only seat in the room that was not piled with books or papers. The walls were bare but there were bowls and vases of flowers in various parts of the room and a skeleton hung loosely jangling in front of a tall bookcase. The girl saw Helen looking at it and said hurriedly, "That's Hector. I'm doing medicine, you see. Would you like a cup of tea?"

"Do you know, I would love one," said Helen.

They were companionably sipping their tea when McDermot came home. As his key was turning in the lock, his sister called out, "In here. You've a visitor."

He stood in the doorway and stared at Helen who stared back. "Good heavens!" he said.

"The police phoned Castledevon. They said you'd been arrested for murder – at least, that's what I thought they said."

He nodded. "Mrs Grossett, but I didn't kill her. I found her dead. She'd been smothered."

141

"Gosh," said his sister. "You must need a whisky." Then she looked at Helen, "You look as if you could do with one too."

"Thanks, Dig. Make it a big one."

"This business is becoming very complicated. Do you think I should just let it drop? Reggie says it would be best to buy off all the phoney claimants with a few thousand pounds and forget the whole thing," said Helen.

"Is that what you want to do? Drop it?"

"Not really. Anyway, I don't think it would work. I feel I've started something I can't stop."

"Well, it's obvious now that whoever is involved won't stop at murder. Make no mistake, Mrs Grossett was killed, and I suspect that has something to do with your business."

"Do you? Why?"

"She must have known something. I was going back to ask her more questions when I found her dead. I was sure she could tell me a lot if she chose."

"But who would want to kill her?"

He shrugged. "Who knows? Maybe her daughter – no, it wasn't the daughter, I saw her going into the Royal Infirmary to visit Mrs Kennedy before I went to Elm Row. Maybe Mrs Maitland. We've got a few suspects."

"But why?"

"If we knew that we'd probably know who."

They had another whisky each and then Val's sister came staggering in with a huge wooden tray bearing three omelettes. Helen felt she had never enjoyed a meal more. When she finished eating, she yawned and said, "Gosh, I'm tired. I'd better head for home. It's going to take an hour at least."

"On your way will you drop me at Elm Row?" asked Val. "The police told me that the neighbours heard some-one speaking to the old woman before she was killed. They might have caught a sight of whoever it was."

"Do you think that's wise?" asked Helen and Dig – which had turned out to be short for Diana – together.

"No, but that's never stopped me before," he said. Then he turned to his sister and added, "Sorry about the Usher Hall. You'll have to go alone."

She sighed. "It started an hour and a half ago, Val. We've both missed it."

It was dark by now and the street lamps were lit, making pools of golden light around the bases of the metal standards. Because a chill wind was blowing from the river, there were few people on the streets, and those who were out walked with their shoulders hunched and their heads down.

Helen's car bowled along, the tyres making a hollow rattling sound on the cobbled Edinburgh streets. Val sat silent beside her staring out of the side window and then he said, "This is a fine car. What sort is it?"

She told him, "A Lanchester."

Then he asked, "How much did it cost you?"

"Four hundred and fifty pounds."

"The yearly salary for three good men."

She shot him a glance. "I bet you earn more than that."

"*Touché.*"

They drove in silence along Princes Street and turned off into Leith Walk. When they reached the line of buildings that formed Elm Row, Val said, "Just stop here and let me off."

She drew on the brake and sat with both hands on the steering wheel staring through the windscreen. "I'd like to come too," she said. "Perhaps it would be better if you have someone with you. You seem to get into trouble when you're out on your own."

He laughed. "All right. Come on. It won't take long, I promise. You'll be on the road to Galashiels before ten o'clock."

143

The building was eerily silent. They climbed the stairs to the first floor where Val knocked on a door and asked the man who answered if he'd seen anyone in the building during the afternoon. "You a policeman?" asked the man.

"No."

"Then push off."

They were rebuffed next door and by the people in the two flats above. A young woman on the third floor wanted to talk and invited them in but it turned out she had nothing important to tell them apart from the fact that she'd heard someone talking to Mrs Grossett a little while before Phemie started yelling for the police.

"Was it a man or a woman?" asked Val.

"A man I think. But I'm not sure."

"Did you see him?"

"No."

On the fourth floor an old man and woman were eager to talk, words tumbling out of them as if they had been dammed up for days.

"Funny people them Grossetts . . . That daughter's very funny . . . Nobody knew where they got their money from . . . She used to go about with our daughter but suddenly she stopped . . . never knew why . . . We heard a man speaking to her after the daughter went out . . . he didn't say much though . . . next thing he was running down the stairs, then someone else came up and the daughter came back . . . what a screaming there was . . . saying the man up there had done it . . . the police took him away."

They had obviously not recognised Val, who asked, "Did you see him? The first man I mean."

"No, but he was a big man, and the other one was skinny. We heard his feet on the floor, though, thump, thump, thumping about."

Val stood up and said, "Thank you very much. I'll go up and speak to Mrs Grossett's daughter now."

"You'll not get her in. She went out with a suitcase an hour ago. As soon as the police took the body away, she was off."

"With a suitcase? She can't be going away for long. Her mother's not been buried yet!" exclaimed Helen.

The old pair shook their heads in unison. "She's a funny girl."

When they were back on the landing, Val said, "I'm going up to check what they said is right. You can go home if you like."

"I'll stick it to the end," she said and climbed the last few steps behind them.

The big man who was searching the flat must have heard the footsteps on the stairs. When Val put his shoulder to the door, it swung open and he almost fell inside only to be caught across the back with a blow from a spar of wood taken from the table. It was lucky for him that he stumbled, otherwise he would have got the blow on the head.

While he was on his hands and knees the big man started kicking him viciously, and Helen – to her own later amazement – dashed into the room, picked up the discarded spar of wood and, swinging it like a golf club, went into the attack. She caught their attacker on the side of the head and made him reel away, swearing viciously. When he turned on her, Val caught him round the legs and brought him down in a rugby tackle. But he was bigger and stronger than they were so he could fight free and made for the door, running full tilt down to the stair and out into the street. Val, hanging out of the window, saw his broad back disappear down the hill in the direction of Leith but it was dark and he couldn't make out any more.

Helen stared at him and was horrified to see that his head was cut and blood was running down beside his left eye. "He's split your head. I'll take you to the hospital," she said but he shook his head.

"No, if you don't mind, take me home. There's one advantage to having a young sister who's studying medicine. I'll give her a bit of practice."

Dig received them calmly and while she was sponging her brother's cut head, Helen said, "I must go home now. My husband will be desperate with worry about me."

The girl looked up and stared at Helen. "So you have a husband?" she asked in surprise.

Then she went back to tending her brother's head and told him, "You're lucky. It's only a scalp wound. It won't spoil your beauty."

When Helen reached Castledevon it was one o'clock in the morning and she found her husband still up and in a state of evident agitation. It was only when she saw the look of astonishment in his eyes that she realised she must be very dishevelled and quite unlike her normal tidy self, for her hair was tousled, a hole had appeared in one of her stockings, and her knuckles were bruised and scratched.

To do him justice, Reggie said nothing about this. Instead he came across the floor and took her coat saying, "Are you all right, my dear? I've been very worried."

How could she tell him that she'd been in a fight with a thug in a flat above Leith Walk?

"I tripped in the street," she lied, indicating the torn stocking. There was dried blood on her leg as well and only when she saw that did the injury begin to hurt.

He accepted her explanation and solicitously helped her upstairs. At her bedroom door he hovered as if he was hoping she would invite him inside but she did not. Instead she kissed his cheek and said, "I'm exhausted. I'll tell you all about it tomorrow. Good-night, Reggie."

At the breakfast table it was obvious Reggie had been doing some concentrated thinking overnight.

"I'm very worried about you, Helen," he began.

146

She'd expected something like this. You could hardly blame him, after all.

"You mustn't worry. I'm perfectly all right."

"No, you're not. Your Aunt Liza thinks we should ask a doctor to have a look at you."

She laid down her knife and glared at him. "What did you say?"

"Liza thinks you're under some sort of mental stress."

"And you agree with her?"

"Not exactly, but you seem to have changed in character over the last few months – ever since your father died, in fact."

"I know. I should have done so long ago."

"Liza thinks you're so set on finding your sister's child because you have no children of your own. I feel that's my fault. I'd like us to try again with our marriage. We seem to have drifted apart rather."

As she stared across the teacups at his heavy, troubled face she felt a pang of pity and sympathy for him. Poor Reggie, he had no idea of what went on in her mind. He knew nothing about her really and only had an idealised picture of the sweet, acquiescent little wife he thought she used to be.

"I was worried about you, rushing off to Edinburgh the way you did," he said.

"I won't go back if you don't want me to," she told him. "But you go to Edinburgh too. Where does your friend live?" she asked, adopting diversionary tactics.

It was possible to read his mental conflict in his eyes. Was she asking what he thought she was asking? He opted for telling her the truth.

"In Drummond Place."

"That's a nice part. She must be well off."

"Her husband was. He owned a big printing works."

She was genuinely interested. "Really? That's good."

"Helen, it's over between me and Eleanor."

147

"Did she finish it or did you?" she asked, casually stirring sugar into her tea.

"I did. I told her that you and I were going to have another shot at our marriage."

The first flash of anger moved her now. "Did you not think you should ask my opinion about that first? You were being a little presumptuous, Reggie."

She left her breakfast unfinished and stormed out to go to Liza's house. As she strode up the stairs to the drawing room it occurred to her that every time she visited her aunt, she was on the attack.

Liza was against braid-edged pillows with a novel lying open on her knees. Helen paused in the doorway and said, "I understand you and Reggie have got your heads together and decided I need a doctor."

Her aunt nodded her grey head. Even so early in the day she was stiffly corsetted.

"I've known many women nearly lose their minds when they are frustrated about not having children," she said solemnly.

"I am not frustrated. I don't want any children. When are all you mother hens going to get that into your heads?"

"You don't *think* you want them. Women in your position seldom do, but you're showing every symptom of mental instability."

"Exactly what are those?"

"Behaving in a very odd way, as you would never have behaved before, keeping secrets, keeping unsuitable company, neglecting your home and your husband – changing your appearance too. You've been wearing some very odd clothes lately."

"I am nearly twenty-seven years old. I have control of my own money. I can do what I like and wear what I like. I should have started behaving very oddly, as you call it, long ago but I didn't have the courage."

Liza shot her a sharp look. "There's a lot of money involved in this Helen . . . all those mills. If Reggie wanted to, he could have you certified as incompetent to manage your affairs. I told him that but he's far too kind to do it. You don't realise what a good man he is. You treat him so badly!"

"You're a bitch! Of course the money is at the bottom of this. It always is. In any conflict between a man and a woman, the man is always right as far as you're concerned and all you think about is money. You're jealous that I have so much and scared that I might give it away to outsiders when you think it should end up with your horrible daughters. And what do you know about my marriage? My husband has kept a mistress in Drummond Place, Edinburgh, for years."

"Oh for heaven's sake, Helen, everyone knows that, and lots of men have mistresses. But he'd never leave you. He probably took a mistress because you've never bothered to make things interesting for him."

"I know why he'll never leave me. It's because I have the money and I pay for all his pleasures. I probably pay for the mistress too if the truth were told." Her voice was bitter.

Liza sighed. "You've become so cynical!"

Helen stormed out again, shouting, "I only came to tell you to keep out of my business and stop filling my husband's head with malicious ideas. When you telephone him to report on what I've said, don't forget to add that if either of you attempt to put any doctor onto me, I'll cut off his allowance and he'll have to find the money for his hunting, shooting and fishing."

She was still fuming as she drove home, asking herself what Reggie or Liza would have said if they knew she'd been at the scene of a murder last night, on the verge of being attacked by a possible murderer! They would have her put under restraint for her own good, she reckoned, and resolved never to tell them the truth.

When she reached Castledevon, Helen telephoned Sutherland, Ross and McQueen and asked if Mr McDermot was in the office. "He's gone out," she was told.

"Does that mean he has been in today?" She wondered how bad the cut to his head had been.

"Yes, he's been in but he's gone out again."

"Tell him Mrs Hunt telephoned and I would appreciate it if he called me back."

It rained all day and she stayed in, staring out of the window at rods of rain showing against the dark green of the gloomy evergreens with which her father had edged the sloping lawns. As the hands of the clock crept round without the telephone bell ringing, she became more and more impatient. When it was four o'clock she stood up to telephone Edinburgh again but sat down sharply when she realised she was being unreasonable. He would telephone when he had something to tell her. There was no reason for him to contact her before that.

Reggie prowled the house, anxiously watching her as if she were a primed bomb that might explode at any moment.

"For God's sake, go and sleep in the library will you," she snapped eventually, taking her eyes off the rain.

He didn't go. "Let's take a trip to Biarritz, Helen," he suggested.

"For goodness sake. I hate Biarritz, all those bathchairs."

"Well, we could go to Monte."

"No, we couldn't. I've got unfinished business here."

He groaned and disappeared.

The telephone rang at half-past six and she shot up in her chair with every nerve in her body quivering. The butler announced, "Mr McDermot on the line for you, madam."

She wished it was possible to take the telephone away

to somewhere less public but it was fixed on a table in the hall and she had to stand there and accept the earpiece from her butler's hand.

"Yes?"

"So you got home safely?"

"Yes."

"I've been looking up some very interesting papers for you. Mrs Maitland had to register children she took in with the local authority and I've had a look at her file."

"How did you manage that?"

He laughed. "By the adroit distribution of some of your money. Don't you want to know what I found?"

"Yes."

"She's been in the baby business since about 1908 but for the last eight years or so she hasn't been active. At the time she placed your sister's child, she was in her heyday. In 1914 she accepted eight children and found new homes for them all. She was very proper in making the returns."

Helen gave a little gasp of interest and said, "Go on."

"Hugo Anderson was the child of the daughter of an Edinburgh cabinet maker who arranged for the baby to go to Mrs Maitland. He paid ten pounds a year for its upkeep for twelve years and another fifteen pounds for the placement with Mrs Anderson who got the boy for ten pounds because he was crippled."

"Poor thing."

"I know. The man who calls himself Billy Cameron was, as I expected, actually Billy Campbell, son of a street hawker. Mrs Maitland got nothing from the mother for that child."

"So neither of them are Leonie's son."

"No. There were three girls and five boys listed as being given to Mrs Maitland in early 1915. I have the details and I'll go to see if the mothers are still at the same addresses. Do you want me to go ahead?"

"Of course."

After she hung up, she realised she had not asked about the cut on his head.

She thought about the unwanted children all next day while she went walking in the woods that fringed her reach of the river. She could not stay out long for fear of missing a phone call which never came. Why have I become so involved with this business? she asked herself. Is Liza right? Am I really frustrated and longing for a child of my own? But even if I do find Leonie's baby it will be nearly twenty-two years old, hardly a baby, and it will be a stranger to me. There's no telling what sort of person it has become, there's no guarantee we'll have anything in common.

Her mind was so distracted that she could not concentrate on reading novels but she spent hours with the newspapers, absorbing news from all over the world. She found most of it utterly depressing, especially the news from Germany where Adolf Hitler was sweeping ahead with legislation banning Jews from public life. Helen knew no Jews but when she read the news bulletins from Germany, she felt a terrible sense of foreboding and wished there was someone with whom she could discuss her concern.

She attempted to bring it up over lunch with Reggie but he said that he could understand that Hitler chap because the Jews had taken over German business and bled the country dry. He was much more interested in the newspaper announcement that Rolls Royce had brought out a superb new car called the Phantom 111 which had a 50 horsepower engine. He talked about this car in tones of such reverence that Helen said rather testily, "Why don't you buy one?"

He looked at her woefully. "They cost over a thousand pounds, Helen. In fact they cost nearly two thousand – one thousand, eight hundred and fifty to be precise."

She knew he was not asking her for the car and felt remorse when she remembered that her father had settled an income of seven hundred pounds a year on Reggie when they married and it had only once been increased – to nine hundred and fifty about five years ago. Her own accession to riches was not shared by him. When he went out after lunch, she telephoned the biggest car dealer in Edinburgh and ordered Reggie the Rolls. It would take a few weeks to arrive, they told her, but she said airily that that didn't matter. "Just get it as soon as possible."

Eight

Old Mrs Grossett was buried in a pauper's grave with no mourners except Val McDermot and his detective friend Colin.

"I thought her daughter would show up, at least," said Val to the other man when they walked away from the cemetery gate.

"She didn't, did she?" was the laconic reply.

"How are you getting on finding out about who killed her?"

"There's not much to go on. Nobody saw anything, nobody heard anything. The people in that building seem to be deaf and blind."

"And scared. Like her daughter. She must be very scared not to show up at her mother's funeral."

"Unless she's glad to be rid of the old woman."

"Where do you think she could hide?" asked Val.

"Anywhere. She's not the sort you notice. She could go to ground up in the High Street, for instance. It's a real warren with all the closes. You can hide like a rabbit down a hole and stay hidden for ever if you're clever. She'll know it well. She was brought up there."

"How do you know that?"

"Her mother had a record. She served a year for doing an illegal abortion when she was much younger and the girl was left on her mother's sister who lived in the High Street. She must have got her hands on some money to be able to flit to Elm Row. It's nothing special either, but it's better than Fleshmarket Close."

"I'm sure that Maitland woman's mixed up in all this. And in Johnstone's drowning as well. I bet he was pushed."

Val sounded angry and his friend looked sharply at him. "Don't get your dander up," he said. "They're hardly going to be missed, either of them."

Val stopped in the middle of the pavement. "Hell, Colin, don't say that. They were people, even if they mightn't have been nice people. It makes me mad that some cynical killer can just knock them off as if they were bluebottles. There must be a reason why they were got rid of – and Maitland's the link."

The detective was unimpressed. "So you say, but we'd need more than your ideas to charge her. We'd need proof and there's nothing to link her with either of their deaths."

"There's her son Danny. I'm sure he was the one that took Johnstone away and it was him too that was searching the Grossett's rooms."

"Could you swear to that in court? You said that flat was in darkness."

"No, I couldn't."

They parted in the High Street and when Colin went into the police office, Val kept on walking till he was back at the Infirmary.

This time it was visiting hour and he was officially permitted to see Mrs Kennedy whose face expressed fear at the sight of him in spite of the reassuring way he tried to smile at her.

"Are you feeling better?" he asked and she nodded. In fact, she was transformed. She was washed, her hair was neatly combed and her face had lost some of its unhealthy colour.

"I hate it here, so they're letting me out soon," she whispered.

"Is that a good idea? Where will you go? Have you seen Phemie Grossett?" Val asked.

"No. Should I have done?"

"I thought she'd have come to tell you about her mother."

The look of fear deepened. "What about her mother?"

"That's she's dead. She was buried today."

"Oh my God, what happened to her? She's older than me of course. She must be nearly seventy."

Val let her have it straight. "She was murdered. Smothered."

The black eyes that stared back at him filled with horror and a sudden certainty that what he said was true. She was frightened but she wasn't surprised.

"Murdered!" she whispered.

"Who did you think would want to murder her?" he asked.

"How do I know? Maybe it was Phemie. They were aye at each other's throats."

"It wasn't. It happened when she was up here visiting you. What did she say to you when she came?"

She wiped twitching hands down over her face as if to clear away all expression and for a while he thought she was not going to speak again.

"What did she come here to say?" he persisted.

A sigh and then, "She said Maitland was going to give her and her mother money to go away. She'd got some in advance and Danny was to take her the rest. Maitland was going to give me some too but I said I didn't want it."

"What was she going to do for the money?"

"Nothing. Just go away. They were going to her uncle in Cowdenbeath she said. She'd told Maitland that so if she's got any sense she won't go anywhere near him. Oh God, I'm feared!"

"What of?"

"Maitland and that Danny."

"Is he Mrs Maitland's son?"

"She calls him Maitland but she hasnae any bairns. He was one she kept for herself for some reason. God knows why. He's a real rough."

"Did she keep many?"

"Oh no, no. Just him."

"Does Mrs Maitland know where you are?"

"I'd be easy to find. The neighbours would tell."

"Why should she want to silence you? What is it that you know?"

Her face crumpled. "I'm dying. The wee nurse told me that I cannae live mair than six months. Why can't I be left to die in peace? Nane o' this was my idea. It was Phemie Grossett's fault. Her and her mother, greedy besoms."

"What is it that Mrs Maitland is frightened about?"

"I'm no' telling."

"Is it because she's afraid of all those well-off families finding out she kept all the money they paid for their fostered children?"

"It's far worse than that."

"So she did keep the money?"

"She probably did. She's an awful woman for money."

"If I can get Phemie Grossett to talk, will you talk too?"

"I don't know."

The bell that marked the end of visiting time began to clang and a nurse bustled along, driving all the visitors to the door. Val leaned over the hospital bed and said, "If I arranged for someone to take you out of here and watch you all the time so's nobody got at you, will you talk?"

"I don't know. I'll think about it. I've nothing to lose now anyway, have I?"

When Val was leaving he looked back over his shoulder at Mrs Kennedy and saw her lying with her eyes closed like an effigy on a tomb.

157

Out in the street again it was a grey afternoon and the trees in the Meadows behind the Infirmary loomed up ghostly and threatening. He shivered and suddenly felt very oppressed by a feeling of evil but he was not finished yet for the day. He had to go to see Mags.

He was angry because Danny had slipped through his fingers. "I should have done something about him before. He'll lie low till the scratches are healed and then they won't be able to connect him with the old woman's murder," he said to himself as he climbed the stairs to Mags' flat where he sat down with her beside her window watching people passing on the pavement far below.

"Mrs Lang's coming out soon but she's scared to come back here because of Mrs Grossett getting murdered. I want her to be where I can keep tabs on her, though," he said.

"We'll watch oot for her. We see everybody that goes up or doon these stairs," said Mags who knew what he was getting at.

"I told her that already but she's still scared."

"She must have a bad conscience."

"Why do you think that is, Mags?"

"I dinna ken. She's been living up there for years but she's aye kept hersel to hersel."

"Does she have any friends that you know about?"

"Just those Grossetts. She's never been yin for friends."

"Who's her landlord?"

"Like us. Cynthia Maitland."

"And Danny collects the rents."

"He does that."

"Mrs Maitland is some woman, isn't she? Tell me about her." Mags could always be relied on for information and she never forgot anything she was told.

"Oh, *Cynthia*, that's a grand name, isn't it? She was christened Sadie but fancied something better. She's a terrible snob. Says she's from a good family, that she went to that fancy girls' school up by the Meadows and her feyther was a church elder. I don't know the truth of it but I do know her feyther was a boozer. Drank anything he could get his hands on and when he died, he left nothing, not a penny piece. Sadie had to leave the school and go into a shop selling stockings. That made her determined to get on."

The sun was warm and Mags got up to open a bottle of beer which she divided between two mugs, handing one to Val and drinking the other herself. The old woman in the bed in the corner gave a little mew when she heard the glass clinking and Mags found a third mug into which she poured some of her beer and some of Val's.

"Ears like a bloody cat. Naething wrong wi' her hearing," she said shortly.

"So she worked in a shop. Which one?"

"Forsyth's I think. But no' for long. She met Harry Maitland – her own name was Downes – and he married her. She's aye been a handsome woman. He was a real gent, a widower, much older than her, and she thought he had money but when he died, it turned out the money was his wife's and he'd only had it for his life. They lived in one o' thae big houses at Newington and it was his wife's too. Folk were real sorry for Cynthia – she'd stopped being Sadie by that time."

"It sounds like she's had a hard life."

"Well, things changed when Harry died. Cynthia had made lots of weel-to-do friends with Harry and she was aye away staying with Mrs This and Lady That. The next thing was her moving to George Square to yin o' the big auld hooses and then to St Bernard's Crescent to that hoose that looks like a funeral parlour and she was in the money."

"How?"

"Taking in bairns that naebody wanted."

Val nodded. "Baby farming."

Mags nodded. "That's it. They went through her hands like stirks in a market. In one door and oot the other. All from the best families, she boasted. You see her pals told their pals and whenever a daughter or a wife found she was having a bairn that was hard to explain, they packed it off to Cynthia."

"I've seen the records she submitted to the council. She never had more than ten babies a year."

"Awa' ye go! Ten a month sometimes."

"Come on, Mags, that's bit much."

"Well, maybe, but she put at least twenty a year through her hands for years. Her over there in the bed has a freend who worked in Mrs Maitland's kitchen and she told us all aboot it. There was a big top room in her hoose – the nursery she called it – and sometimes it was fu' of cots and baskets but they never stayed long. The only yin she kept was Danny but she didnae get him as a baby. He came when he was about five or six."

"Where did the babies go when they left her?"

"All over the place. Oot they went onywey."

"Is your mother-in-law's friend still around?"

"Oh aye, she lives below us. I'll shout doon and ask her up."

The woman who came up in response to Mags' summons was tiny, almost a dwarf, but with a sharp, lively face and a quick tongue which was easily loosened by the opening of another bottle of beer. Her name was Sal; she came from one of the families that had lived in the High Street since time immemorial and knew everybody.

"Aye, when I was a lassie I worked for Mrs Maitland. My mam knew her because mam was aye pregnant and used to take some of the wee bairns for suckling."

"Did she ever keep any of them?"

"No' for long. They'd be taken away when they were strong enough and if they werenae strong, they were taken away quicker. That Mrs Kennedy on the top flair used to come for them sometimes."

Mags said, "You never telt me that before."

"Didn't I? I must hae forgot. Her and the midwife worked thegither. They took the wee yins."

"The midwife. Mrs Grossett . . . Lilian Grossett," interrupted Val.

"That's right. Lil. She was a cold-hearted bitch that yin. I've seen her tuck a bairn under her airm and go off without a blanket on it in the bitter weather."

"Tell him aboot working in Mrs Maitland's," urged Mags.

"Weel, I was aboot ten and she took me on in her kitchen. I washed the pots and ran the messages for the cook. Thon cook was a big besom. She used to say to me that I was lucky I wasnae one o' the bairns folk brought in because I'm that wee and I'd be one of the chuck oots, as she ca'ed them."

"Chuck oots?" asked Val.

Sal cocked a sharp eye at him, making him think of a cheeky blackbird. "Well, they didnae a' live to grow up," she said.

"What happened to them?"

"They disappeared. I mind once askin' why there was never a funeral when a bairn died and the cook said they didn't die in Mrs Maitland's hoose. That would be bad for business."

"Where did they come from?"

"Sometimes servants brought them, sometimes the midwife Grossett brought them, sometimes the mothers came with them. That was aye sad. I've seen lassies going doon the steps greeting like their hearts would break because they'd left their bairns behind. I mind one woman who came with her lawyer and a bairn wrapped up in a lovely shawl. She kept going back and knocking on the door, asking Mrs Maitland to be sure the bairn would be well looked after. It was yin that disappeared – it went the next night. It was a lassie, ye see, there was never such a demand for lassies."

A sinister picture was beginning to take shape in Val's head and he looked at Mags who he could see had come to the same conclusion.

"They'd never know, would they?" he asked.

"Not unless they tried to see the bairn again, and they could be shown any bairn of the right age, couldn't they?" Mags replied.

Val stood up. "The police said they'd had their eye on Mrs Maitland from time to time. I wonder what for? I think I'll just go over and ask."

It was Sergeant Henderson behind the desk again. "Oh aye, Val?" he said in greeting.

Val leaned his elbow on the desk and said, "I'm involved in a case and that Mrs Maitland's name keeps coming up. What do you know about her?"

"Everybody knows Mrs Maitland up here. She owns a lot of property in the High Street, flats and rooms mostly, and she lends money to folk sometimes."

"That's not illegal."

"No, she's very careful. When she lends money she charges terrible interest though. Folk end up owing twice as much as they borrowed if they don't keep up their payments. Some of them die with the money not paid off."

"But the police wouldn't watch her for that."

"If anybody doesnae pay their rent or their loan payments, they can have some unpleasant visitors. That's what we hear about. They get their furniture broken up, women get knocked about, or worse – folk wait for them in dark closes, that sort of thing."

"Sounds like the right sort of jobs for Danny."

"Aye, we've had Danny in a couple of times but we've never kept him because we can never find any witnesses.

Folk seem to forget what they saw or heard or even what's happened to them."

"And Mrs Maitland sails on. Does she ever come up to the High Street?"

"Not her. It's all done for her. She has men working for her – the most important ones are Danny and Joe Quinn. Joe's aye in the Queen's Head across the road. You'll find him there but be careful. He's been known to carry a knife has Joe."

The Queen's Head was the most sordid sort of drinking den, situated halfway down a little close. It was only one room with sawdust scattered over the floor and the woodwork in front of the bar all scraped and scuffed where the customers' boots had bumped against it. No effort had been made to give the place any character, or to keep it clean, and Val screwed up his face in disgust when he stepped inside.

Three men were sitting at a table in a corner; one was leaning on the bar and two were leaning against the far wall engaged in what looked like a rising argument.

"Where can I find Joe Quinn?" Val asked the barman who nodded his head towards the solitary man at the bar. "That's him," he said.

Val walked across and said, "Joe Quinn? Can I buy you a drink?"

"Onybody can buy me a drink. I'll have a double whisky," said Quinn who was a shifty-looking character incongruously clad in a long dark overcoat and a Homburg hat that had seen better days.

When the glass was in his hand he stared at Val and said, "I've seen you before."

"In the court maybe. I'm an advocate."

"Oh aye. That's where I've seen you. Touting for business, are you?"

"No, looking for information."

"That doesnae come cheap."

"I'll pay if the information is interesting."

"Ask away then."

By this time the whisky glass was empty and had to be refilled.

"I'm involved in a property case and I'm trying to find out the names of the principal owners of property in the High Street. The biggest landlords, you know."

"Well the Kirk owns a lot. You ken that already maybe."

"Does it?"

"It owns maist o' the pubs. Funny that, isn't it, when they're aye preaching against the evils of drunkenness."

Val laughed. "I suppose it is. Have another whisky. Who else owns property?"

"There's a lot of grand families have it as their family inheritance and their lawyers administer it – dukes and lords and that sort. All I know about them is the names of their factors."

"Aren't there any private people who own property?"

"Aye, one or two." Quinn reeled off a number of names but Maitland wasn't among them. Val was forced to say, "I heard there's a woman that owns a lot."

"Mrs Maitland?" asked Quinn. "She's been selling up recently. She's retiring."

Val pretended only casual interest. "I suppose she's done well over the years."

"I couldnae say," said Quinn.

"You work for her, do you?"

"Sometimes."

"Funny thing for a woman to do."

"Why?"

"Well, she wouldn't be able to turn heavy on anybody that didn't want to pay their rent, would she?"

"Mrs Maitland never needs to turn funny on anybody."

By this time Quinn was on to his fifth double whisky

and becoming slightly slurred. Val laughed. "Somebody else does it for her, do they?"

"You mean something by that?" asked Quinn belligerently.

"No, I just wondered how she managed. By the way, do you know a woman called Georgina Kennedy? She's one of Mrs Maitland's tenants, I believe."

"No," said Quinn and swigged his whisky down.

"I was wondering where I could find Danny today," went on Val, who could see his companion was on the verge of leaving.

"Then you'll have to go on wondering because I'm no' going to tell you," was the snappy reply.

When Quinn had weaved his way out of the pub, the barman leaned over the counter and told Val, "Danny was in here with him last night. But dinna let on I told you."

"Thanks," said Val and ran out into the close after Quinn who he could see was heading for the High Street.

There was a lot of people about for some reason, crowding the pavements. Two ragged children were selling sweetmeats tied up in coloured paper from a big wicker basket on the pavement and an old woman with a barrel organ pulled by a white pony had attracted a considerable crowd because of the cheerful music she was churning out. Val was sure that the inebriated Quinn would never see him in the throng, so he stayed quite near to his quarry's heels.

They went down the High Street to the Tron Kirk where Quinn crossed the road but then came back again, ran across the North Bridge and shot down a tiny close beside a bookshop. The swiftness of this manoeuvre took Val by surprise and he started to run as well. He was still running when he entered the darkness of the close and almost fell over Quinn who was waiting for him in the shadows.

An arm was thrown round his neck from the back and

when he saw the glitter of Quinn's knife he cursed himself for being stupid. It took more than six doubles to slow down a villain like Quinn.

"I don't know why you're following me but you'd bloody well better stop it, Mr Advocate," hissed Quinn into Val's ear. "And to give you some reason to remember what I say, take this."

Almost gently, he slid the point of the knife down Val's right cheek. It didn't hurt at first but within seconds it began to sting and blood poured out of the cut. While Val was standing with both hands on his face trying to staunch the flow, his assailant disappeared.

"You silly bugger, Val. I told you Quinn carried a knife," said Sergeant Henderson when he saw the blood dripping through Val's fingers as he staggered into the police station office.

He came round his counter and prised the injured man's hand away to see the wound. "Neat," he said and then asked, "Do you want to make a statement? Do you want me to send out a man to bring him in?"

"No. I'd rather he was going about where he could be watched making his contacts. I don't want to charge him."

"Well, I think you're daft. You'd better not be the one watching him or he might not be so cautious where he cuts you next time. Sit down and I'll send you up to the Infirmary in a car. I dinna think you're able to walk it."

The doctor in the accident department was quite complimentary about Val's injury. "This'll make a very nice scar," he said as he stitched.

"I'm glad you're pleased."

"Like a Prussian duelling scar, really. Distinguished."

Two stitches were inserted and a dressing put on the wound before Val went home to India Street, where his sister showed very little surprise at his appearance.

"Let's have a look at it," she asked and when the wound was revealed, she echoed the casualty doctor's enthusiasm. "The chap who stitched you did a good job. What a neat scar it'll make."

"Not you too. You medics seem to think of it as a fashion accessory," he snapped.

She laughed. "Prussian officers try to get scars like this. You do it by accident."

"I'm not a Prussian, I'm happy to say."

"I hope it doesn't ruin your credibility. with your revolutionary friends," laughed Dig.

"Don't joke about that. I'm really serious. When this case is finished I'm planning to go to Spain," he said irritably. He wouldn't let her dress the wound for him next day and took himself back to the hospital to have the blood-soaked dressing changed. That was how he happened to be leaving the Infirmary at the same time as Mrs Kennedy.

He saw her in front of him heading for the main gate. She was walking very slowly and carrying her little bundle of possessions tied up in a square of cloth. He overtook her and put his hand on her shoulder. "I'll carry your bundle for you," he said.

She almost jumped round to face him but when she saw who it was, she relaxed.

"Have you been waiting for me?" she asked.

"No. I've been in the accident department. I cut myself." He pointed to the dressing on his face. If she thought it a strange place for a self-inflicted injury, she said nothing.

"They've let me out. I dinna want to die in there," she told him dolefully. "But now that I'm out, I'm feared."

"Where are you going?"

"I dinna ken."

"I'll take you back to your room above Mags'. You'll be safe there – as safe as any place, at least. I've asked them to look after you."

She didn't object and took his arm as they walked down George IV Bridge towards the Lawnmarket. They didn't speak as they walked along and once when he looked down at her, he saw there were tears on her cheeks.

The tears began to flow more copiously when they reached Mags' flat. "I've come home to dee, Mags," said Mrs Kennedy.

"Och come on in and dinna talk daft," said Mags comfortingly, so he left them.

When *The Times* ran the notice appealing for information about Helen Hunt's mother, Lady Kitty Rutherford's long life was drifting to an end.

Confined to bed, she lay propped up by pillows, occasionally staring out of the window at the view she had loved for so long, but mostly just dozing.

Her daughter, granddaughter, and the red-haired girl who was her companion tended her lovingly and every morning one or other of them read interesting items out of the newspapers to her.

When the notice about Milly Gates was read, she opened her eyes for the first time for days and said, almost in her old voice, "Tell me that again!"

After listening for a second time she closed them again, sighed and said, "Poor girl!"

"Who? The Gates woman?" asked Kitty's daughter Marie, who was the reader that morning.

"No, her daughter, the one who put that notice in – Helen Hunt from Castledevon. She badly wants to find her mother but I doubt if she'd get much comfort if she succeeded."

"You know where Mrs Gates is, don't you?"

"Yes, but I promised not to tell. Mind you, I'll be dead soon. When that happens send a note to Helen Hunt and tell her where her mother is. The address is in my book, don't forget."

"Oh, Mother," said Marie. "You're not going to die soon."

"Don't be silly," replied her mother. "I'll be dead before the week's out."

And she was.

Helen went to the funeral, just one of a vast crowd of people who came from far and near, but the only one from the intensely self-protective and snobbish section of society to which she belonged.

The next morning, her butler brought in a note which he said had been hand-delivered. When she opened it, all she found inside was her mother's name printed in foreign-looking capitals – 'MILLY GATES' – and on the next line, in script, 'can be found at 16 Roland Way, Chelsea, London. She has no telephone.'

Reggie had gone off golfing at Gleneagles with some of his friends but she left him a message.

"I've gone to London to find my mother," she wrote. That night she caught the sleeper train from Galashiels to London.

It arrived in the capital at half-past six, and when Helen lifted the blind of her first-class sleeper, she saw a deserted, sinister-looking King's Cross Station platform. Her courage almost failed her, but gathering strength and resolution, she rang for the attendant, who found her a porter. He in turn loaded her bag into a waiting taxi.

"Roland Way, Chelsea; number sixteen," she said, and settled back to watch the metropolis – which was beginning to look exciting and vibrantly alive even at that time of the morning – sweep past the window.

Roland Way was a mews behind a line of imposing red sandstone houses. The roadway of the mews was cobbled like the stable yard at home and most of the buildings in it had once been stables and carriage sheds, but were now garages with little houses above them. Some of the

169

houses had pots of flowering geraniums at the front doors and lacy curtains at the windows. Number sixteen had flowers too, though they looked as if they were in need of watering.

A milkman driving a horse and cart was trundling his way down the mews when Helen's taxi drove in. He had just put a bottle of milk on number sixteen's step when Helen stepped down from the cab, paid her fare, asked the cabby to bring out her bag and looked for a bell. There wasn't one, so she knocked on the door panel with her gloved fist, conscious of the curious milkman watching her.

Nothing happened, so she knocked again. There must be someone in, she thought, otherwise why have milk delivered?

"Knock louder, missus. She'll be asleep, she don't get up till dinner time," cried the milkman with relish from across the roadway.

So she fairly hammered on the door and that caused a rattling to break out from the window above her head. It shot open and an angry-looking woman stared out.

"What the hell is going on? I paid you yesterday," she demanded, glaring across at the milkman.

"Ain't me, Mrs Fawcourt," he said, pointing at Helen who was standing on the step with her head craning upwards.

The angry woman, whose greying hair was loose and tousled, bent farther over the sill and shot a fearsome look at the nuisance. "You've got the wrong house. Go away," she snapped.

"Is this number sixteen?" asked Helen.

"Yes. Go away."

"I haven't got the wrong house then. Are you Milly Gates?"

There was a very still and silent moment when nothing in the mews, nothing in the whole of London, it seemed

170

to Helen, moved or made a sound. Then the woman in the window said, "Not now."

"But you were. Please let me in. I'm your daughter."

The milkman was still watching in evident interest when the woman in the window withdrew her head and came clattering downstairs.

All night long, in the clattering, swaying train, Helen had lain sleepless visualising this meeting, hoping that it would not be too emotional to bear, afraid that her mother would faint or shed uncontrollable tears. She'd hoped she wouldn't break down herself when she felt her mother's arms around her for the first time in so many years.

While the woman inside the house wrestled with the bolts of the door, Helen stood shivering on the step. Tears pricked her eyes already, her arms longed to reach out for her mother and her whole body ached to be embraced and wept over.

When the door opened she took a tentative step forward, weeping already, but her mother stopped her with the words, "Bring that bottle in from the step, will you? It'll go off if it's left out there."

Shaking, Helen bent down and picked up the bottle, and with her bag in her other hand, followed the woman up a narrow hallway and into a small kitchen.

Milly Gates was tall and slim still with a mass of hair that was rapidly losing its colour. With her back towards her daughter, she said in a casual voice, "Do you smoke?" When she turned round she had a cigarette in her mouth and was holding a lit match to its end.

Unable to speak, Helen shook her head.

"Didn't think you would. Are you going somewhere?" This was said indicating Helen's bag.

"I'll go on to a hotel later," Helen told her and this seemed to be a relief. "I wanted to find you first," she went on. Her whole body was still aching to be hugged but she quickly realised that wouldn't happen.

"The Ritz is good," said Milly, drawing on her cigarette, "and I presume you can afford it now that Howie's dead."

"You know about that?"

"Yes, a lawyer wrote to my bank. He said my annuity would still be paid, though."

Helen looked round the kitchen. It was cramped and rather squalid with dirty dishes in a sink beneath the little window. "Do you need money?" she asked. "I'll be glad to give you anything you want."

"Is that what you've come for? I don't need anything." Helen watched as the woman who had given birth to her rattled about, filling a kettle and putting it on a gas ring. "Must have coffee," she said almost to herself, and looking at Helen, "Do you have time for some coffee?"

"Please." She needed coffee badly.

Her mother leaned back against the sink and crossed her arms as if fending off any demonstration of affection. "You look like your father," she said, "you've got his eyes."

Helen blinked, no longer wanting to weep. "Why did you leave me?" she asked point-blank.

Milly shrugged her fine shoulders. "I knew you'd be all right. You were always Howie's favourite and my sister Agnes doted on you. She was far better with you than I ever was. I never cared much for babies as a matter of fact."

"Was I my father's favourite?" Helen found this hard to believe, remembering Howie's indifference towards her.

"Oh yes. Leonie was too like me. She even looked like me."

Milly, unconsciously coquettish, put a hand to her unruly hair and brushed it back from her face. "She was very pretty."

The coffee was made and poured into big cups before

Helen spoke again. "It's Leonie I've come about really," she said.

Milly stubbed out her cigarette and lit another. "Yes. Why?"

"After Father's funeral a young man turned up and said he was Leonie's son. Then another one wrote and said he was too. My lawyer is trying to find out which one is genuine. She did have a baby, didn't she?"

The second cigarette was glowing well when Milly said, "Yes."

"Did the baby have a club foot?"

"A club foot? Of course not."

"You're sure?"

"Certain. It was a fine child, the midwife said. That Maitland woman wouldn't have taken it otherwise."

"Didn't Leonie want to keep it?"

"Oh no. Nobody would ever have married her if she had a baby, would they? She knew that and she wanted a rich husband. Why did you want to know about the club foot?"

"Because one of the claimants to father's money has a club foot."

"Then he's a fake. Don't give him a penny. Did your father leave money to Leonie's child?"

"Yes, he left him half the mills."

Milly laughed. "Trust Howie, guaranteed to cause trouble even after he's dead. So the other claimant gets the lot?"

"I'm afraid not. We've found out he's not genuine either. There's some mystery about what happened to my sister's child. I thought you might be able to clear it up, that's why I advertised for you."

"Did you? Where?"

"In *The Times.*"

"I hardly ever bother to read newspapers."

"I thought perhaps one of your friends might have seen it and told you."

173

"What name did you ask for?"

"Milly Gates."

"Nobody here would know me as that. I call myself Milly Faucourt now. Faucourt was a Frenchman, an artist, very good. There's some pictures he did of me upstairs. Do you want to see them?"

They carried their coffee cups upstairs to a large room where Milly pointed out three large canvases of a glowing, golden-haired nude sprawling along a green sofa. "That's me," she said proudly. As Helen looked at her mother's portraits she thought the artist had caught her mother's personality exactly, for he'd made her look like a predatory tigress waiting to put out a paw and snatch its prey.

"They're very good," she said cautiously. "Is he still painting?"

"He's dead. But he left me a lot of pictures. I sell one now and again when I need cash," said Milly complacently. There was not a trace of regret for the dead Faucourt in her voice. Helen wondered if she'd ever felt genuine affection for anyone, but then remembered Kitty Rutherford had said her mother had to be dissuaded from killing herself after Leonie died. She wanted to find out about that.

"Why did my sister drown herself?" she asked.

Milly's face hardened. "Who told you that?"

"The editor of the local newspaper. He was at the inquest and he knew the policeman who found her body."

"It wasn't recorded as suicide."

"But she did drown herself. Why? Was it because she had to give away her baby? If she felt so bad about it, couldn't you have got it back?"

"The baby had nothing to do with it."

"But you must have thought it did. You told Kitty Rutherford that you wanted to kill yourself too. Was it because you made her give the baby away?"

174

"Kitty Rutherford should have kept her mouth shut. I didn't make Leonie give the baby away. Nobody did. She wanted to. That woman Lang, the housekeeper, said she knew a woman that would take it and find it a good home. Leonie was too young to have a baby. She was still a child herself and she was having a good time."

Numbly Helen nodded, remembering what she'd been told about her sister having seemed happy the summer before she died. "So why did she do it?" she whispered.

"Don't be silly, Helen. It was because of the father of course. She found out about him."

"The father," whispered Helen. "Who was the father? Nobody knows; nobody has been able to tell me."

"I thought that was what you came here to talk about."

"Not really. I came about the baby."

"I can't help you about that. I was there when it was born but I wasn't there when they gave it away. Your father did that with Leonie."

"But you know who the father was."

"Oh yes, I know."

They stared at each other, willing the other to speak first. Surprisingly it was Milly who gave in. "It was one of the grooms. Fred Lang."

"Lang? The same name as the housekeeper. She was Lang, wasn't she, but she calls herself Kennedy now."

"Is she still alive? I heard she married some fellow who died in the war. Fred died there too, at the Somme in 1916. He was her brother. They both came from Camptounfoot. Father liked employing local people if he could and Fred had worked for us since he was a young lad, since before I got married."

"What was he like?" asked Helen.

Milly looked jumpy, and it was suddenly noticeable that she was growing agitated. Though the cigarette she was smoking was only half burned down, she stubbed it out and took another from a red and black packet

175

of Craven A that she pulled from her dressing-gown pocket.

"Don't you remember Fred? He used to lead you round on a little Shetland pony."

Helen had completely forgotten the pony, rubbed it out of her mind with a lot of other memories of her earliest years, but now it came back – the terrifying feeling of being perched up on its back, the smell of its sweat and of her own fear, for she hadn't liked ponies and still didn't.

But now she remembered Fred – a smiling dark face, big hands; a kind man. "Only a little bit," she said.

"Leonie liked him," said Milly bitterly. "She liked him a lot. I don't suppose I can blame her. He was something special. I don't think I ever saw a more handsome man. He turned your spine to water when he looked at you, couldn't help it, really. He handled women like he handled horses, gently. It could have gone on for years but Leonie took it too seriously. She didn't want to marry him – she was too much of a Gates for that – but she didn't want anyone else to have him. Her father was trying to marry her off to another of those mill families' sons and she'd have done it, if she and Fred could have carried on like they'd been doing."

"But he married somebody called Amy, one of the maids, didn't he? Was that why . . . ?"

"Amy Robertson, the scullery maid. She was his cousin and he'd been betrothed to her for years. He didn't marry her till after . . ." Milly's eyes were hard and distant-looking.

"Was it because of Amy that Leonie killed herself?"

"Amy? Of course not. It was because of that bitch Cunningham, the governess."

"Was he having an affair with her too?" Helen was geninely astonished, remembering the stiffly corsetted Miss Cunningham.

"Of course not. He wouldn't look at *her*. She was after your father and she thought if she told about me, she had a chance of getting him. She didn't know Howie though. He'd only marry for money or status and when he married me, I had both."

Helen reached behind herself and found a chair into which she sank but without taking her eyes off her mother. Milly was sitting down now too and talking as if she was alone, almost unaware she had an audience.

"It was a very hot day, very erotic weather if you can understand that . . ." She looked at Helen and shrugged as if she doubted Helen would have any idea of what she meant.

". . . I went across to the stables. Fred was in his shirt sleeves, filling hay nets. There was a wonderful smell. I didn't speak, just took his hand and we went up into the loft. I didn't know that governess had followed me. But she went back to the garden where your father and Leonie were lying on chairs under the big walnut tree. You were there too, don't you remember?"

Helen put her hands up to her face, for she was beginning to remember and what was coming back terrified her.

"I knew Fred was the father of Leonie's baby. I didn't mind really. It didn't matter. She'd led him on and he couldn't resist women, but he was mine really. He'd always been mine. Howie didn't know about him though; he'd have sent Fred away. We told him the baby's father was some chap she'd met when she was hunting in Leicestershire, some whipper-in. And Cunningham didn't know either. Only Leonie, Fred and I knew."

Helen wished she could tell her to stop, for now she didn't want to hear the rest, but Milly was determined to go on.

"Cunningham told your father to go to the stables. I can imagine how she did it, sneaking up to him, whispering,

177

making innuendoes. He'd know what she meant. He'd always suspected me. Leonie followed him and they found us. It was pretty obvious what we were doing. We were stark naked."

Helen closed her eyes. She'd been there too. She'd seen her mother sitting up in the hay and Fred, like a white marble god, beside her. The memory was shockingly vivid and immediate as if the incident had just happened and had not been buried in her subconscious mind for so long.

She also remembered her sister screaming and launching herself at her mother, talons out, scratching like a maddened cat. People had to pull them apart and then someone came – perhaps Aunt Agnes – and took Helen away from the corner of the stables where she was hiding.

"Oh God," she whispered.

The woman sitting beneath a nude portrait of herself shrugged. "It was very nasty," she admitted.

"What happened then?" asked Helen.

"Your father fired Fred. I never saw him again. I didn't want to really. It was one of those urgent, passionate things that burn out eventually. Howie couldn't understand, but then he was never full-blooded like me."

"But Leonie? What did Leonie do?"

Milly turned away and walked towards the door. "That night she drowned herself."

Nine

Helen did not go to the Ritz. She spent the day with her mother and that evening took a cab back to the station where she boarded the train home to Scotland.

Throughout the journey she did not sleep but sat upright, huddled in the corner of her sleeping bunk, and thought about Milly Faucourt, the woman she found it difficult to remember was her mother.

Milly had signed a statement for McDermot saying that Leonie's baby was not born with any physical defect and giving its date of birth as December 10th, 1914. She also told Helen that Howie had arranged to pay an annuity of £50 a year for the upkeep of his daughter's child until it reached the age of fourteen. She did not know for certain that he continued to pay this after she left but she would not imagine him backing out of such an arrangement as he was an honourable man.

Helen, remembering his anguished deathbed attempt to tell her to find the child, believed too that he would have gone on paying.

As the two women sat talking together on that golden summer day, Helen was able to observe her mother with the same detachment as she would view a stranger whom she had only recently met. This she found absorbing and not as upsetting as she would have expected. It was a rare experience, she realised, to be able to scrutinise one's parent with such detachment, and in a way it freed her from her past.

She did not like Milly Gates, she very quickly realised; she did not like her and she certainly did not understand her. Milly had no attachments and no real affection for anyone except herself. People were valued only for what they had done for her and she showed absolutely no curiosity about Helen's life; was only vaguely interested in the fact that she'd married Reggie Hunt, whose parents she knew, and never broached the subject of why Helen was childless. Neither did she want to know about her sisters and she received the news of Agnes' death without any emotion.

People did not matter to her, Helen realised, and was shocked that her mother's chief memory even of the unfortunate Fred Lang was only that he had been a superb lover. "The best I've ever had, and believe me I've had several," she had told her daughter.

Her Achilles heel, however, was Leonie. She could not be drawn on the subject of her dead daughter or on why she told Kitty Rutherford that she too wanted to die. Otherwise she had managed to divorce herself completely from the past and, because she was a hedonist, was able to live entirely in the present.

Watching her, listening to her, Helen wondered how dour Howie had coped with such a basically amoral character. How angry he must have been yet how he must have missed her when she left! No wonder Castledevon had always seemed like an empty, echoing ghost house whilst she was growing up.

Once the shock of hearing the plain unvarnished truth was over – for Milly did not put a gloss on the facts – instead of being saddened or disappointed, Helen was relieved to realise that they were not going to delve painfully into the past. When they parted, it would not be with tears. Milly had no wish to worm her way into Helen's heart and gave the impression that when she left Castledevon, she had closed off that part of her life, like someone slamming shut one of the leather-bound books in Howie's library. What she felt about it all was an enigma that she was not prepared to reveal.

Before she left the mews house Helen wrote out a cheque for £1,000 and handed it to her mother. "Please take this. I've far more than I need," she said.

Milly looked at the neat writing, folded the paper carefully and put it in her pocket. "Thank you, darling," she said. "I'll use it to go to Paris. There's a man there I'd like to see again. And there's something I'd like to give you."

From behind a sofa she hauled out a framed crayon drawing of a naked woman with her hair tumbling down around her shoulders and over the abundant breasts that she was flaunting proudly. "It's me," she said, looking at herself admiringly. "Faucourt liked that one best of his drawings." She always referred to the painter only by his surname and seemed detached about him too, though she'd told Helen that they had lived together for more than fifteen years.

Helen stared at the painting and thought that the painter who so cleverly captured her mother's pleasure-loving character had been equally detached about Milly. "What was he like?" she asked.

"Tall, dark; I like dark men. I used to say he looked like a hawk . . ."

"No, I mean what was he like as a person?"

"As a person?" Milly seemed slightly flummoxed. "He adored me. Frenchmen make splendid lovers, you know."

Helen didn't know and didn't want to think about it so she hurriedly asked, "Do you miss him very much?"

"Of course, but you get used to being on your own. I quite like it really."

The picture was wrapped up in brown paper and was conveyed by her to the train and then on to Castledevon, where she gave orders that it should be hung in the drawing room, displacing a dark and gloomy landscape that had been there since she was a child. She watched while this job was going on and was amazed at the transformation the new picture, with its glowing Provençal colours, made to her house.

"When the business is all over I'll redecorate the whole place. I'll change my life," she decided.

When Reggie came back from his weekend at Gleneagles later in the evening, he was not even aware she'd been to London until she told him. Then she took him into the drawing room and showed him the picture. "Look what I brought back from London," she said.

He goggled at it, aghast. "Do you think this is the right place for it, Helen?" he asked.

"Yes, don't you like it?"

"Well, it's not the sort of thing . . . she's a fine looking woman, I suppose, but . . . I liked the old picture better though."

"This is by a very distinguished painter, a Frenchman called Faucourt."

"It would be by a Frenchman," said Reggie heavily.

"Actually it's of my mother."

"Oh my God, Helen. You can't leave it hanging there!"

"Why not, for heaven's sake?"

"The servants! And imagine when people call, when fellows look at it and ask, 'Who's the girl?' We can't tell them it's your mother."

"Then say you don't know. I like it and I want to keep it there at least for the meantime till I get used to it."

Valentine McDermot almost did not recognise her when she turned up in his office next afternoon. She looked very excited, much younger and a good deal less conventional than when they first met. She was wearing a new coat, a flowing cream-coloured thing with a succulent fur collar that she clasped round herself with one gloved hand as if, he thought, she was a fan dancer about to whip it off to tantalize an audience.

Words were bubbling out of her when she stepped into the room and before she sat down she was saying, "You'll never guess where I've been. To London and I met my mother. I got her to write out a statement about Leonie's son and she's told me all sorts of things. I know the name of the father too."

Val stood up and offered her a chair into which she threw herself. "Haven't I done well?" she gasped, looking up at him through the speckled eye veil of a minute hat. She smelt of French perfume.

You've come a long way in a short time, Mrs Hunt, he thought with amusement as he walked back to the other side of the desk and sat down too.

"Let's begin at the beginning. So you've seen your mother?" he said.

She leaned forward, hands clasped on her knees. "Yes. I tried to get in touch with you but I went off in a hurry. Lady Rutherford sent me her address. It arrived after she died so she didn't break her promise not to tell. As soon as I got it I went up to London."

"She was pleased to see you?" he prompted.

She stared at him through the veil. He noticed that she was wearing the diamond earrings that sparkled when they caught the light. Only real diamonds sparkled like that, as if there were tiny fires inside them. He didn't approve of such ostentation.

She said something that he didn't catch and when she saw he'd missed it, she said it again . . . "I really don't know if she was pleased to see me. I don't think she'd ever have come looking for *me*. But I was pleased to see her. I felt so much better afterwards . . . as if a shadow had been taken out of my life. It's hard to explain. I think it's difficult for people to see their parents objectively sometimes. I found it very useful. Have you got a mother, Mr McDermot?"

"She's dead. But I was very fond of her. She died two years ago."

"Oh, I'm sorry. That was tactless. You must miss her."

"Yes, but that's got nothing to do with the matter in hand. I take it you told your mother about the business up here."

"I did indeed. She wasn't very impressed. But she said that Leonie's baby definitely didn't have a club foot, so that eliminates Anderson."

Valentine sat with his chin in his hand staring at her and said, "Pity. I liked him better than Cameron. Is your mother prepared to go to court or to swear a statement about the baby?"

"She wrote it all down for me. Isn't that enough? I don't think she wants to come back to Scotland ever again. She's washed her hands of the past completely."

"And of you?" He shouldn't have said that perhaps, he thought.

"She washed her hands of me a long time ago," she said. Then she looked hard at him across the desk. "What have you done to your face?" she asked in a changed tone.

"I had a slight disagreement with a man in the High Street."

She looked shocked. "Fighting?"

"Not really. Just asking questions about Mrs Maitland."

"I don't want you to get hurt over this business, Mr McDermot," she said.

"A lot of people have been hurt already, I'm afraid. Mrs Grossett and Mr Johnstone have got themselves murdered and I've got Mags and her family hiding Mrs Kennedy or she'll be the next to go."

"Kennedy! The old housekeeper. My mother told me something very important – Mrs Kennedy's brother, Fred

Lang, was the father of Leonie's baby. He was a groom at Castledevon and he was killed on the Somme – that was 1916, wasn't it?" She wondered if she should tell McDermot about her mother's involvement with Lang and the true reason why Leonie committed suicide, but she decided to keep that to herself. It wasn't relevant.

He sat back in his chair, his lean face lighting up. "I knew she was in it up to her neck!" he exclaimed. "Did your sister kill herself because of him? Did she want to marry him and they wouldn't let her – or was it because he married the girl called Amy?"

In spite of her good intentions she heard herself saying, "No, it was because he was having an affair with my mother too and she found them out."

He let the chair legs thud onto the ground and stared at her. "Your mother?" he asked. "She must be quite a lady."

Helen stiffened and said nothing.

"Did they fire him?" he asked.

"I believe so."

"Poor sod. Beseiged by over-enthusiastic women. Very dramatic."

"How do you know it wasn't all his fault?" she hissed.

"I'll find out and let you know," he said.

She stood up. "I'm beginning to think we should let this business drop. Neither of the people who've claimed to be my sister's son is genuine. I don't like the way we're getting involved in other things . . ."

"You drop it if you like, but I've got interested now and I've also got annoyed, very annoyed. I don't think it right for people to get murdered by thugs like Danny Maitland just because they know things that would embarrass or even incriminate a rather nasty woman. I'm out to get Cynthia Maitland, Mrs Hunt, and I don't care if you keep me working for you or not."

She had to admit that she wanted to find things out too.

She wanted to find her sister's baby. She stared bleakly at him. "We seem to be at cross purposes, Mr McDermot," she said.

"I think we probably always were, don't you? Do you want to discontinue our agreement?"

After a long pause she shook her head. "No. I'm ready to go through with it to the end, even though things are turning up that I didn't expect."

"The skeletons are falling out of your family cupboard," he agreed.

She pulled her fine coat around her. "I don't care about that really; I'll get used to it. Now that I've told you what I found out from my mother, I've other things to do in Edinburgh today."

He looked caustically at her. "Shopping?" he said.

She bristled. "Actually, yes. I'm going to buy a Rolls Royce for my husband's birthday present." She had the satisfaction of seeing his jaw drop.

She had been out of his room only for a few minutes when his desk telephone rang. When he picked it up a woman's voice came rasping over the wire.

"Is that Mr McDermot?"

"Yes."

"This is Miss Grossett, Phemie Grossett, the one whose mother was killed."

He gripped the receiver tightly. "Yes, Miss Grossett."

"Listen. I want to see you. I've got things to tell you but I canna come into the town. D'ye know St Bernard's Well on the Leith Water?"

"Yes." He had played round the Well as a child with his little sister.

"Meet me there at five o'clock – and bring some money. I've got to get away."

"How much money?" he asked, but she had rung off.

A Rolls Royce, she'd said. She was going to buy a Rolls

Royce. There was only one place in Edinburgh where cars like that were sold and it was in the Haymarket.

He ran into the front office, pulling on his raincoat as he went. "Can I borrow your bicycle?" he asked the office boy who nodded in amazed agreement.

Then he was off, pedalling madly along Queen Street. He had to catch her.

He saw her Lanchester parked in the forecourt of the garage showroom, jumped off the bike and negligently let it fall on to the tarmac. She was in the front office with a smoothly dressed salesman, studying brochures.

"Mrs Hunt, I've just had a very strange phone call from Phemie Grossett. She wants a meeting this afternoon – at five o'clock. She's going to tell the truth at last, I think."

She stared at him wide eyed. The eyes were very blue, he noticed for the first time.

"Do you want to come?" he panted.

The salesman was standing up, trying to push him out of the office door but he resisted. "Do you want to come?" he repeated.

"Yes," she said, dropping the brochure onto the desk top. "Thank you, Mr Laing. The dark blue one please and have it here as soon as possible."

"And send that bike outside back to the office of Sutherland, Ross and McQueen in Queen Street," Val added.

"Yes, do that too," she agreed.

Then she walked out after him.

"Where to?" she asked, looking at her watch. It was almost four o'clock.

"St Bernard's Well."

"Where's that?"

"I'll show you." He climbed into the passenger seat of the car beside her.

"She says she wants money," he told her as they drove along Palmerston Place.

"How much?"

"She didn't say. Enough to get out of Edinburgh."

"Oh. There's a bank. It's still open. I'll get some from there." She stopped the car and ran into the bank just as a clerk was preparing to close its heavy front door.

In ten minutes she was back with a wad of notes in her hand. "How much have you got?" he asked, taking it from her.

"Two hundred. I thought she'd better go abroad."

He laughed. The idea of Phemie Grossett as a foreign traveller was irresistibly funny.

"You can't just hand her a fold of money like that. She'd get killed for it before she was half a mile down the road." As he spoke he was quickly putting a little pencil tick in the corner of each note.

She groped under the car seat and brought out a paper bag. "I'll put it in this, then." It was a Jenner's paper bag and he laughed again. "Nothing but the best, as usual," he said.

They got to the iron gate leading to the Well at half-past four and walked along the river bank towards it. It had been built over a century ago as a spa, dispensing health-giving water to the citizens of Stockbridge, and was a strange, stone structure like a scaled-down Greek temple. Pillars supported a round dome, which stood on a built-up plinth that had to be ascended by stone steps. Another paved roadway ran higher on the bank behind it and it was surrounded by gardens laid out with variegated shrubs and trees – a pretty, quiet place now, popular only with nannies and their charges or old ladies walking pet dogs.

There was no one else around except a man throwing sticks for a Labrador that plunged into the Water of Leith to retrieve them. The desultory sun that had shone all day now retreated behind a bank of cloud which made the well and its surroundings look extremely gloomy and suddenly sinister among its clustering trees.

Helen sat down on the top step of the flight to the well itself, which was beneath the dome, and Val walked a bit farther up the river and stood behind a large tree. He had half the money in his raincoat pocket because he'd persuaded Helen that two hundred pounds was an excessive pay-off for Phemie. Lying on the step beside her, Helen had the paper bag packed with the rest of the money.

At five o'clock exactly the first drops of rain began to fall and Phemie Grossett appeared on the corner of the path leading from Stockbridge. She was wearing a dark-coloured cape, like a nurse, and her old felt hat.

Looking anxiously over her shoulder, she hurried nearer to Helen, who stood up at her approach. "Have you got the money?" she asked.

Helen brandished the bag. "I've brought you a hundred pounds."

"Give it to me."

"Oh no. First you must tell me what it is you know. It might not be worth anything."

"It's about your sister's bairn."

"Yes?"

"It was a wee boy and he was given to Mrs Maitland by my mother and your sister."

"Yes? Where did it go?"

"It's dead. It died at two weeks old."

"Two weeks. Just after Leonie gave it away. What happened?"

"She killed it. It was a troublesome one, aye greeting, aye being sick. She got rid of it."

Helen sat down on the step with the paper bag falling from her hand. Phemie picked it up and backed away.

"Wait. She. Do you mean Mrs Maitland or your mother?"

"Maitland. My mother's job was to look after the babies and get rid of the bodies if necessary."

Val had joined the women now and he asked quietly, "How did she get rid of the dead babies?"

"There was a special place in the High Street my mother told me about. I've got the key here in my pocket."

"Tell us where and you'll get another hundred."

Just then Helen shouted "Val!" and pointed to two men who were running towards them along the river path. One of them had bright red hair and Val saw that the other was Quinn. Phemie saw them too and, snatching the money, she leaped down the bank and plunged into the river which fortunately was running low. Throwing water up all round herself she crossed to the other side, clambered up the steep bank, clawing at tree roots for purchase, and disappeared into the undergrowth.

Joe Quinn plunged in after her but Danny headed for Val and Helen who took one look at him and turned to climb up the steps to the roadway above the well. Fortunately for them the man with the dog was there too, talking to a woman with a baby in a pram.

Hauling Helen by the hand, Val ran. Danny ran behind them but he was heavy and out of condition so they soon outpaced him. When they reached the main road a tramcar was passing. They jumped on to the platform and had the satisfaction of seeing Danny coming puffing out of the end of the lane that led to the Well as they clanged up the hill to safety.

"What do you think'll happen to the Grossett woman?" panted Helen.

"God knows," said Val. "What did she tell you?"

"That Mrs Maitland killed the baby when it was two weeks old."

"I thought as much. God I'd like to nail that woman," he said grimly.

'The body of Euphemia Grossett, aged 38, was found yesterday evening lying in the Water of Leith by two

190

schoolboys on a fishing expedition. It is thought she fell from the bank of the river, adjacent to Ann Street. Miss Grossett, who was an office cleaner, lived with her late mother in Elm Row, Leith Walk. Her mother, Mrs Lilian Grossett, 62, was found dead in bed two weeks ago,'

ran a small item in the first edition of the Edinburgh Evening Dispatch at lunchtime of the following day.

Val was reading it in his office and he stood up, throwing the paper on the floor. "They got her," he told his clerk.

"Got who, sir?"

"Phemie Grossett. They got her like they got her mother. They're eliminating the evidence. They've got to be stopped." In the doorway he paused and said, "Phone Mrs Hunt and tell her Miss Grossett's dead."

"Oh dear," said Helen when the news was broken to her. "Was Mr McDermot very upset?"

The clerk was pedantic. "I wouldn't say upset, exactly, madam. He did seem rather angry though. He went rushing out, madam. He said they'd got to be stopped."

"I think I'd better come to Edinburgh. I'll go to the police station to tell them what I saw. If he comes back tell him that."

The clerk hung up the phone, shaking his head with disapproval. Only since Valentine McDermot joined the firm did Sutherland, Ross and McQueen start dabbling in cases like this one.

Sergeant Henderson thumped his hand on the desk at the sight of Val McDermot. "Not you again!" he cried.

"It's about Phemie Grossett. The body they found last night in the Water of Leith. She was murdered by the same lot that killed her mother."

"And who's that?"

191

"You know as well as me. Danny Maitland and that Joe Quinn. I saw her yesterday when she was running away from them. They must have caught her."

"You are always around these days when something unpleasant happens, aren't you? How's your face?"

"It's all right and I'm serious. I was at St Bernard's Well meeting Miss Euphemia Grossett at five o'clock yesterday afternoon and I saw her being chased by Maitland and Quinn."

"And what did you do then?"

"I ran away too. I had Mrs Hunt with me and Maitland came for us so we ran. The Grossett woman ran across the river and went up the steep bank on the other side. We thought she'd got away."

"They think she fell from the top of the steep bank beside Ann Street. She was found beneath the rocks there, lying in a pool."

"I bet she was pushed."

"Speculation," said the sergeant. "There was no sign of a struggle. Her neck was broken. It really looks as if she just fell."

"Did she have any money with her?"

"She had some coins in her pocket . . ." He turned up a list on his desk. "Seven shillings and threepence ha'penny, a handkerchief, a tram ticket, a pan drop, a comb, a key – that's all."

"She was given a hundred pounds in marked notes by Mrs Hunt a few moments before she plunged into the river."

"*Marked* notes?"

"I marked them with a pencil in the corners. I've also got the numbers."

"I don't suppose there's any point asking why?"

"Not yet, but I've a feeling you'll get to hear about it in time."

He was about to leave the office when he suddenly

turned round and came back. "That key. Has anybody tried it in her flat door?"

"I don't think so."

"Can I try it?"

"Oh God, Val, you'll get me hanged. Here you are. Take it round to the locksmith and get him to copy it for you, then bring it back. Take it off the counter when I'm not looking." Then he walked to a side office. When his back was turned, Val took the key. Within fifteen minutes he returned, laid the key on the counter and left again.

Sergeant Henderson was about to go off his shift when Helen Hunt entered the office.

"I want to make a statement about the late Miss Grossett," she said.

"Your friend's been in already," said the sergeant.

"Which friend?"

"Mr McDermot."

"Well, I want to make a statement too. I've just seen the newspaper and it infers she was killed in an accident. She wasn't. She was murdered."

The sergeant lifted the flap top and ushered Helen into the Inspector's office where she showed an admirable ability to remember details as she recounted the events of the previous afternoon. There were two things she didn't tell them – the first, because she did not know about it, was that Val had marked the notes. The second was that Phemie had told her Mrs Maitland killed Leonie's baby. She said the child she had been looking for was dead, but not how.

When she returned to Castledevon, Reggie was sitting in the library with his chin in his hands staring at the fire.

"Helen," he said when she went into the room, "have you any idea how many times you've gone to Edinburgh recently?"

"Not really, Reggie," she admitted. "But it does seem as if the car knows the road by heart."

He held up his hands and enumerated her trips on his fingers. "Today, yesterday, two days before that – four times in one week. You're never at home."

She sat down beside him. "I'm sorry, Reggie. But it's nearly over. It really is. I know now that Leonie's baby is dead."

He looked up in surprise at how calmly she was taking this. "It's dead? When did you find that out?"

"Yesterday. But we've suspected something like that for a while."

"We?"

Her use of 'we' surprised even her. "Mr McDermot, my lawyer, and me, I mean."

Reggie nodded and then he asked, "Helen, is something going on?"

"What do you mean?"

"With this man McDermot. Is something going on with him?"

"Of course not. He's working for me."

"It's a strange relationship."

She stood up in fury. "I don't even like the man. He's quite impossible. You have the most rotten mind. You think everybody's like yourself."

Reggie shook his head. "I'm confused, Helen. I don't know where I am. I never see you. Your aunt says you treat me like a pet dog."

"My Aunt Liza! If you mention her name in this I will hit you, Reggie. I really will. How can she say that when I have ordered a new car for you? I wasn't going to tell you about it till it came, but I've ordered you a Rolls Phantom! It should be here soon. Would I do that if I thought of you as a pet dog?"

He looked up mournfully. "You might."

She felt sorry for him again and wished he didn't have the power to do that to her. His fair hair was thinning and his cheeks were drooping like a bloodhound's. Reggie

194

was losing the looks that had once captivated her. "Oh, don't be silly," she said. "I'm tired. Have a nightcap with me."

Surprisingly he shook his head. "No thanks, but Helen – let's go to bed together tonight. It's been such a long time since we slept together."

She was not prepared for the feeling of revulsion that this suggestion aroused in her and she had to fight to hide her reaction from him. Years ago, when she was burning up with resentment because he preferred his mistress to her, she would have leaped into his bed but no longer.

"I'm very tired, Reggie," she said carefully. "It's a long drive and my head is aching. I wouldn't be much of a lover, I'm afraid."

He shook his head as if what she had said confirmed his worst suspicions, padded over to the decanter that stood on a little table by the fire and poured himself a large brandy.

"It was very good of you to order me the Rolls, my dear," he said politely.

The big key did not open the locked door of the Grossett flat in Leith Walk so Val knew what he'd got. He was getting near to the end of the riddle.

His next call was on Georgina Kennedy. A lock had been fixed on her room door and he had to wait for a bit while she interrogated him but when he was admitted, he saw that she was much slimmed down and without the liverish yellow tinge in her complexion. In her new guise she had regained some of the stately quality she would have presented in the past when she walked though the rooms of Castledevon like a queen.

Sober now, she had taken the trouble to comb her hair neatly and her threadbare clothes had been patched by Mags who was an expert needlewoman. Because she had a caller, Mags' little daughter brought up a brown earthenware teapot full of black tea and two cups.

"My mam says open the door and yell down if you want any more," she told them and ran off again.

"They've been very kind," said Mrs Kennedy to Val. "It's all thanks to you for asking Mags to look after me; but I'm worried because I canna pay her. Phemie said Mrs Maitland was sending me some money but it's never come."

"And for that you ought to be grateful, because the person that brought it would be either Joe Quinn or Danny and they wouldn't just be acting as messenger boys. Mags' family won't let either of them up this stair anyway. I told them not to. I want you to stay alive," Val told her.

"What for?" Her voice was dispirited.

"So you can tell me all you know about Mrs Maitland's baby farm. What happened to the babies that didn't find homes?"

She rolled her eyes. "Dinna ask. I canna tell you."

"Why not? If I don't get an answer I might just walk down the stair and tell Mags not to bother watching you any longer – and then you know what would happen. Danny would be up here like a flash, putting you out of harm's way. Make no mistake, he and Quinn killed Phemie Grossett, though the police have written it off as an accident, and I'm sure he did in old Mrs Grossett as well. You'd have an accident too. What kind would you like? It would probably be a broken neck from a fall down the stairs, I guess."

She put her hand up to her throat. Then she said, "That would be quick. What does it matter about me anyway? I've no' got much longer to live. That would just mean it came quicker."

He sat forward staring fiercely at her. "Don't talk rubbish. You're looking much better and you're feeling better too, aren't you? Come the spring, you'll be wanting

196

to get out again – but you'll never be able to leave this room till something's done about Mrs Maitland and Danny. You're the only one that can do it, aren't you? You're the only one left that really knows what went on."

"I'm too feared."

"But if you don't tell, you'll always be feared. Every knock at your door, no matter where you go, could be the last one you'll ever hear. I know now that your brother fathered Leonie Gates' baby – and I know it's dead long ago. Tell me what happened to it."

She gulped and her eyes filled with tears. "Are you sure Fred's bairn's dead?"

"Phemie told me it was. She said her mother got rid of it. Tell me how."

She said with frank terror, "But what would happen if I told? Would they put me in jail too? They might even hang me."

"Hang you? Why should they hang you? People only get hanged if they're murderers."

"Well, I'm no' a murderer, but other people were."

Val held his breath. It seemed as if she was about to start talking but she shook her head. "I'm feared," she said again.

He tried another tack. "If you give valuable information it's possible to make a deal with the court. You'd be treated with leniency because of the information you gave the prosecution."

"Would I? Are you sure?"

"Positive. I'd fight your case myself."

"But I'd have to go into court and tell what I know. She'd be there watching me. She'd put the evil eye on me. I know she would."

"That wouldn't matter. She'd be locked up."

"You don't know how evil she can be. God knows what would happen to me if I talked."

197

They were getting nowhere, but he knew she was the key to their mystery.

"Do you remember working at Castledevon? Tell me about it," he said.

The black eyes fixed on his face. "It was a grand place, and a grand position for me. I was only twenty-eight, that's young for a housekeeper, and I was that proud when Mrs Gates took me on!"

"I'm sure you were very good at your job."

"Yes, I was good and I was honest. I didn't fiddle the books or anything like that. Some housekeepers do, you know. It was unfair of them to send me away. They wanted me off the place because of what I knew, because I knew about the baby – not because of Fred. It wasn't his fault. None of them were letting on about Fred, not even to each other. If Fred hadn't done what he did, I'd have still been at Castledevon maybe. I think that was the happiest time of my life, when I worked there." She wiped her eyes with the back of her hand and stared bleakly at Val.

"But you said what happened wasn't his fault."

"I don't think it was really. He said they both threw themselves at him, especially the mother. She used to go across to his room in the middle of the night and get into bed beside him – what man could resist that?"

"Tell me about the baby," he prompted.

"A lovely wee laddie. If he'd been allowed to grow up he'd have been a fine boy."

"But he wasn't allowed. Who stopped him?"

"Maitland or Mrs Grossett. I don't know which one. They thought no more of killing a baby than some folk think about drowning kittens. I wasnae there. I wouldn't have let her kill it and I wouldn't have taken the body away to hide it. Grossett must hae done that on her own. She was a bitch, a devil inside."

"How did they kill the babies?"

"That was easy. They were smothered like Grossett

198

was smothered. That's strange, isn't it? Serves her right. Or they were starved. Some o' the poor wee things lay in their cots like kittens mewing away for food and they just walked past without a sideways look."

Val felt nausea rising in him but he had to maintain cool composure. "How many were killed?" he asked.

The question seemed to make Georgina snap back into reality. She stared around as if afraid of being overheard and shrank back in her chair. "What have you made me say?" she asked.

"Nothing I didn't guess already," Val told her. "How many children were killed?"

"God knows. I never knew what was happening till Fred's baby went there. When I went back to see it, she told me there had never been a Gates baby but of course I kent fine there was. It was Lilian Grossett who let the thing slip. She'd been in with Maitland from the start. I only got involved because one of the houses in Edinburgh where I worked as a parlour maid had a lassie who fell pregnant and they wanted rid of it. They took it to Mrs Maitland and the lady's maid told me all about it. When Miss Leonie was in the family way, I told her mother where to go. I was trying to help."

"But why is Mrs Maitland scared for what you could tell if you don't know anything particular?"

"God forgive me for this! God forgive me, but afterwards when I needed money for drink I used to go with Lilian Grossett when she took the bodies away. I know where she took them. Oh dinna ask me anything else. I can't tell you any more. I can't even bear to think about it."

"Will you tell me where it is?"

"I cannae go back there . . . I never want to go there again."

"Just tell me."

"I cannae. I'm scared. Oh go away and leave me be."

"I'll go now but I'll be back," he said, standing up.

Fate played into his hands. That night Mags and her family were wakened by a tremendous shouting and banging coming from the top floor. When her two burly sons ran up the stairs, they found a man trying to push Mrs Kennedy through the window of her room. The intruder was stopped just seconds before he succeeded in his evil purpose and if it had not been for the fact that the woman's strength had returned sufficiently for her to put up a fierce fight, she would definitely have been dead.

Mags' boys manhandled the attacker downstairs and after giving him a thorough beating, threw him out onto the street. In their society people administered their own justice and no one thought of calling in the police, an oversight which Val McDermot deplored next morning when he was told about the dramatic events of the night.

"Was it Danny?" he asked the victorious boys but they shook their heads. "No, it wasnae him and it wasnae Joe Quinn either. It was a little rat that used to hang around the pubs in the Canongate and'll do anything for a bottle of whisky. We asked him who'd sent him but he wouldn't say so we beat him up," said the oldest brother.

When Val went up to see Mrs Kennedy, he found her shaken, bruised and very frightened.

"I told you, didn't I?" he asked. "If they'd sent two of them, you'd have been out of that window before the boys heard the noise. Next time you might not be so lucky. You'd better try to have them all locked up before they kill you."

She was weeping, wiping her discoloured face with shaking hands. "All right, all right, I'll tell you. It'll ease my conscience if nothing else. Like I said already, sometimes feeble bairns died naturally, but if they didn't they were helped and then Mrs Maitland always got Lilian Grossett to take away the bodies. After I started to drink heavily I helped her. They were so wee we could carry them in a basket."

"Where did you take them? To the sea?" Val knew that the fate of many unwanted babies was to be left lying on the shingle of the Forth estuary where either the water or the weather did its terrible work.

"No. It was easier than that. There was a special place, a cellar that Lillian knew, at the bottom of a building in the High Street, at the foot of Paton's Close where her sister lived then. We put them in it. She lived on the ground floor at the back and she had a key for a cellar that nobody else knew about. You know there are whole streets of houses in the cellars of some of those old buildings in the High Street. There's another town down there."

He nodded. "So I've been told. Some of them were walled up at the time of the plague."

She was looking at him with huge, haunted eyes. "And there's skeletons of cats and rats – and people. You'd no' get me going down there again."

"But you went with Lilian Grossett. How many times?"

"About ten I think, over a period of maybe five years. Sometimes we took two bairns. She could manage on her own but she preferred to have company. It was a bad place to be on yer own."

"Were you paid for going?"

"Maitland gave me a couple o' florins each time, but she also let me live in this flat. It's her property, you see. So was the cellar."

"Were the babies boys or girls?"

"Both, but most often wee girls. Bonny wee things some o' them."

"And Mrs Grossett did it alone sometimes?"

"Yes she did, but not often. Only in emergencies. She wasnae as scared of the cellar as I was though. She said it would have been worse if we were digging for coal. But even she liked having me with her."

"Did you dig graves for the children down there?"

"No. The floors were nearly all laid with stone slabs but there was a bit of the cellar with long stone benches down both sides. We just wrapped them up in their swaddling claes and laid them doon. The rats got them sometimes but one of the last times I was there, I reckoned there must have been about a dozen bodies in the cellar. I was glad when Mrs Maitland retired. There's been naething put there for about fifteen years now."

Val clapped his hands together. "Right, now we've just got to find it again."

She shook her head. "You'll no' get in. Lilian had a key and it opened the doors. I never had a key."

Val dug into his pocket and brought out the key. "Don't worry about that," he said. "Just tell me where the place is."

She drew him a little map. The entrance was down one of the herring-bone closes that went off the High Street in a slanting fashion. "Go half-way down and you'll come to an old arch. Look up and you'll see a carving of a thistle over your head. Then turn to your right and there's another wee entry. Go up it and you'll come to the first door. It's very dark but the lock's on the right-hand side. Go through to the back room and you find a locked door and then behind it a line of steps going down. At the bottom there's another door that's locked too, but the same key opens it. Then there's another line of steps going down again, a passage going straight ahead and a door with a beam over it. You have to lift the beam. It's heavy. Then you're in the first bit of the chamber. The bairns are hidden farther along. Mind and take a lamp. There's no light doon there and no' much air either. God, it'll be terrible down there now."

"I'm going to have a shot at it anyway," said Val. "And whilst I'm away there's something for you to do.

You must try to remember the names of any people that you know gave bairns to Mrs Maitland. We've got to find at least one other family than the Gateses whose child disappeared without trace."

Ten

V al McDermot telephoned Helen Hunt next morning and told her, "It's nearly finished. Mrs Kennedy told me where the babies' bodies are and I'm going there today."

Helen felt breathless with excitement. "Can I come too? I must come. I must."

"No, sorry. I'm going with the police. It's not the sort of thing we can do on our own and it's probably going to be very nasty. I'm not looking forward to it."

She was sobered and brought back to earth by the solemnity of his voice. "Where are they?" she asked.

"In a cellar in the High Street. The sort of place where, unless you knew it was there, they could stay hidden for centuries. That's if what Mrs Kennedy has told me is true. I'll let you know the outcome when it's all over."

When he hung up she decided that she could not wait for a telephone call. She'd go to Edinburgh and wait outside his office.

In order not to arouse too much interest or suspicion among neighbours who might also be tenants of Cynthia Maitland and could alert her to what was going on, the four-man police squad arrived separately at the High Street building dressed as Council workmen and Val, too, turned up alone.

The back ground-floor flat was empty and the door yielded easily to a jemmy. There were only two rooms, bare of furniture, built on what looked like an overhanging crag staring down at the roof of Waverley Station.

Georgina's description of the location of the hiding place was remarkably accurate. In the second room, what looked like a cupboard door proved to be locked. When Val slipped the key he had taken from Phemie Grossett's possessions into the lock, it turned easily and they found themselves looking in at a stone-walled alcove and a flight of steps going down into the bowels of the earth.

They entered the stairway, one after the other, each man holding a torch, for it was stygian black. The leader counted out the steps. "Seventeen, eighteen, nineteen, twenty, twenty-one – how many of them are there? – twenty-two . . . here's the end. And another door."

The same key opened it and they filed along a narrow stone walled passage with a barrel-shaped roof from which lines of green slime dripped. When impatience was beginning to set in again, they found another door, this one of battered-looking wood with a big beam across it and held in place by iron hoops. They lifted out the beam and propped it up in a corner. Then they opened the door.

What they found on the other side made them all draw in their breath with surprise. It was a short section of street, walled at both ends and full of little shops – each one open at the front like a booth and with living quarters at the back. Inside were counters and even a chair here and there. Hanging from the beams of one were the feathered corpses of game birds, and a dried out flitch of ham. Another had shelves at the back along which were lined bales of cloth that, when they were touched, disintegrated into fine powder. The corpse of a cat lay in a corner, just black fur and white bones.

Some of the shops had the names of the owners written along the stone lintels – Landels, Smith, Purvis. Guttered candles, surrounded by hardened wax, stood on counter tops, and fine drift of dust covered the floor.

"Christ," muttered one of the policemen. "When would this be closed up?"

Another, who was studying a line of boots in a shoe-maker's booth, said, "About three hundred years ago judging by the style of the shoes."

"They must have got out in a hurry," said a third man.

"If they got out," said Val. "When the plague struck, people panicked. If this street was badly hit, they'd wall it up with the sick still inside and anybody left here would have to take their chance."

This was a sobering thought to a group of men many feet below the surface of the street and the open air, with only two doors providing an escape for them. They looked at each other, their torches raking the sinister shadows and one of them said, "Well, let's get this over. Where did she say the bodies were, Val?"

"She said they were at the back, laid out on stone shelves. In what sounded like a wine cellar or something to me."

A man who had been walking ahead with his torch making raking beams of light across the vaulted stone roof gave a shout. "There's a lot of barrels up here. It looks like a wine shop."

They crowded after him and stared into a dark cavern along the back of which barrels were piled on their sides. A wooden trestle table filled the front and they had to edge round it to get inside. Over their heads hung a garland of what had once been green bay, put there to sweeten the air – though it had proved no protection against the plague.

It turned out that the line of barrels formed a wall between the outer and the inner shop. Behind it was, as they had been told, a cellar with stone benches. At the end of one was a huddle of what looked like silkworm cocoons, only bigger. The torches sought them out and stayed fixed on them while the men stared. Then one voice said softly, "That's them I bet."

They approached gingerly, each man reluctant to be the first to touch. Though they were hardened by having seen many horrible things, the thought of dead little children piled up like mummies was frightening for them. Eventually one man put down his torch and lifted one of the bundle off the top of the pile. It was wrapped in what looked like a white bedsheet that he took some time to unwind, untwisting and untwisting while the others watched, hardly daring to breathe.

Then the man retched and put it down. "Christ," he exclaimed. "It's a body right enough. Let's take some of them back for the doctors to look at. This isn't a job for us."

There were eleven little corpses but each man gathered up only one, carrying his burden carefully as if the child inside the wrapping was still alive and might waken at any moment. They did not wait to make any more extensive search of the sinister place for they had found what they wanted and that could be done later. They then retraced their steps till they found themselves again in the flat at ground level with natural light flooding through the windows. When they saw that, there was not a man among them who did not give a huge sigh of relief.

Sergeant Henderson in the police station was shaken out of his usual levity by the spectacle of the white wrapped bundles. "Are they really bairns?" he asked in disbelief.

"Yes," said Val, "and I know who's responsible for them being there."

"Who?"

"Mrs Cynthia Maitland, queen of the money lenders."

"She's a hard nut," said the Sergeant, "but you can't go around saying things like that without being able to prove it, and from the look of those bundles they've all been dead quite a long time." The coverings on the children, which had looked startlingly white in the darkness of the cellar, proved in the open air to be stained and discoloured.

"I'll prove it, don't you worry," said Val.

It was well past lunchtime but, though he normally had a good appetite, today the thought of food nauseated him and he walked down to Princes Street Gardens to sit alone on a bench in the chilly air staring down at his own hands that were gripping his knees. You can do such a lot with hands, such a lot of good or such a lot of evil, he thought. Which hands smothered the life out of the little babies now lying in the police station? It was up to him to find out and to make them suffer for what they'd done. The taking of such innocent lives seemed even more reprehensible than the killings that were going on – and which he was sure were about to become worse – all over Europe.

He took his hands off his knees and knotted them together. 'When this is over I'm going to Spain,' he told himself. 'I'm getting out of Edinburgh, away from all those feelings that have come crowding in on top of me recently.'

He was sitting on the south side of the railway line and lifted his head to stare across at Princes Street and the rising streets behind. 'It's beautiful but it's sterile and too safe. It's too money-conscious,' he thought.

Then he remembered Helen and her projected purchase of a Rolls Royce. 'Typical!' he said bitterly. 'She thinks she can solve any problem with her money – buying her husband a car, giving two hundred pounds to Phemie Grossett . . .

'Women like her shouldn't have access to so much money,' he told himself as he got up and prepared to walk to India Street, for he had suddenly felt that his skin was caked with the dust of the sunken street. It was in his hair, beneath his clothes, under his fingernails, and he longed to be clean, really clean. He wanted to scrub himself so that not an atom from the hidden street stayed with him.

He sat in a steaming bath tub for an hour, always running more water in when the original supply got cold. He had emptied into it a packet of his sister's pink bath crystals and now he washed his hair with her Amami shampoo, lathering it in and rinsing it out by lying on his back and letting his head float on the surface of the water. He tried to keep his mind empty but all the time it was working away at the next thing to be done, at the case he was going to construct against Cynthia Maitland.

When the last of the hot water had been used up, he got out of the bath and towelled himself dry. He was alone in the house and could walk from room to room naked, his long brown legs covering the landing in three strides. He was suddenly filled with a rush of energy and wished he could set out for Spain there and then but Mrs Hunt's business had to be concluded first – besides, the money he'd earn from that would fit him out well for his travels. He envisaged himself in a suit of khaki and a dashing beret, a red silk scarf tied round his neck. He'd buy a gun and some ammunition, a brandy flask and a good cigarette case. He might even buy a car, but not a Rolls Phantom. Heigh ho, roll on Spain, he told himself as he tied his red tie.

Helen, who had been sitting in her car for over two hours, saw him striding along Queen Street and found that the sight seemed to interfere with her breathing.

'My God, I hope I'm not developing heart trouble,' she thought, leaning back against the car seat back and inhaling deeply. Howie had suffered from heart trouble and was always having attacks during which he thought he was being stifled. He carried a brandy flask to refresh himself when those episodes took place. 'I'll buy a brandy flask too,' said his daughter to herself.

Val had not seen her – or if he had he was not

acknowledging her – so she had to open the car door and call to him. He turned with one hand on the iron balustrade and glowered at her.

She leant out of the car and asked, "What happened? I couldn't wait. I simply had to know."

He walked across the pavement and leaned down to talk to her. "We found eleven bodies."

She gasped. "Eleven! How awful. What happens now?"

"The real trouble starts. We've got to prove Mrs Maitland killed them."

"Mrs Kennedy said she did, didn't she?"

"We've only her testimony about that. She didn't actually see her do it. Mrs Grossett who probably did see her is dead; so's Phemie, who must have been told about it by her mother. Mrs Kennedy is living on borrowed time as well. If Mrs Maitland's men don't get her, that cancer probably will. It's important that the whole thing comes to court while she's still alive and able to give evidence."

Helen's eyes were searching his face. "You don't sound very optimistic about the outcome."

"I prefer realism to optimism."

"I think I do too, but surely the forces of right can win sometimes. Surely Mrs Maitland will have to pay for what she's done. All those little children! It's unthinkable."

"The forces of right can sometimes be very lazy. They have to be given lots of helping hands," said Val, straightening up.

She got out of the car and came round to stand beside him on the pavement. "What are you going to do first?" she asked.

"I've been thinking about that. It's Mrs Kennedy again, I think, and then I'll have to find someone who will admit to having given a child to Mrs Maitland so we can follow it up and discover if it survived or not. We know your sister's child didn't but it might have

died naturally. Mrs Kennedy said it was very 'fine',
didn't she?"

"But what are the police doing?"

"They're having the bodies examined but I doubt that
will tell them much. All of them have been dead for at
least ten years. There'll be no way of ascertaining how
they died unless they have broken bones, and according
to Mrs Kennedy the preferred way of getting rid of them
was smothering them – which doesn't show, of course."

"Are you going to see Mrs Maitland?"

"No. Not yet. The whole thing has to be kept quiet
till the police are ready to move on her. I hope she has
no idea what's happening. We were very careful about
how we went in and out of the house so's nobody would
see us."

She looked earnestly up at him and asked, "Are you
still working for me?"

He stared down at her. "Do you want me to? You've
found out what happened to the baby you were looking
for. That's the end of it as far as you're concerned,
isn't it?"

She shook her head. "No. I thought it would be but it
isn't. I want to see that wicked woman punished too. If
you have to spend money building up a case against her,
charge the costs to my bill."

"All right. I'm going to see Mrs Kennedy now. Do you
want to come?"

"Yes, I do. I'll drive."

He climbed into the car without a protest.

It was difficult for Val to look at Georgina with the same
detachment and sympathy as he had in the past because he
kept imagining her carrying dead babies into that horrible
hidden street down below the foundations of the houses
on the High Street. How had she done it? For drink, she'd
said. Val liked a glass of whisky or a bottle of good wine

but the thought of being so obsessed, so desperate for alcohol that your need overrode every scruple or principle you ever possessed, was hard to comprehend.

She was not so alert today as she had been the day before. Her face was grey and drawn which made him remember again the grave diagnosis the hospital had given her. If she was going to be Nemesis to Mrs Maitland, he'd have to move quickly.

"We found the bodies," he told her. "Just where you said they'd be. Your directions were impeccable."

"I'll never forget that place. I still have dreams about going back there," she said mournfully.

He nodded in agreement. "It was horrible. I think it was a plague street. It probably dates back to the 1600s."

She shuddered. "A few people in the High Street know it's there but they won't go near it because they say it's haunted."

"It deserves to be haunted," said Val bitterly remembering the pathetic pile of babies.

"Oh, I mean it was haunted before we started going down there. A young woman is meant to walk along the street looking for someone. Lilian said she saw her one day."

"And that didn't stop her going down?" asked Helen in amazement.

"She was a hard case was Lilian," said Mrs Kennedy.

"Have you remembered any names of people who gave babies to Mrs Maitland?" asked Val. This was crucial for his case.

She reached out and found a spectacle case on the window ledge beside her. "Yes, I wrote them down. I remembered two. The first was the place where I worked when I was a lassie. It was in Charlotte Square with a family who had a house near Inverness as well. They came down to Edinburgh twice a year. There was a daughter and she was called Annabelle. She was the one who fell pregnant and the lady's maid told me about them giving the baby to Mrs Maitland."

Val was writing in his notepad. "What was the family's surname?" he asked.

"It was double barrelled. Finnieston-Stewart. I don't exactly remember how they spelled it but the father was very important in some bank or other."

Val was staring at her in astonishment. "Finnieston-Stewart?" he repeated.

"Yes."

"They're my mother's cousins."

"That's good, you'll be able to ask them about the baby," said Helen but he glared at her. "Could you ask your cousins something like that? Of course you couldn't. Somebody else will have to do the asking."

He looked across at Georgina Kennedy who was reading the piece of paper she'd taken from her spectacle case. "There was another one. A woman Lilian told me about, a Miss Chalmers, who turned up at Maitland's on her own with a wee baby. She was a missionary and very religious. Before she left the baby she put a wee cross on a chain round its neck. It was a little boy, Lilian said."

"What kind of a missionary?"

"I don't know. Church of Scotland probably. Mrs Maitland was a great one for the church, always giving them donations, and after she bought the St Bernard's Crescent house she let them use her garden for sales of work and things. She was very keen on the mission to India."

"That's a start," said Val scribbling this down as well.

He stood up. "You've done very well. You don't know of anyone else who might be able to help, do you? Anyone working in Mrs Maitland's house perhaps?"

She shook her head. "Not really. She always used to have an old, very crabbit maid called Nancy who knew a lot, but I doubt if she'd talk to you. Her sister worked in a place I had just before I went down to Castledevon."

"She's not there now," said Val. "The maid when I called on Mrs Maitland was a pretty little thing, very far from crabbit. You stay up here now, and keep your door locked. Mags' boys are going to watch the stairs day and night."

The woman in the chair by the window shuddered. "I was nearly away the other night. He was trying to throw me out o' the window. If he had done, people would have said I jumped, wouldn't they?"

"They probably would. Don't think about it."

When they went back downstairs, they called in at Mags' and then descended to the street. There was a crowd of urchins around Helen's car which was being guarded by two younger members of Mags' family, who were given two threepenny bits for their trouble. As they drove away, chased down the road by shrieking children, Helen said to Val, "Do you think either of those people she told you about will provide the information you need?"

"I don't know but I've got to try, haven't I? I can't ask my mother's cousins though. You'll have to do that for me."

"*Me*?" She was astonished at the suggestion.

"Well, you're always saying how you want to help and this is a perfect job for you. Dress yourself up in all your finery, drive your big car and descend on them. They're terrible snobs."

"What do I say?"

"It's best to stick as close to the truth as possible. Tell them that you're looking for your sister's child and why. Say something like you need their help to be introduced to Mrs Maitland – something like that. It'll come to you."

She sent a letter on her best personal stationery asking

for an interview about a personal matter with which the Finnieston-Stewart ladies might be able to help.

"They'll check up on you, but they do a lot of charity work and they'll probably think you want to see them in connection with that," said Val.

A very guarded letter came back saying Helen might call at eleven a.m. next Friday morning when Mrs Finnieston-Stewart would be able to spare her half an hour.

"They're a prickly pair but keep your head and you'll be all right," said Val when he saw her off. It was only a short walk from Queen Street to Charlotte Square where the Finnieston-Stewarts lived and Helen looked cool and unflustered when she was shown into an enormous drawing room that faced south over the gardens in the middle of the Square.

Waiting for her were two women, one grey-haired and patrician with a look of Queen Mary, and the other in middle age with her fair hair wound round her head in two plaits that gave her the look of a German peasant in an operetta.

They assessed Helen's clothes the moment she stepped into the room, their eyes raking her from top to toe. That gave her confidence because she knew what she was wearing was of the highest quality.

When her coat was taken from her, she sat in a high-backed chair and crossed her legs, knowing that her stockings were of the sheerest silk and her shoes brand new.

She began by telling them who she was – Helen Hunt, born Helen Gates, daughter of mill magnate Howie Gates of Galashiels. They'd never heard of him, so she elaborated on the extent of his business empire and then dropped her voice to say how, when her father died in the spring, it was discovered that her late sister had given birth to a child that was lost.

The two listening women looked at each other. "Lost?" said the mother.

"I mean she gave it away for adoption when it was born. My father has left it a legacy – a large legacy in fact – and for months now I have been trying to track it down."

Mother and daughter watched her carefully, neither of their faces betraying any real sympathy.

They did not help her when she came to the difficult bit either. "During my research I found out that my sister's child had been sent for fostering to a Mrs Maitland who lives in Edinburgh. She undertook to place it with a good family and when the boy was fourteen he was to be apprenticed to some respectable trade. Unfortunately my lawyers have been unable to find him because Mrs Maitland now denies ever having had any connection with him, though I know that my father paid her a stipend for his upkeep for fourteen years."

The mother looked stonily at Helen and said, "It seems to me, Mrs Hunt, that what you are telling us is something that should be dealt with by your lawyers. It has no connection with us. Who is representing you legally?"

"A Mr McDermot of Sutherland, Ross and McQueen."

"Valentine McDermot? He's the son of mother's cousin," said the younger woman.

"Did he send you to us?" demanded the mother, whose face was reddening.

"He suggested that you might be able to tell me if the baby you sent to Mrs Maitland for fostering is still alive," said Helen boldly, for she guessed that they expected her to say something of the sort.

"Valentine has always been a mischief-making boy. His mother was a sweet person who married a mad Highland laird – Sir Roderick – a maniac of a man and absolutely penniless. His son takes after him. I do hope he hasn't sent you here in some sort of blackmail attempt."

"Blackmail? Good heavens no. All I want is information."

The daughter was wringing her hands but the mother

was still very much in control. "What makes you imagine we would know anything about fostered babies and this Mrs Maitland?" she demanded.

Helen took a chance. "Because Mrs Maitland was required by law to make returns of the children she placed and your name was on that list," she lied.

"Oh, Mama," cried the daughter. "She promised our names would never be known!"

"Annabelle, control yourself," snapped her mother, but Annabelle could not. "I was only eighteen. I didn't know anything. It was a little girl and the father had gone to India . . . Every time I pass a girl of the right age in the street I wonder if she might be mine."

"Be quiet, Annabelle!" shouted her mother and the daughter sank back in her chair weeping.

Mrs Finnieston-Stewart stood up like an avenging angel. "I don't know why you came here to cause trouble for us. What happened is in the past and we have put it out of our minds completely."

Helen stood up too. "Several of the children Mrs Maitland took for fostering were murdered. Mr McDermot is trying to bring a case against her. He needs witnesses."

"He certainly won't get us," said Mrs Finnieston-Stewart, opening the door and showing Helen into the hall where a maid servant was waiting with her coat.

Back in Queen Street, she sank into a chair beside Val's desk and said, "They'll never admit it."

He drew a line through their names on a paper he had on the desk and said, "Too snobbish. Too afraid of their reputations – even if Maitland killed Annabelle's baby, they'd never give evidence. Edinburgh snobs!"

"You didn't tell me your father was Sir Roderick McDermot," she said.

He glared at her. "Does it matter? Do you think any better of me for it?"

She stammered, "N-n-n-no, of course not. It's just that you said you were a Communist and I thought . . ."

"That I was the product of the slums, is that it? I am a Communist and when this case is over I'm off to Spain to fight Franco."

The Church of Scotland offices on George Street had an address for a retired missionary called Marjorie Chalmers. They told Val that she lived in rooms in a house in St John's Road, Corstorphine, coincidentally not far from Hugo Anderson and his mother.

He rode out to the suburb on the top of a tram, wondering all the way if he should have given this sensitive commission to Helen too but she had not telephoned for two days and he suspected that she would not take on another commission after the Finnieston-Stewart fiasco. After all, she had hired him to do her investigating for her.

The house sat four square on a patch of ground, fronted by a rigidly laid out garden and a line of trees behind the low wall that cut the garden off from the street. There were fringed white blinds on all the windows, each one drawn down to exactly the same level. The door brass was glittering and the step so immaculately pipe-clayed that he was fearful about standing on it.

A woman in a blue patterned cross-over overall answered the door to him. Miss Chalmers was at home but gentlemen callers were not permitted in the residents' rooms. If he waited she would enquire if Miss Chalmers wished to speak with him. What was the name? He passed over his card and said he'd wait. He was confident he'd get a hearing since lawyer's cards were difficult for most people to resist.

A few minutes later the door opened again and the formidable keeper of the gate announced that Miss Chalmers would see him. She stood back and allowed him to enter the hall and then opened the door to a sitting room where two very ancient ladies sat in bath chairs staring bleakly out of the little gap beneath the window blinds of the two windows. He wished them good morning but neither replied.

"Are you Mr McDermot?" asked a soft voice behind him after few moments and he turned round to find a stout, rather florid woman in her late fifties smiling at him. Her front teeth were crooked, her cheeks apple red, her grey hair an unruly frizz and her eyes sharp like a curious bird's.

"I am," he said putting out his hand. "And you're Miss Chalmers."

"Indeed I am. Why do you want to see me?"

From the corner of his eye he could see that the old dames in the bath chairs were both listening intently. It would not be possible to ask what he needed here.

"I was wondering if you and I could walk up the road and have a cup of coffee together so we can discuss our business in private."

She did not need persuading. "That would be nice. I'll get my coat," she said.

They went to a hotel where there was a lounge with basket chairs and potted plants and privacy. Val liked Miss Chalmers with her bluff country woman's face and her matter-of-fact manner so he knew he was not going to prevaricate with her.

"I need your help, Miss Chalmers," he said, and launched into an account of how he was engaged by Helen Hunt to find out about her sister's baby and the events that led from that. She listened in silence, only making little clicking sounds of surprise and shocked disapproval when he talked about the deaths of Mrs Grossett and her daughter. As he described the cellar where the babies' bodies were found however, she seemed to shrink into her chair and her face lost its high colour.

Finally he came to the bit when he had to explain why he had sought her out.

"A woman who worked with Mrs Grossett gave me the names of some people who placed children with Mrs Maitland. Your name was among them. I hope you are able to help me because it is essential to prove that Mrs Maitland was running an extensive business and that babies she pretended for years were alive and thriving were in fact dead."

"Is my little boy dead?" The question was whispered.

"I don't know. Tell me the details and I'll try to find out."

She lifted her coffee cup with a shaking hand and, without asking her, Val signalled to the waiter and ordered two brandies. The alcohol seemed to steady her and she said, "I was working in the mission in Poona. I was there for ten years and towards the end of my time I became sick with dysentry. The doctor who treated me was the most wonderful man I had ever met. He was an Indian, a Maharastrian called Jadhav Srivastava, and we fell in love. But he was married of course.

"When I began to get better, a letter came ordering me to go to Bombay and then back home because they had a posting for me in Africa. We were both distraught but I had to obey orders. We had not done anything wrong till then but when it seemed that we would never meet again . . . we slept together, Mr McDermot. Do you think that was very terrible?"

Val shook his head. "Not at all. I think it was very sensible."

"Have you ever been to India?" she asked.

"No."

"The hot nights are so wonderful, so luxurious somehow. And there are flowers that only give out their perfume in the dark. It's easy to do things there that you'd never do here."

He nodded and she went on, "It didn't last long but it was wonderful and eventually I had to go down to Bombay and get on the boat. I think I cried for most of the voyage and I felt rather ill but it was not till I was back in Edinburgh that I realised what was wrong with me. I was having his baby."

"What did you do?"

"I had a cousin living here and I went to her. She was horrified. She said the Church would throw me out if they knew. I'm not a rich woman, Mr McDermot, all I had was what I earned and that was never very much. All my family apart from the cousin were dead – I was old to be having a baby, you see. I was forty-three."

"What year was it?"

"1921. I arrived home in March and the baby was born in July. I called him Krishna. He was the most beautiful colour, golden brown."

"How did you get in touch with Mrs Maitland?" asked Val with a sinking heart for he could guess that a mixed-race boy would have little chance of surviving the Maitland selection process.

"The midwife was called Grossett. My cousin hired her and I had the baby at home. I was meant to be still recuperating from my dysentry, you see, and that was not a lie because I was quite ill for a long time. Mrs Grossett told my cousin that she knew of a woman who would take the child. All I had to do was pay sixty pounds. I raised the money by pawning some rings and brooches my mother had left me. I never wore them. They were kept in the bank so I didn't mind."

"Did you have to pay any more money than the sixty pounds?"

"No. Mrs Grossett said it was customary for people to pay what they could afford every year for the upkeep of the child but because I was a missionary, Mrs Maitland would overlook that and try to find a well-off family that would give my baby a home. I thought she did that because she was a religious woman."

"It must have been awful for you to part with the child."

"It was but I was quite ill after the delivery and really didn't know what was happening. When I was fit again, he'd gone, but I had him for three whole weeks. I held him in my arms and he was so lovely, Mr McDermot, a perfect child and so good natured, just like his dear father. I put a little chain with a cross round his neck so that Jesus would take care of him. I pray that He did."

Val said nothing, just patted her hand. She sighed and went on, "So I went to work in Africa and came home at last a year ago but Mrs Maitland was very unhelpful and told me nothing about Krishna. My cousin had died while I was away but that house along the road where I live now belongs to another woman who used to be a missionary. She takes in old ladies and I get a cheap room in exchange for helping her. She'd throw me out if she knew about Krishna."

They walked back along the road companionably with her hand resting on his arm and when they parted she looked up at him and asked, "Will you let me know if you find out anything about my wee boy? Will you tell me even if the news is bad?" He promised that he would.

Back in the centre of Edinburgh he took himself up to the police station where the autopsy results on the children awaited his attention. The police had recovered the remains of the children all aged between two weeks and six months. They had been wrapped in old bedsheets – one of which miraculously had a legible laundry mark which the police were currently checking. None of the corpses had anything to distinguish or identify them except one little boy who wore a cheap, rolled gold cross on a chain round his neck.

Val left the police office in a raging fury and went

back to his office where he lifted the telephone to ring Helen.

"Have you lost interest in this business?" he snapped when she answered.

"No, of course not, but I've been busy down here . . ." She didn't tell him that she had been briefing her Galashiels lawyer about a divorce from Reggie and trying to summon up the courage to break the news to him and the family.

"Well, since I haven't seen or heard of you for days I thought you might like to know that I found the missionary Miss Chalmers. One of the dead babies is hers because she put a cross round his neck."

"It's upset you. I'm sorry. Did you like her very much?"

"What does that matter? The important thing is that she's a material witness and she'll give evidence I think because she's a brave woman."

All night he worried about how he was going to break the bad news to Miss Chalmers and next morning, when he reached his office, he found Sergeant Henderson, on his way home after a night shift, waiting for him.

"You ken that laundry mark on the sheet one o' the bairns was wrapped in?" he asked.

"Yes."

"Well, it's from the laundry Mrs Maitland uses round the corner from St Bernard's Crescent."

Val clapped his hands together. "That's great. What are you going to do?"

"A couple of the lads have gone there to bring her in for questioning. Come up to the station later on and we'll let you know how it's gone."

He took the tram once more to Corstorphine and walked about among the village shops till he judged it was a suitable time to go back to the house where Miss Chalmers lived. When she saw him standing on the step, she knew why he had come and quietly went to fetch her hat and coat so they could walk down by the old church together and he could tell her what she dreaded hearing.

"I'm sorry but your son is dead."

She nodded slowly with her head down. "How do you know it was him?"

"Because of the cross you told me about."

She looked up with tear-filled eyes, "He was still wearing it?"

"He was only about four weeks old when he died, Miss Chalmers."

She stopped short in the middle of the pavement. "He was three weeks old when I gave him to her and he was very well then. She killed him, didn't she? She took my money and she killed my baby."

"I'm afraid so."

"What are you going to do?"

"The police are going to charge her. Will you accuse her of killing your son? Will you give evidence? I'll fight the case for you for nothing."

Her eyes searched his face. "You're very angry, aren't you? You're an idealist, Mr McDermot."

"Yes, I'm angry. What the Maitland woman did fills me with rage. But I need witnesses. I need women who will stand up and say they gave her their babies."

"You understand why they don't want to, of course."

"Yes."

"If I give evidence I'll lose my room and my job and my name will be blackened among my friends in the church."

"I know I'm asking a lot. I'll understand if you can't do it."

"But I can and I will. I can still feel the weight of my baby in my arms. I can still see his sweet wee face in my mind. I'll do it."

They parted on the church steps and she went inside to pray.

Eleven

H elen was not entirely sure why she wanted a divorce but one thing was certain, she was decided on it.

For days she had tried to open the subject with Reggie but to no effect for she always quailed from delivering the final blow. Instead she found herself behaving in a querulous, spoilt fashion that made her ashamed.

When she received the phone call about the missionary woman's baby however, something hardened in her and she marched into the library where her husband was dozing and said sharply, "Reggie, I want to speak seriously to you."

He sat up, mild-mannered as ever and said, "Yes, my dear."

"I want a divorce."

For a moment it did not register and he kept on staring but then he blinked and said, "A divorce? Because of Eleanor?"

"No. I know you haven't been seeing her recently and in fact I'm sorry about that because everyone tells me what a nice woman she is. No, I want a divorce because we aren't right for each other."

"Is there anyone else?" asked Reggie going across to a side table and pouring himself a brandy.

She shook her head. "No. I don't want to be married to anyone. I want to be on my own because I feel that I haven't taken time to grow into a woman. I want to be independent."

"You are independent," her husband said. "You have your own fortune."

"It's not because of that. And I'm not going to let our divorce affect you financially. You'll still have your position in the company and still draw your salary – in fact, I'll make it bigger. I just want us to go our own ways. Please, Reggie, this is very important to me. I'm not the same woman as I was a year ago."

He nodded. "That's very true. How are we going to do it? I wouldn't want Eleanor named. I'll hire a woman and go away with her and then you can sue me."

She let out a gasp of relief. "Oh Reggie, you really are the nicest man I know."

"Pity you don't love me though, isn't it?" he said.

Eleanor, the ex-mistress of Reggie Hunt, was sitting in the window of her Drummond Place drawing room when she saw him coming along the pavement and her heart leaped with delight. When he was shown in she was standing in the middle of the floor with both hands outheld.

"Darling, how wonderful to see you again," she said. She was not the sort of woman who went in for recriminations or accusations; not the sort to ask him where he had been for the best part of three months. She was pleased to see him and showed it.

He walked over to her and held her in his arms. She was a tall woman, almost as tall as he was himself, and they stood like that for some time with his face sunk into her neck and her hands stroking his hair. "Dear Reggie," she whispered and it was like healing balm to him.

"It's all over with Helen and me," he told her some time later when they were having a companionable drink. A sun red as a blood orange sank over the tree tops of the gardens in the middle of the Place.

Eleanor was a nice woman and she never miscalled her

226

lover's wife but she patted his hand soothingly. "That's a pity. Tell me about it," she invited.

"I've not been to see you because I tried to patch it up with her but she's been behaving so oddly, Eleanor. She's off on some wild goose chase looking for her sister's illegitimate baby. She found her mother in London and came back all dressed up like a fashion plate and now she's after the child. She's hired an Edinburgh lawyer to help her and we've had the police phoning the house about him being found in the flat of a murdered woman, all sorts of peculiar goings on. Now she says she wants a divorce but she's promised there's no other man involved and I believe her. She's not really interested in that sort of thing."

Eleanor shook her head. "Perhaps she should see a doctor. It sounds to me as if she's frustrated at not having a baby."

"That's what her aunt says but when I suggested it to Helen she flew off the handle. The last thing she wants is a baby, she said."

Eleanor, mother of two grown sons, shook her head sagely. "They all say that at first. Does she know you're here, Reggie darling?"

"Oh yes. We're getting divorced. All very amicable but we mustn't admit that or the courts won't wear it. The awful thing is that I can't be angry with her because she's really being very nice to me. She's ordered me a Rolls Phantom, Eleanor, and you know how much they cost. But in a way I feel as if she's buying me off, giving me toys as if I was a little boy or something . . ."

She knew how much a Rolls Phantom cost and her eyes widened in surprise. "A Rolls! Good heavens. Are you sure she's not having an affair? What's her lawyer's name?"

"It's like an actor's name. Valentine McDermot. She says she doesn't like him."

227

"I knew his mother, Lady McDermot. Such a sweet woman but the father's mad. She had two boys and a girl. He must be the younger one, a bit of a rebel at school I think. A real worry, takes up all sorts of ridiculous ideas, wears red ties and says he's a Communist. The father never comes to Edinburgh, spends his time up north fishing and shooting and that sort of thing. They're rather poor."

"Doesn't sound quite Helen's sort. He's not an actor?"

"Not an actor."

"I'll do what's necessary. I'll go off to a hotel some-place with a woman and she can sue me for adultery. Then you and I can get married. I wouldn't drag you into it, Eleanor."

She leaned across and kissed him. "You are the sweetest man in the world. Helen's a lucky girl and doesn't know it," she told him.

The sight of two burly policemen on the threshold of number twenty St Bernard's Crescent threw the household into a panic. Cynthia Maitland was still in bed and her son Danny was sleeping in the top-floor nursery, out of the way of prying eyes because he was being sought for questioning about the deaths of Phemie Grossett and her mother Lilian and his face bore the scars inflicted on him by his victims.

When he went charging downstairs to find out why his mother was screeching so much, he walked straight into the arms of a policeman who arrested him. "We've been looking for you, my lad. Where's your friend Joe Quinn?" he said.

When Danny was taken back upstairs to get dressed, he made a bungled attempt at hiding a roll of money which was taken to the police station with him and which turned out to be the notes Val had marked before he gave them to Phemie. Though this interested the police, they could not keep Danny in custody because he said he found the notes at St Bernard's Well and no one could prove he hadn't.

Cynthia Maitland, after an initial outburst, behaved with great restraint when asked to accompany the officers to the police station for questioning and sailed out of her house dressed in a leopard-skin coat and a black hat with cock's feathers sweeping down across one cheek. No one could say she did not go in style. She and Danny sat in silence in the police van, not even looking at each other. When her son was led away to a different part of the police station, she heard him saying to one of his escorts, "It's all up to her. I'd nothing to do with it," and she knew Danny was liable to turn King's evidence.

That night she was charged with murdering two children who had been given into her care under the assumption that she would find them homes. The first was the son of Marjorie Chalmers and the second was the son of the late Leonie Gates.

"This is absolute nonsense," she said calmly in response to the charges. "Both of those children died of natural causes and I defy you to prove otherwise."

"Oh well," said the detective closing his notebook. "If we don't get you for those two we'll get you for the others."

Val had been in the police station all day was jubilant when the charge was finally made. "We'll have her up for the first time tomorrow and then after that it's up to you legal boys to make your case," a policeman told him.

It was half-past ten when he emerged on to the pavement of the High Street and stood staring up its long, sinister, steel grey length. Far away in the distance he saw the light of a telephone box and headed for it. Helen Hunt would want to know what had happened.

She was sitting alone in the library beside a dying fire, pondering her situation. That afternoon, under the curious observation of the servants, Reggie had taken himself and his many bags off to Edinburgh where he would stay from now on and she had Castledevon all to herself. Tomorrow, she had been thinking, I must go to Liza's to tell the news. After that the telephone wires all over the district will be zinging with excited callers discussing me.

At that moment the phone in the hall set up an insistent ringing. She opened the library door and stared at it. Who could be phoning at this time of night? Perhaps it was Reggie who had forgotten to take something with him. Because Simes would be in bed, and was probably lying cursing at the sound of the bell above his head, she padded across the hall in her stocking feet and lifted off the receiver.

"Hello."

"McDermot here. They've arrested Mrs Maitland. She's in the cells and so's Danny. He had my marked money on him but that's not enough proof he killed Phemie of course. He could just have picked the money up. But he's scared silly and information is pouring out of him. It's wonderful." He sounded as a excited as a small boy.

"What's going to happen now?" she asked.

"Well, Mrs Maitland'll come up tomorrow but she should be remanded in custody. They won't let her out on bail in case she bolts – which she would of course."

"What time tomorrow?"

"Any time after half-past ten."

"I'll come up, I think. I've never seen her, you see."

"Please yourself. You'll see plenty of her in the future, I hope."

"Why do you hope that?"

"A good long case. Great fees. I'm appearing for the prosecution," he laughed.

"I'll see you tomorrow then."

"Probably not. I'll be busy."

"Oh. Good-night and thank you for calling."

"Good-night. It's good news. You're pleased aren't you?"

"I'm very pleased," she said politely. "Good-night."

Instead of going to Liza's the next day, Helen took the train to Edinburgh. She was tired of driving. She sat in the corner of the first-class carriage and stared bleakly out of the window at a grey world outside. The trees would soon be leafless. Almost a year had passed without her noticing. The thought of the approaching festive season filled her with terror.

How I wish I had somebody to love, she thought but immediately drove the idea away as being sentimental self-indulgence. She had lots of friends and acquaintances who, when they heard that she and Reggie had split up, would inundate her with invitations. At least that was what she hoped.

The court was crowded and smelt of sweating people. She shouldered her way into the courtroom where Cynthia Maitland would appear and perched on a bench at the back, watching while a succession of offenders was hauled up out of a hole in the ground, trotted past a magistrate and put back downstairs again.

It was nearly noon before Mrs Maitland appeared and at the same time a door at the back of the court opened and Val McDermot stepped in to stand beside a policeman with his arms crossed over his chest.

Helen sat forward in her seat and studied the woman whose prosecution she had initiated, conscious that she had brought about her downfall almost by accident really. If she had been let in on the family secret about Leonie's suicide years ago, she would not have been so shocked when Phemie Grossett and Billy Cameron made their bungled attempt at claiming part of her father's fortune. She would only have put her lawyers on to them and seen them off at once.

Cynthia Maitland looked very cool, very composed, beautifully dressed and as sinister as a cobra. When the charge was read out, she said quite clearly that she was not guilty and an elegant advocate popped up from a front seat to announce he was appearing for Mrs Maitland who should, he said, be granted bail. This request was, however, refused by the sheriff, and the case was sent to the High Court. It was now out of the jurisdiction of lower officials and would in future be heard by a solemn judge in a full-bottomed wig with a black silk cap ready to hand beneath his desk top. The machinery of the law had begun to turn.

When Mrs Maitland was taken back down below, the court emptied in a sudden rush. It was if an avalanche of people were all trying to get out of the door at once. Newspaper reporters ran, all eager to get to their offices or to the nearest telephone first for this was a sensational story. When Helen looked round for Val he had gone as well, swept away in the mêlée. Perhaps he had not even seen her.

She went to the Café Royal and ate oysters alone. Then she went back to Galashiels on the train. That evening she drove to Liza's and dropped her bombshell, deliberately very casually, over a drink. "By the way, Reggie's left me. We're getting a divorce."

"Well, I can't really say I'm surprised. You've always treated the poor man in a very offhand manner," said her aunt.

"That's rich. Poor man indeed. He's the one that's having the affair. I'm the one that's divorcing him."

"I always say a man stays at home if he's being well looked after."

"I might have expected you to say something like that," said Helen angrily and stormed out of the house again.

No sooner had the door banged behind her than Liza was on the telephone to all the relatives and Colin in

Leeds. They'd be shocked, horrified and thrilled at having such a juicy bit of gossip to chew over. Not one of them would blame Reggie for the break-up of the marriage. Helen was difficult, would be the consensus of their opinion. What really exercised their minds, however, would be the question of money. Would Reggie be able to keep on his job at the mills? Would Helen allow him to do so or would she turn vindictive?

She was correct; the telephone wires buzzed and hummed for the rest of the evening and most of the next day.

Twelve

It took several weeks for Val to prepare his case against Cynthia Maitland and Helen heard nothing from him till one autumn morning when she received a telephone call.

Standing in the hall of Castledevon, she felt a little sick when his voice rang out over the line. Perhaps, she thought, it was because he brought back memories of terrible things – Phemie Grossett running away at St Bernard's Well, the squalid flat where Mrs Kennedy lived . . .

He didn't waste time with preambles. "You'll have to give evidence, is that all right?"

"Yes, of course."

"I need your mother too. I wrote to her but she hasn't replied and there's no phone."

"I don't think she'll come. She said she never wants to see Scotland again."

"She must come. Her evidence is crucial. Go and get her."

It was an order.

Milly, fortunately, had not gone to Paris to find her mysterious man and was still living in the same untidy state in Roland Way when Helen once more found herself on the doorstep.

"Oh, it's you again," said Milly, looking out of the window in response to the early-morning knock.

Inside the house Helen asked, "Why didn't you reply to my lawyer's letters?"

234

"Because I'm not going to Scotland to give evidence about something I'd far rather forget."

"You have to. You must. The Maitland woman is a killer. She had Leonie's baby killed, she took money for it for years though she knew it was dead. She killed other babies too. She can't be allowed to escape justice."

Urgently Helen grabbed her mother's arm as she spoke and Milly looked at her in surprise. "Good heavens, this has really upset you. Why are you so involved?"

"Because of my sister, because of her baby . . ." Helen was on the verge of tears.

Milly shrugged her daughter's hand off her arm. "If the woman hadn't killed the baby, we might never have known what happened to it anyway."

"Wouldn't you have wondered?"

"Not particularly."

"Please, please, think about this. The child was Leonie's but it was also your lover's child. There's other innocent children involved . . . there's a woman missionary who gave up her son. She's going to give evidence though the publicity will probably ruin her. Don't be so *selfish*!"

Milly looked genuinely surprised. "Selfish? Me? I'm not selfish. I'm not greedy. I could have got far more money out of Howie than I did but I never tried. I didn't ask you for money, did I?"

"That's not what I mean. I mean try thinking about other people instead of yourself all the time. Come to Edinbugh and give evidence. It'll only take a couple of days."

"But I won't go back to Castledevon. I won't go anywhere near Galashiels. When I took the train out of that station in 1915, I swore I'd never go back," she told Helen. "I couldn't wait to get away." Milly was so vehement that Helen realised her mother was probably frightened to go back.

"All right, I'll rent a flat in Edinburgh for the duration of the case. You won't need to go out of the city, I promise."

Reluctantly Milly went north with her daughter next day.

The Maitland case was attended by the maximum publicity. Day after day the newspapers ran front page headlines about the 'Baby Farm Killings' and all Edinburgh was agog because many people there knew Mrs Maitland, who had presented herself in society as a pillar of propriety.

There were also people in smart drawing rooms who read the stories with extra horror for they could have added charges to the list of Mrs Maitland's crimes if they were not anxious to keep their own family skeletons well hidden.

Helen rented a flat in Heriot Row for the duration of the trial because she wanted to be present every day. She shared it for a while with her mother, but Milly could not be persuaded to stay on after her evidence about the birth of Leonie's baby was delivered. Fortunately for Helen's patience this was given fairly early in the proceedings and the defence did not want to cross-examine Milly.

During her week in the city she behaved with ill-grace, refusing to meet her sister Liza and not going out. She preferred to spend her time staring out of the flat window, complaining about the weather, about the lack of gaiety in Scotland's capital and about the unfashionableness of people passing by on the street.

Helen too had an early appearance in the witness box for she was called to explain how the whole investigation started; at her instigation after Phemie Grossett and Billy Cameron visited Castledevon after her father's funeral. The trial was an enthralling experience for her. She watched Cynthia Maitland, she watched the expressions on the faces of the jury, she listened intently to every word uttered by the witnesses and tried to imagine the sort of impression they were making on the judge and the jury.

Billy Cameron appeared, brought back from Glasgow

where he had fled after the collapse of his attempt to extort money from Helen. He told how he had been talked into the impersonation plan by Phemie.

"She persuaded me I really was the old man's grandson. She was after big money but I'd have been happy with a few hundred. I shouldn't have listened to her," he said dolefully.

Val, almost unrecognisable in wig and black gown, behaved in court like the actor Reggie had been convinced he was. He struck attitudes, pointed fingers, raised and lowered his voice in dramatic cadences and altogether held his audience spellbound.

Helen watched him entranced and before she left, Milly said, "Where did you find that lovely McDermot man? What a gift to womankind. Snap him up, my sweet, before someone else does."

Helen bristled. "I hired him as my lawyer. Our relationship is strictly professional. When this is over we'll never see each other again."

Milly looked into her face and sighed. "You do take after Howie, don't you?"

Georgina Kennedy was still alive when the case began, but she was growing visibly weaker every day. Though she knew that her evidence would incriminate her in illegally disposing of the dead babies, she was adamant that she wanted to clear her conscience and tell the truth. "Then I'll die happy," she told Val who pointed out to her what her giving evidence meant.

When the time came for her to appear in court, Mags' boys had to carry her downstairs and along to the court in a sort of a litter, with Val hovering over her, worried in case she would not be able to stand up to the ordeal.

She mustered the last vestiges of her strength however to deliver damning testimony. She remembered specific dates, specific names, specific babies – even babies whose real families had not appeared to give evidence themselves. To Val's secret satisfaction, one of them was the Finnieston-Stewart family.

Detail piled upon detail, including things she had not told Val. In a faltering voice she described the horror of the underground cellar, leaving nothing out, not even the smell, and she did not spare herself or make excuses for what she had done.

"I needed drink. I'd have done anything for drink. I knew what we were doing was wrong when we hid those bairns in the cellar but Cynthia Maitland gave me four shillings every time and that was all I could think about. I don't know where they'd been putting the bairns before or where they put them after because they kept changing the places, and when I got my job working in the brewery I wouldn't go with her any more, but I know about that place beneath the High Street and I'll never forget it."

As she was speaking, Cynthia Maitland sat glacial in the dock eyeing her coldly but she never flinched or faltered. Georgina was in the witness box for two days and by the end of it she looked near to death. She must have known how close her end was for she was fired with a kind of fury to reveal all she knew about the killing of the unwanted babies. The case she made against Mrs Maitland looked irrefutable but when Helen said as much to Val after her last appearance, he shook his head,

"Don't get over-confident. The defence have still got to get their hands on her."

After each day's session, Helen would look for Val outside the court. Sometimes she missed him but occasionally they would meet and then she walked north with him, stopping when she reached Heriot Row and he went on to Queen Street. They discussed the events as they went. Both of them were impressed by Cynthia Maitland's chilly composure.

"I don't think she has any conscience at all," said Helen.

"Real criminals and people who make a huge success in life often don't have much in the way of conscience, they can't afford it," Val told her. "I bet your father who made all that money didn't have much of a conscience."

"Neither does my mother come to that," said Helen.

"So where does that leave you?" laughed Val.

"I'm a throwback," Helen told him.

One night they were walking through driving sleet, the first of the year, when Val suddenly stopped outside a brightly lit little bar in Frederick Street and said, "Let's go in here and warm up for a bit. They've a ladies' snuggery."

The snuggery was empty and they drew two chairs up to the fire, holding their feet in front of the dancing flames till the soles of their shoes steamed.

"Don't let's talk about dead babies," said Helen. "Tell me something else. How's Dig?"

"Boring. She's fallen in love with another medical student and they sit in the flat staring longingly at each other and making halting conversation about diseases and horrible operations. I stay out as much as I can to make it easy for them to fall into bed together. Once they do that they'll be much better company."

Helen laughed and Val said, "How's your husband?"

"He's all right." Why could she not bring herself to tell him about the divorce?

"Was the Rolls a success?"

"Oh yes!" Reggie had telephoned in raptures about the car which she had arranged to be sent to him in Drummond Place and then he had written a fulsome letter of thanks that read like the sort of letter polite children send after Christmas.

"What's the next present you're going to give him?"

She took the plunge. With a bright smile on her face

239

she said, "A divorce, perhaps," but he thought she was joking and threw back his head with a laugh.

Danny Maitland and Marjorie Chalmers were Val's last witnesses. Danny exhibited not a jot of loyalty to the woman who had brought him up.

Yes, he said, he knew about the babies in the attic. They'd been up there when he was a little boy and for many years after. Yes, he knew Mrs Maitland got rid of some of them, by smothering mostly. He didn't help get rid of the bodies – he was too sly to admit to that, which would have made him an accessory to murder – but he knew she paid women to do it. Mrs Grossett was one and there had been others who took babies to the seashore and left them there.

When Val asked him if he was implicated in the deaths of Johnstone, Mrs Grossett or Phemie, he looked the picture of injured innocence. "Of course not," he said. Since it was impossible to prove, there was no point pursuing the matters. These deaths would be left unpunished.

The last witness for the prosecution was Marjorie Chalmers who swore the oath in a fervent voice and clutched the Bible like a talisman. She told her sad story and then wept when she reached the part about putting the cross around her baby son's neck. "I thought it would protect him," she sobbed.

Helen, listening, felt tears welling up in her own eyes and when she looked across at the jury she saw some of them were weeping too. 'I don't care if Val thinks I'm acting like Lady Bountiful, I'm going to do something about that poor woman,' she told herself and when she went home, she instructed Mr Stevens to send £200 to Miss Chalmers and also to buy a good property in Edinburgh and give it to her. This was to be done anonymously, or with a plausible cover story, because Helen feared that if Miss Chalmers knew who had given her money, she would try to give it back. If she had a good house then instead of looking after old ladies for her friend she could do it herself.

The defence dragged out the proceedings for another two days, bringing in church-going friends of Mrs Maitland's to testify to her charitable nature and her kindness, but after the evidence of Danny and Miss Chalmers, they were fighting a losing battle.

At last the final day came and Helen sat in a court where the atmosphere crackled with tension waiting for the jury to return with their verdict.

She scrutinised their faces as they filed in – solemn looking men and three chastened women with eyes reddened by weeping. None of them looked in the direction of the dock where the accused sat in a silver-grey coat and tight-fitting hat, her red lips a scarlet slash in her white face.

When the judge asked the foreman of the jury to give his verdict, he said, "Not guilty of murder, my lord . . ." The audience gasped. ". . . but guilty of manslaughter and an accomplice to murder." The gasp turned to a sigh of relief and approval.

The judge's speech when he delivered his verdict was so sonorous and solemn that it made the blood of his listeners run cold.

"You," he told the prisoner in the dock, "have been implicated in a series of heinous crimes against innocent and defenceless children. You extorted money from the parents or guardians of those children on false pretences and continued to do so after they were dead. There are no words strong enough to express the grievousness of your sins."

For the first time Cynthia Maitland showed emotion. Her face was trembling as she stared at the bewigged man on the bench, but he did not spare her.

"The penalty for crimes like yours is death," he said,

"but the jury have seen fit to temper their verdict with mercy and, because of the confused nature of the facts behind this terrible story, and because of your age and the respect with which some of your friends appear to have held you, I am prepared to sentence you to life imprisonment. You will never again set foot in the outside world. Take her down."

The little crowd of witnesses that met on the pavement outside the court was chastened and far from jubilant. Georgina Kennedy was not there. Her health had failed so rapidly after she gave her evidence that she could not endure another day in court.

Danny had disappeared and so had Billy Cameron. Joe Quinn had not been seen in Edinburgh for months.

Marjorie Chalmers was outside the court, however, weeping and thanking Val. Helen wished she could tell her about the house and the money that was on its way to her but to do that would remove the effectiveness of the anonymity.

Eventually Val and Helen were left alone and they looked forlornly at each other for a few seconds.

"Goodbye, Mrs Hunt," he said and stuck out his hand towards her. The moment she took it, she jumped for she felt as if she had grasped live electric wires. The shock tingled up her arm and nearly made her cry out. Mutely she stared down at their entwined hands wondering what was happening to her. Val was staring down too and she wondered if he had felt the same strange sensation.

It was difficult to speak for a moment but when she could summon up a sound, all she could say was, "Goodbye. You were magnificent. What will you do now?"

He shook his head, her hand still in his. "I don't know. Another case'll come along eventually, probably, but I'm really thinking of going to Spain."

"Everybody will want you after this. You're the hero of the hour." Her legs were trembling slightly and she was afraid that her turmoil of feelings would show on her face.

He shrugged. "You deserve the glory as much as I do. It all started with you wanting to find your sister's child. I hope it's not been too painful for you."

The bleakness of her future prospects stilled her rapidly beating heart. "What will you do in Spain?" she asked.

He was in one of his aggravating moods. "Well, I won't sun myself, that's for sure. I'll probably get killed. There's big trouble there and I quite fancy getting in on it."

"Do take care," she whispered.

A journalist who was waiting to talk to Val approached with his notebook open as they unclasped their hands.

"Goodbye then," they said together.

"I hope we meet again," she said.

"I hope so too."

Then he turned to speak to the journalist and when he turned back he saw her walking off up the pavement, very small, like a doll, straight-backed and proud, dressed in luxurious fur that was soft to the touch, sparkling with jewellery and smelling of Chypre. He wished he could run after her and go through those unsatisfactory farewells all over again, lift her off her feet and hug her. But you didn't do that to another man's wife. For the first time Val wondered about Reggie – what a queer fellow he must be, just a voice on the telephone, never around.

What he did not know was that as Helen walked away she was crying.

Thirteen

Georgina Kennedy died a week after the trial finished and the next night Helen dreamt of her, not bloated and ill as she was in court but young and fresh faced, bustling and efficient, the Georgina Lang who once presided over the domestic arrangements of Castledevon. She turned towards Helen and, with a smile, handed her a chocolate bar in shiny blue and silver paper. "That's for a good girl," she said.

The Scotsman gave the date of the funeral as two days hence, at two p.m. in Greyfriars Church and Helen decided to go. On the appointed day she ordered the car and dressed herself in a luxurious fur coat and a tiny hat with a spotted eye veil that was really too coquettish for such a solemn occasion. Then she said to Simes that Manson, the chauffeur, should drive her. She was going to see Georgina out in style.

They reached the iron gate into Greyfriars churchyard at five minutes to two – Manson was always good with timing. There was no sign of life anywhere and light snowflakes like goose feathers were drifting down from a steel grey sky.

"It's snowing," said Helen with concern in her voice. "You'd better go back to Galashiels at once, Manson, or you might not get home tonight. You know what that road over Fala Hill is like."

"But what about you, madam?"

She had not yet given up the Heriot Row flat so she

said, "I'll stay in Heriot Row. It's going to take a few days to sort out the things there anyway. I'll telephone and tell you when to come up for me – if the road is open. If it isn't I'll stay up here in Edinburgh till it is. I'll be perfectly all right. Now off you go, Manson. I don't want you driving into a snow-drift near Heriot. I'll find a taxi when the funeral's over."

He did as he was told and she turned to walk up the gradient into the churchyard. On the far side of the expanse of tip-tilted graves, she saw a forlorn little cluster of people standing beneath the drooping branches of a leafless elm tree. One of them was very tall and stood with his hands in the pockets of his overcoat and a long striped scarf dangling from his neck. The sight of him made Helen's head swim and she thought she was going to stumble and fall but managed to retain her equilibrium as she walked over the frozen grass.

There were only five people waiting to send the dead woman off – Val, Mags, the little woman Sal from downstairs at Mags' place and Miss Chalmers, as well as a black clad minister holding a Bible. The coffin lay on the grass beside a gaping grave. Snow drifted slowly and softly down, settling noiselessly on their heads and shoulders.

The minister was reading the service for the dead when Helen approached. She saw Val look up and an expression of surprise cross his face at the sight of her. He obviously had not expected her to attend.

In less than ten minutes it was over and the mourners were galvanised into life, stamping their freezing feet and throwing their arms around themselves in an effort to make their blood flow faster. She saw Val pull some banknotes from his pocket and give them to the minister, then he detached himself from the group and walked across to her.

"Did you pay for her funeral?" she asked.

"Yes – well no, actually, you did. I took it out of the profits. I thought the poor thing shouldn't go into a pauper's grave. Do you mind?"

"No. But I haven't paid your bill yet, and I might not if it's too outrageous." She was trying to joke but he took her seriously.

"Suit yourself. I don't care really. I'm going to Spain next week."

They could say no more because Mags came over and said, "What about a wee dram? There's a bar on the corner with a snuggery that we could go into."

"I'm going back to the office," said Val. "But you ladies go if you like. I'll pay." He reached into his pocket and brought out more money with a sharp look at Helen.

Miss Chalmers, who was shuddering with cold, said, "Not for me, thank you very much, Mr McDermot. I'll have to go home. My ladies will be waiting for their tea. Did you know I'm going to open my own boarding house soon? It was like a miracle. A very distant cousin, whom I've never met, read about the court case and bought it for me. Wasn't that wonderful?"

"Wonderful," said Val and Helen together.

"Och well," said Mags, taking the money from Val's hand and looking at him and Helen, "I'll just have a drink on my own with wee Sal here. You two'll be going off thegither I suppose."

They looked at each other and a strange feeling came over Val. Helen Hunt was so intensely annoying with her fixation about money. She'd probably fight like hell over that bill, which, he had to admit was on the heavy side but, as he had once told her, he would use the surplus for deserving cases. It had buried Georgina, after all. Yet though she annoyed him, he couldn't help feeling a great wish to spend time with her.

He looked at her feet in flimsy black suede shoes on the soaking grass. Water marks had already appeared round the edges of the soles. "You can't walk anywhere. Your shoes are soaking," he said.

She looked down at them too. "I'll take a taxi. Did you say you were going to Queen Street? I'm going to my flat in Heriot Row and I could drop you on the way."

"All right," he said, surprisingly humbly for him.

In the taxi, they made bright, strained conversation.

"When are you going to Spain?" she asked.

"Soon. After Christmas. Dig's getting married on Christmas Eve."

Her face lit up. "Oh, I am glad. Please tell her I wish her every happiness."

"You're very enthusistic about marriage," he said.

"Am I? I suppose I am really . . ."

He grinned at her. "About that bill, Mrs Hunt. Send it back if you think it's too big. I'll tell my clerk to take a couple of hundred off it."

By this time they were turning into Queen Street. Helen could see the steps leading up to his office door in front of them. "It doesn't matter," she said, for her anger about the bill had miraculously disappeared. "Give the surplus to your good causes. I don't care."

He was leaning forward with his hand on the door handle and turned to stare at her. Their faces were only inches apart and for a moment she thought he was going to kiss her. Instead, he sat back down in the seat again as if he'd been punched in the stomach and said, "Oh, that's good of you, thank you very much . . . thanks a lot. I did load it on a bit. Thanks." He didn't seem to know what he was saying.

Then he stuck out a hand to shake hers and when she took it she gave a muffled little cry because again the sharp sensation like an electric shock shot up her arm the moment their hands touched.

And he felt it too for he shook his fingers as if they were tingling. Then he threw open the taxi door and ran across the pavement to the sanctuary of his office. He did not look back as he disappeared through the big door.

He couldn't work that afternoon and at half-past four he slammed shut the book on his desk, stood up, put on his coat and scarf and headed for India Street where he found his sister in the kitchen making toasted cheese for her adoring lover who was hovering over her, trying to kiss her neck. It was obvious that they wished he had waited a bit before he returned home and their expressions of disappointment made him determined to stay, so he sat down and started to tease Dig.

"Don't know you it's bad for your digestion to eat cheese before you go to bed? It'll give you bad dreams. Are you getting married in white? Have you picked out a name for the first baby yet?" Questions like these, he knew, made his sister furious and finally she snapped at him, "What's the matter today then?"

"Nothing. I went to a funeral, that's all. Oh, by the way, that woman Mrs Hunt was there and she sent you her best wishes. She thinks it's grand you're getting married. Seems very keen on the institution."

"I liked her," said Dig, "and so did you, don't pretend. She'll have her eye on bigger game than you, Val, but she was nice," said Dig.

He glared, "Mrs Hunt is a respectable married woman."

"Not any more she isn't, or at least she's trying not to be," said Dig. "Didn't you read your newspaper today? I thought you legal men read every word of *The Scotsman*."

"I don't know what you're talking about." He hadn't been bothering much about the newspapers recently, he had to admit.

"Her name's in the paper." Dig's finger was on a close-printed column at the bottom of the page that she snatched up from the seat of a chair and shoved under his nose . . .

He read . . . UNDEFENDED DIVORCES.

Near the top of the column were the names of Reginald and Helen Hunt of Castledevon, Galashiels.

There was a sort of explosion in his brain and he remembered the night they'd sat in the little bar with their shoes steaming and he'd asked what she was giving her husband for Christmas.

'Maybe a divorce,' she'd said. My God, she hadn't been joking.

"Thank you Dig, you're a clever girl," he cried, throwing the paper down and slamming out of the house in a sudden access of energy.

When she reached the little flat in Heriot Row, Helen opened the windows to let out stale air and went into the kitchen, where she found a bottle of champagne that she'd bought to celebrate the ending of the trial but had never opened. It was icy cold, just right for drinking now, so she inexpertly unpopped the cork, letting most of it froth out on to the floor, and poured some into a thick tooth mug.

"Here's to me!" she cried aloud and swigged it down. It tasted wonderful and she sat down waiting for the legendary heart-lifting effect of champagne to sweep over her but it didn't. Instead she started to cry.

"I've never felt like this about anybody before," she told the empty room. "When I touched his hand I thought I was going to give off sparks. Why did I let him go like that? Why didn't I throw my arms round his neck and kiss him? God, I am a fool. I'll never get another chance. He'll go off to Spain and I'll never see him again."

The more she thought about that, the more horrific her visons became. She saw him lying mortally wounded behind some battlements. She saw him in the arms of an exotic Spanish gypsy. The champagne seeped into her bloodstream and made her imagination take fire.

She was at her lowest ebb, mingling champagne with

tears, when there was a knock at the door. Barefoot, red-eyed, and carrying the champagne bottle, she padded across the carpet to open it, not knowing who to expect on the other side and not much caring either.

He was standing on the mat with his hair tousled and his coat half-buttoned.

"God, it's cold out there. We're in for a blizzard," he said, stepping inside and taking the bottle from her hand. Then he put his arm round her waist and swept her up so that their faces were on the same level.

She clung to the lapels of his coat with both hands and didn't say a word. Their faces were inches apart again and this time he did kiss her. "I don't give a damn about your money. I don't care what people will say," he told her between kisses.

She laughed, "That's not very flattering. Maybe they'll just say we were made for each other."

"Both awkward cusses, you mean. Yes, maybe they will." And he kissed her again.

After a bit he carried her over to the sofa and laid her down saying, "At least I've not been electrocuted this time. Did you feel what I felt when we shook hands this afternoon?"

"Yes. It was wonderful," said Helen.

"Let's try again. This time we might light up the whole city," he said and lay down beside her.